T0106527

A killer wants Lilly Echosby to roll over and play dead…

Lilly may be losing a husband but she's gaining a toy poodle. That could be seen as a win-win, since her new adopted pooch Aggie (named after Agatha Christie) is cute and adorable, and Lilly's dirty dog of a spouse is cheating on her with a blond bimbo—except for one problem: Albert Echosby's just been murdered, and Lilly is the number-one suspect.

With the cops barking up the wrong tree, it's a good thing her best friend Scarlett "Dixie" Jefferson from Chattanooga, Tennessee, decided to take a break from the dog club circuit to pay a visit, along with her own prize pair of poodles. With help from Dixie, her defense attorney daughter, and a blue-eyed man in blue with a K-9 partner, Lilly is determined to collar the real killer. But when a second murder occurs, it's clear they're dealing with one sick puppy…

Books by V.M. Burns

Mystery Bookshop Series
THE PLOT IS MURDER
READ HERRING HUNT
THE NOVEL ART OF MURDER

Dog Club Series
IN THE DOG HOUSE

Published by Kensington Publishing Corporation

In the Dog House

V.M. Burns

LYRICAL UNDERGROUND
Kensington Publishing Corp.
www.kensingtonbooks.com

To the extent that the image or images on the cover of this book depict a person or persons, such person or persons are merely models, and are not intended to portray any character or characters featured in the book.

LYRICAL UNDERGROUND BOOKS are published by

Kensington Publishing Corp.
119 West 40th Street
New York, NY 10018

All Kensington titles, imprints, and distributed lines are available at special quantity discounts for bulk purchases for sales promotion, premiums, fund-raising, educational, or institutional use.

Special book excerpts or customized printings can also be created to fit specific needs. For details, write or phone the office of the Kensington Sales Manager: Kensington Publishing Corp., 119 West 40th Street, New York, NY 10018. Attn. Sales Department. Phone: 1-800-221-2647.

First Electronic Edition: August 2018
eISBN-13: 978-1-5161-0787-2
eISBN-10: 1-5161-0787-X

First Print Edition: August 2018
ISBN-13: 978-1-5161-0790-2
ISBN-10: 1-5161-0790-X

Printed in the United States of America

Acknowledgments

As always, I want to thank my agent, Dawn Dowdle at Blue Ridge Literary Agency and my editor, John Scognamiglio for their faith and patience.

Thanks to my dad, Benjamin Burns, my sister, Jacquelyn Rucker, for the emotional support and many prayers. Thank you to my niece Jillian for the social media support and encouragement and thanks to my nephew, Christopher for the fashion advice.

I have been blessed with a number of friends who have supported me in so many ways, whether it was listening to crazy hair brained ideas, brainstorming plot ideas, or talking me off the ledge when things got too tough. Thanks Kellye Garrett for answering a million questions. Thank you to Debbie Bennett for the ideas and moral support. Thanks to my Seton Hill University Tribe, Anna, Alex, Lana, Michelle, Patricia, Jessica, Matt, Penny, Jeff, Dagmar, Kenya, Gina, and Crystal for the accountability and support. Thanks to Patton Musick for letting me know I wasn't crazy and encouraging me to keep writing. Thanks to the Barnyardians (Jill, Lindsey, Chuck, Jamie, Stephen, Tim and our fearless leader, Sandy) for being so amazingly supportive. Thanks to Deborah Hughes, Tena Elkins, Jamie Medlin and Grace Dixon, best training team ever. There is no way this book would be finished without my two good friends, Shelitha Mckee and Sophia Muckerson. Thank you for always supporting me as I pursue my dream and pushing me forward toward new levels.

Thank you Dru Ann Love, Colleen Finn, and Karen Owen for the support and for everyone who has helped to share, and promote my books.

Special thanks to my wonderful friends at Echo Dog Club in Buchanan, Michigan for the encouragement and support throughout the years when I was training and competing with my poodles. If it wasn't for the wonderful memories I have with ECHO, I wouldn't have come up with the idea for the series.

CHAPTER 1

"YOU TWO-TIMING LOW LIFE WEASEL!"

I'd always prided myself on being in control and maintaining my dignity, but I was on the verge of not only humiliating myself, but committing physical violence.

"Mom, calm down." Stephanie placed her arm around me and helped me back into my seat.

I glared at my soon-to-be ex-husband, thankful there was a large conference table in between us. He refused to make eye contact, looking everywhere but directly at me. The twenty-year-old home-wrecking hussy sitting next to him looked bored. The bleached-blond, heavily made-up twig was actually filing her fingernails.

I was shocked he'd had the nerve to bring the floozy he was leaving me for to the meeting with our lawyers to discuss divorce proceedings and the distribution of assets.

Less than five minutes ago I was on the verge of tears. My marriage of twenty-five years was ending. That was until Albert walked in with his lawyer and his super-slim girlfriend, who happened to be younger than our children. I shouldn't have been surprised. Even though he'd said he still loved me, I knew there was someone else. Wives always knew. When he started working out, dyeing his hair, and spending lots of late nights at his car lot, I should have known. He said he needed something new. Turned out the "something new" was a twenty-year-old dancer who was younger than both of our children.

Little Miss Home-Wrecker stopped filing her nails and smacking her gum long enough to yawn, and that set me off again.

"Are we boring you?"

She looked at me with a snide curl to her lip and a shrug of her shoulders, and before I knew what came over me, I was halfway across the table with my hands wrapped around her throat. It took three people to pry my hands off her scrawny little neck.

"You're crazy," she croaked.

"I *am* crazy, you little bimbo."

She backed up to the door. "I'll be in the 'Vette." She marched toward the door. "And the name is Bambi." She turned and left.

The white-hot rage that propelled me across the table subsided, and I allowed myself to be placed in my seat.

Albert stood in place, torn between his current wife, who was all but frothing at the mouth, and his girlfriend, who'd just walked out. He made his choice when he turned and walked out.

His attorney followed not long afterward, leaving Stephanie and me alone in the conference room. We sat in silence for what felt like a long time but was only minutes. Then I hopped up from the upholstered wingback chair and paced in front of the large plate-glass window that looked out over the city of Chicago onto Lake Shore Drive. I was so angry I wanted to swear, but I'd never said the kind of words I saw spray-painted on the sides of buildings or scratched onto the walls in public restrooms. I was raised to believe well-bred ladies didn't use those types of words. I trained my children that the English language was so rich, a well-educated person should be able to express themselves without resorting to those types of words. Today, I learned I was wrong. Well-bred ladies *did* use those types of words. In fact, I felt like stringing all of them together and saying them loud and repeatedly. Nevertheless, close to fifty years of training and Catholic school guilt didn't dissolve in an instant.

Instead, I said the harshest word I was capable of, "Rassa-frazzin'-fragdaggle-blasted-tater sauce!"

"Mom!" Stephanie feigned a look of shock, but couldn't prevent her lips from twitching or her eyes from sparkling. However, the look was brief, given the magnitude of the occasion.

"I'm sorry, dear." I stared at my daughter, embarrassed I'd lost control in front of her. "I shouldn't have said those things about your father. Or tried to strangle his...whatever she is. This has to be hard enough for you, watching your parents split up, without your mother losing control like that."

"You've got to be joking. You should be furious. You should be swearing, *with real curse words*, throwing furniture and slashing his tires. Maybe not trying to kill the girl—at least not with so many witnesses." She smiled briefly, but then she banged her hands on the desk, causing a glass of water to shake, sloshing water onto the table. "Get angry and let it out. I know I would."

Old habits die hard. I hurried to the table, grabbed several tissues, and mopped up the water before it could stain the lovely mahogany table that dominated the room.

Stephanie sighed as she watched me clean. "You've spent your entire life cleaning up after other people—Dad, David, and me. After twenty-five years of marriage, he leaves you for a woman younger than me, and here you are, still cleaning up. You shouldn't let him get away with it." She reached across and grabbed my hands, preventing me from continuing. "I'm not going to let him get away with this."

I stared at the determined look in my daughter's dark eyes and the set of her chin. For an instant, instead of the polished, intelligent, high-powered Chicago attorney, I saw the scrappy tomboy who got sent home from school for beating up the neighborhood bully when he tried to steal a younger kid's lunch money. Stephanie had always been a defender of the poor and downtrodden. At twenty-five, she was still doing it. I felt a moment of pride, knowing I'd had a hand in creating such a strong, beautiful woman. My conscience pricked when I remembered that her father had also contributed to making her the woman she was.

"I shouldn't have allowed you to get involved like this. You shouldn't take sides. He's your father. I—"

"Mom, stop." She grabbed me by the shoulders and gave me a shake. "He is my father and I love him. I always will, but you always taught me it was our duty as good citizens to stand up for what was right and to fight for justice for those unable to fight for themselves." She smiled. "That's why I became a lawyer."

I pulled her close and hugged her. When we separated, we both needed tissues to wipe away the tears. We sat down and composed ourselves.

Stephanie pulled some notes from the large folder on the desk. "Daddy's attorney is asking for the house, the car, everything. He claims, as the sole provider, he's entitled to all of the assets."

I swallowed the lump in my throat. "But your father never wanted me to work outside of the home. He said my job was taking care of my family."

"I know. Don't worry. I won't let him get away with that." She scanned the papers. "He claims business hasn't been good, so he can't pay alimony or any type of spousal support." She tapped her pencil on the table and mumbled, "We'll see about that."

"I don't want anything from him. I kept my CPA license, and I can always find a job."

"Mom! That's not the point. You worked harder than anyone to help him build his business. You even did the books for years, plus you raised two kids, cooked, cleaned, and sacrificed. You deserve better than to be tossed aside after more than twenty-five years, like an old discarded newspaper."

Stephanie looked out the window.

She spent several hours explaining things and making phone calls to Albert's attorney. By the end of the day, she had a smug, satisfied look, which told me she'd gotten more than she'd given up in the negotiations. Between the shock of learning the man I'd pledged my troth to over twenty-five years ago not only wanted to call it quits, but he'd been unfaithful, too, had my head pounding beyond anything mere aspirin could soothe. Stephanie wanted me to go to dinner with her, stay overnight, and take the train back to Lighthouse Dunes, Indiana, in the morning, but I wanted to go home, while I still had a home to go to.

The South Shore commuter train ran between Chicago and South Bend, Indiana. Lighthouse Dunes was about forty-five miles west of South Bend. The ride from beginning to end took two hours and twenty minutes and was popular, especially in the summer months, for Indiana residents to go to baseball games, museums, and shopping without the hassle of dealing with the often bumper-to-bumper traffic and parking in the Windy City. For me, the ride provided time to sit and think.

When Albert first moved out, I was in denial. I felt like a statistic. At fifty, I was part of the 40 to 50 percent of marriages that end in divorce. Initially, I thought he just needed a little distance to realize he was making a mistake and would eventually come home. I spent the first few months cleaning the house and working out. I even read magazines and books on how to rekindle the spark. I actually replaced my warm flannel pajamas with flimsy negligees. Initially, I was embarrassed by the sheer fabric, which left nothing to the imagination. However, I had to admit they were perfect for coping with hot flashes and night sweats. After six months, the divorce papers arrived. That was when I burned the magazines, tossed out the books, and cried. I cried a lot. When my credit cards were declined and I could no longer get money from our bank account, I called Stephanie. I suspected there was another woman, but I never dreamed she would be so young.

As the train sped through the night, I looked out the window as the trees and buildings sped past. In many ways, that ride mirrored my life. It felt like yesterday I was a new bride, in love and confident our love would conquer anything. Then came the children. Stephanie and David were the joys of my life. One minute they were chubby little babies, and the next they were graduating from college. The years rushed by as quickly as the scenery outside my window. In all likelihood, my life was more than half over, and what did I have to show for it apart from two children who were now adults with little need for me?

I leaned my head against the cool window and pulled my coat tight. I didn't realize I was crying until the woman next to me handed me a tissue.

"Honey, whatever he did, it ain't worth all them tears."

I took the tissue and stared at my neighbor. She was a large African American woman with a round, kind face and a head full of thick gray hair. "Excuse me? How did you…"

She laughed a low, throaty chuckle that caused her eyes to crinkle at the corners and her belly to shake. "You wanna know how I knew you was crying 'bout a man? Or, how I knew he wasn't worth them tears?" She laughed again. "Only a man can make a woman cry like you was crying. And, baby, ain't *no* man worth crying over." She leaned close. "Tears are a precious commodity. You shouldn't waste them on someone that done you wrong."

I sat up straight. "I don't know what you're talking about."

She shook her head. "Alright, why don't you tell Miss Florrie what's bothering you."

I stared at the strange woman, who didn't seem to think anything strange about asking personal questions of a complete stranger on a train.

Miss Florrie looked at me expectantly. Her soft brown eyes were patient and kind, and before I realized it, I was telling her about Albert, our life in Lighthouse Dunes, Stephanie and David, and even my pitiful excuse for a garden.

Miss Florrie listened patiently without interrupting. She listened and nodded at the appropriate places and *tsk*ed her disapproval at the right time.

When I finished my tale, I felt spent but calmer than I'd felt in months. I looked at Miss Florrie and waited for her pronouncement. Part of my brain wondered why I cared what this stranger thought. However, another part of me was more than curious.

Miss Florrie sat quietly for several moments. Then she smiled. "Well, you been done wrong, that's for sure, but ain't nobody on this earth gets off without no trouble. I reckon you done had yo share. Now, whatchu gonna do 'bout it?"

I blinked. "What do you mean?" The irony of telling my troubles to a complete stranger on a train hit me. I had no intention of reenacting the Alfred Hitchcock movie where two strangers met on a train and committed murder for each other.

She must have read my mind, because she laughed again. "Honey, you ain't got no cause to worry 'bout Miss Florrie." She chuckled. "I like watching dem old movies too, but I ain't 'bout to kill nobody." She laughed.

Her hearty laugh and sincerity made me realize I was being ridiculous.

"Your husband left you." She stared intently at me. "Whatchu gonna do now?"

I shrugged. "Well, my daughter is an attorney and she's working on negotiating for support and the house—"

"You mean that house you just told me you can't stand?"

I stared at her. "Yeah, that house."

"Why you want it? Seems to me that man done you a favor."

"I don't understand."

"Well, you don't like the house. He wants the house. Why fight for a house you don't want?"

I shrugged. "I guess it's the principle of the thing."

"Pshaw. You gotta pick yo battles, and that one ain't worth the energy. Now, I ain't saying you just give him the house. No. You entitled to a fair share. He should pay you half of what the house is worth. Then you take that money and you do the things you've always wanted to do."

"What things?"

She laughed. "Baby, only you can answer dat." She chuckled. "But I can tell you, if it was me and I had a chance to start over, I'd leave this snow and cold and move someplace warm."

I smiled. "Florida?"

"Noooo." She shook her head. "Florida is too hot and humid for me, plus they got gators in Florida. Miss Florrie can't do no gators."

There was something lyrical in the way she spoke. Florida sounded like *Floor-y-da*, and I wanted to smile.

She shook her head. "Naw, I got a sister lives in Chattanooga, Tennessee. I ain't seen her in ten years. I'd move there."

"Chattanooga? I have a friend in Chattanooga, my roommate from college."

"Where 'bouts?"

I shrugged. "I'm not really sure. I've never been there. We were best friends in college, but we drifted apart," I said vaguely. "You know the kids came, and well, we just lost touch."

Miss Florrie looked at me as though she could see through my soul. Heat rose up my neck, and I knew I was blushing. She saw through all of my lies, but she didn't say anything.

Instead, she shrugged. "It's warm most of the time in Chattanooga. It gets hot in the summer, but that's okay with me." She leaned closer. "The older I get, the harder it is for me to take the snow and cold." She shivered. "I feel the cold down in my bones and it gets in my soul. The long, cold winters do somethin' to folks. They gets depressed and sad with all dat snow and cold." She shook her head as though shaking away the memory of the cold. "They got mountains and lots of green in Tennessee." She nodded. "Yep, if it was me, that's what I'd do. I'd buy me a house and a little building where I could start a restaurant down south and start over. Life is too short to be unhappy."

"A restaurant? Are you a chef?"

She chuckled. "Naw, I ain't no chef. You gotta go to school to be a chef. I'm just a cook. Been cooking all my life." She sat straight and tall. "Pretty good at it too, if I do say so myself."

"What if you move away and you don't like it?"

Miss Florrie laughed. "Baby, that's easy. I'd sell the house and the restaurant and try someplace else, and I'd keep trying until I find my happy place."

* * * *

Later, when I sat in the cold cookie-cutter house Albert insisted would be a great investment, I thought about what Miss Florrie said. I thought about finding my happy place. If I was honest with myself, I hated the house. I'd always hated it. Almost all of the houses looked exactly the same. The same builder built most of them, and there were only three different plans in the entire subdivision. The same house, but with different color siding, shutters, or brick façades. I hated the fact the house had very few windows. I hated that the neighborhood association dictated my life, right down to the type of plants I could have, and refused to allow a fence. They even had rules about the type of Christmas decorations I could put up. I'd always wanted a dog, but the association would only allow invisible fences. At one time, I thought about fighting them, but Albert was allergic to dogs anyway, so it all became a moot point and I eventually gave up. If I moved, I could get a house with a fence and I could get a dog. Heck, I could get several dogs if I wanted. The children were grown and had both moved away, Stephanie to Chicago and David to New York City. There was nothing holding me to Lighthouse Dunes. No job. No husband.

The idea of moving away and starting over had sounded scary on the train. However, in the still silence of an empty house, the idea took root and started to grow. I walked through the rooms, full of furniture and memories of a life that was no longer my reality, and realized I didn't particularly care about any of the furniture. The pictures of the children were the only things

I valued, and I could take those with me. At that moment, I decided to take control of my life and find my happy place.

"But where to go?" I spoke into the cold, dark, empty house and waited. Thankfully, there was no answer. I sat at my computer and typed, *Where should I live?*

I didn't honestly expect an answer. However, my browser returned a list of sites with quizzes to determine the best place to live, based on my responses. I was pleasantly surprised and spent several hours taking online quizzes. I got responses for everywhere from Spain to Texas. One of the sites provided a list of ten best cities based on my answers, including climate, housing, and demographic information. I browsed the list and was excited when Chattanooga, Tennessee, showed up in my list as one of my ten places. I clicked on the link and stayed up until the wee small hours of the night looking at houses and jobs and reading as much as I could. Spain sounded exotic and fun, but my Spanish was *malo, muy mal.*

Chattanooga had a lot going for it. It was in the United States, for one, and I wouldn't need a passport or shots. Like several other states, Tennessee had no state income tax. The cost of living seemed a lot lower than in Indiana. Plus, it didn't snow very often. Add that to the fact I knew at least one person in Chattanooga, which catapulted it to the top of my list.

It turned out the Internet was good at finding long-lost friends too. I tracked down an e-mail address for my friend Scarlett Jefferson. Scarlett and I met during our freshman year of college and had been fast friends. She was a southern belle with a wicked sense of humor and a sharp mind. Her mother had been a huge fan of *Gone with the Wind*, so much so she'd named her two children Scarlett and Rhett. Despite the moniker, Scarlett got along well with the Yankees at Northwestern University and made tons of friends. Everyone called her Dixie, and we'd remained friends and roommates for our full four years. However, after college she moved back to Tennessee and married her high school sweetheart, Jeremiah Beauregard "Beau" Jefferson, and I fell in love and married Albert. We wrote for a few years and talked on the telephone, but Dixie and Albert never got along. Albert thought she was too opinionated and outspoken. Dixie never trusted Albert. Turned out she was right. While I was still riding high from the excitement of my decision to start over, I fired off an e-mail before my courage failed, stating I was thinking about moving to the Chattanooga area and was curious if she could recommend a good Realtor. I pressed send and promptly shut down my computer. I wasn't sure if anything would come of this, but I was determined to find my happy place.

CHAPTER 2

I fully expected the crazy idea of moving to Tennessee would have faded in the bright light of a new day. However, the next morning I found myself even more excited than I was the previous night. In fact, when I sat down with coffee, I noticed a new e-mail had arrived. It was from Dixie. She was ecstatic to hear I was considering moving to Chattanooga. There were a lot of capital letters and exclamation marks, along with an entire row of happy face emoticons. She declared it fate that she was actually only a few hours away attending a Poodle Specialty, whatever that was, in Lansing, Michigan. She was going to be staying in the area for another week to attend an Obedience workshop and would drive down and maybe we could have lunch or dinner.

I promptly responded I would love to get together and sent my address, my cell phone number, and directions. I had plenty of room and invited her to stay here while she waited for the workshop. Message sent, I drank my coffee and tried to remember the last time I'd seen Dixie.

Later, I called Stephanie and told her what I wanted. Initially, she was unsure, but when I shared my plan to move someplace warm and sunny and start over, she thought it was a great idea. She told me to leave all of the legal arrangements to her, which I was happy to do.

I got dressed and started on my tasks. My next-door neighbor was an elderly retired police officer who suffered from dementia. Bradley Hurston had retired from the Chicago Police Department and moved to Lighthouse Dunes to stay with his sister after her husband died suddenly. Mr. Hurston had once been very active, coaching the boys' baseball team and teaching self-defense classes to the women in our neighborhood. I still remembered his suggestion to S.I.N.G. if we were ever attacked. SING was the acronym he used to help us remember the four areas to attack—solar plexus, instep, nose, and groin. He was now confined to a wheelchair, where he spent his days looking out his front window with a pair of binoculars.

I got the lawn mower out of the garage and cut the grass. It had been a very wet spring, and now that summer had arrived, the grass was growing very rapidly. When I finished my yard, I cut Mr. Hurston's grass, as well. His son usually cut his grass when he was in town or arranged for someone to do it, but he was a cop, too, and I knew he was often tired when he got home from work. Plus, he had a family and a yard of his own to mow. So, I'd made a habit of cutting Mr. Hurston's yard whenever I cut mine. Besides, it was the least I could do for someone who'd been so committed to serving and protecting our community.

When I was done mowing, I edged both yards and swept up the grass clippings. The neighborhood association frowned on grass clippings left on the sidewalk. Three hours later, I was hot, sweaty, and covered in grass clippings, but both yards looked great.

The front door opened, and Marianne Carpenter, Mr. Hurston's sister, smiled and beckoned me to come in.

Marianne Carpenter was a petite woman, barely five feet tall. She was probably in her mid-sixties but looked older. I suspected that was due to her hair, which was thinning but which she dyed a vibrant orange, along with an excessive amount of makeup, which highlighted rather than concealed every wrinkle. She was a timid woman who liked flashy clothes, large gawdy pieces of jewelry, and pink slippers. "You must be worn out. Come inside and have some lemonade."

I was itchy from the grass clippings and suspected the odor that made its way to my nose every few seconds wasn't something being carried by the wind, but was me. Nevertheless, I'd learned that declining Marianne's offers was in poor taste. Her eyes filled with tears and she became offended. So, I made my usual half-hearted protests and went inside.

Bradley Hurston was seated in front of the living room picture window. He had always been a big man. Now he seemed small and shriveled up. His skin sagged, and the few hairs that remained stood out, making him look like a mad scientist.

"Hello, Mr. Hurston. How are you today?"

He gave me a glassy stare. "I saw you. I know what you did. I've got my eye on you."

This was his standard greeting. He repeated those same words to everyone he met, repeatedly.

I nodded and followed Marianne to the kitchen. The layout of the house was a mirror image of my own, which always threw me off. My natural instinct was to turn left to go to the kitchen instead of right. After more than twenty years, I still veered to the left, bumped into the console table, and stubbed my toe. I went into the kitchen. Marianne was sitting at the circular wooden table with a pitcher of lemonade and a plate of cookies.

"Have a seat and take a load off." She smiled.

I sat and took a long drink. The lemonade was a mix, and it was so sweet I could feel my blood sugar rise. However, I was thirsty, so I chugged it down. Marianne Carpenter was the world's worst cook. Her cookies were so hard I once used one as a wedge to level my kitchen chair. When she offered, I used my standard response, "Those look delicious, but I'm dieting."

I wasn't overweight. I'd describe myself as "big boned." I was five feet four, one hundred fifty pounds, but compared to Marianne, I looked like the Jolly Green Giant. She was conscious of her figure and very conscientious of mine. She was extra-sensitive about everything else, but she understood dieting.

"Of course, dear, I didn't mean to be insensitive. Please forgive me. I've never had to watch my weight, but I do understand." She patted my hand.

I plastered a fake smile on my face and dug my fingernails into my palm to prevent myself from flinging the glass of lemon-flavored sugar water at her.

"How are you holding up?" She leaned across the table and whispered with the look people wore to console family members at a funeral.

"I'm doing well. How are you?" I pretended I didn't know she was referring to the fact that my husband had left me for a younger woman.

"Well, of course you're fine." She patted my hand again. "I'm praying for you two. In fact, when the pastor had altar call Sunday, I stood up and shared your situation with the congregation, and our pastor put your names on the prayer list at church."

I dug my fingernails deeper and bit the inside of my cheek. "You did what?"

She smiled proudly, then hopped up and pulled a calendar off the refrigerator and brought it to the table. "Not only that, but I asked our prayer circle to keep you both on their prayer chain. There are people praying for you every hour of every day." She looked at the sheet. "I'm scheduled from five to five thirty every morning." She pointed her long, bony fingers at the time slot on the calendar.

I stared at the sheet until my eyes blurred and a vein throbbed on the side of my head. I stood up so quickly I nearly knocked over the chair. "Thank you for the lemonade, but I have to go."

"You're welcome, dear," were the last words I heard as I rushed out the back door.

As I marched home, I told myself over and over again, "She meant well." However, the idea of sharing my marital situation with the entire church in a small town like Lighthouse Dunes was the equivalent to posting an ad on the front page of the *Chicago Tribune*.

It took the rest of the afternoon before I calmed down enough to step outside. However, I needed groceries, and unless I went to the store, I'd be forced to order pizza again and the delivery boy went to Marianne's church. I shouldn't be embarrassed. I hadn't done anything wrong. Albert was the one who cheated. He was the one who had an affair. He was the one who had left me for a bleached-blond Barbie doll who was young enough to be his daughter. Nevertheless, I found myself looking askance at everyone I passed at the grocery store and the gas station.

When I got home, I was surprised to find a large RV parked in my driveway. I pulled up next to it, and the door opened and out jumped a tall, thin woman with big Dolly Parton hair, tight jeans, lots of jewelry, and holding a tiny black poodle.

"Lilly Anne, I know I should have called." She hugged me, careful not to squash the poodle. "I was so excited to get your e-mail this morning, I hopped in my RV and hightailed it up here to see you." She pulled back and looked at me. "I hope that's okay?" she said in her sweet southern drawl.

I smiled and gave her another hug. "Of course it's alright, Dixie. I'm really happy to see you too. Please, come inside."

She handed me the dog. "You don't mind I brought a few of my dogs along, do you?"

I juggled my grocery bags and held the little shivering fluff ball to my chest. "Of course I don't mind. I love dogs, but I thought you had big poodles."

She opened the side door to the RV and out pranced two large black poodles that appeared to be shaved closely in many places, but where their coats were longer, the hair was wrapped up as though they were getting a perm. They had bright-colored wrappers hanging from their ears, and the hair atop their heads was a conglomeration of scrunchies and rubber bands. On the ground, the dogs came to my waist. They were big and carried themselves regally, regardless of the ridiculous wrappers and bands.

There was something in their bearing that proclaimed, *I don't care what you think of my appearance. You are beneath me.*

"I do have standard poodles." She placed a lead over one of the dog's heads. "This is Champion Chyna, the Ninth Wonder of the World."

I raised an eyebrow at hearing the name.

Dixie shrugged. "That's what I get for letting my nephew and his fraternity brothers choose the name." She patted the dog. "I just finished her at the specialty, so that made the win even more special."

She scratched the dog behind the ear, and Chyna looked as though her eyes would roll back in her head. "That's her registered name, but her call name is Chyna." She put a lead around the other dog. "And this is Champion Galactic Imperial Resistance Leader, call name Leia."

"Wow. That's a mouthful."

She smiled. "The registered name is just for shows. Breeders try to come up with unique names that will make a statement with the judges. The call name is what we actually *call the dog*."

"I get it. So, Chyna and Leia?"

She nodded. "You got it."

I held out the fluff ball in my arms. "And who is this?"

She smiled. "I have no idea. One of the breeders rescued her from a puppy mill. Her husband went bonkers when she came home with another dog, apparently fifteen was his limit. She asked if anyone would be willing to take her."

"She looks awfully small." I stared at the other poodles relieving themselves on the shrubs that separated my house from my neighbor's. I cringed at what Bradley Hurston would say when he saw me again.

Dixie must have noticed my cringe, because she quickly grabbed the dogs' leads. "I'm sorry. I forget not everyone is a dog lover."

"No, it's okay."

She pulled bags out of her pocket and cleaned up the deposits and walked them around back to the garbage cans. When she came back, she opened the RV door to return the dogs, but I stopped her.

"You aren't going to leave them outside, are you?"

She looked skeptical. "Well, I don't want to cause trouble."

"You're not causing trouble. Bring them inside."

She searched my face and then opened the door and called the dogs. They pranced out, and we all marched into the house.

"They're very well-behaved. They're both completely housebroken and, after an entire weekend of shows, they're worn out and will eat and sleep for days." She turned to me. "However, I'm not sure about the little one. She isn't really a puppy. She's probably about two years old, but I suspect she's spent the majority of her short life locked in a crate, pushing out litter after litter."

I frowned. "That's horrible."

"Unfortunately, not all breeders are responsible dog owners. For some, these cute little things are merely a commodity to be used to generate cash." She scratched the dog's head.

"So, if she's two, then she's fully grown?"

Dixie nodded. "She's a toy poodle. Poodles come in three sizes: toy, miniature and standard." She scratched the small fluff ball behind the ear. "This is a toy. Toys are the smallest and shouldn't be more than ten inches from the withers."

"The withers?" I asked.

She smiled. "From the shoulder to the ground. Dogs between ten and seventeen inches are miniatures. Anything over seventeen inches is a standard." She pointed to the other two dogs, which had eaten a large bowl of dog food and were now lying on the floor fast asleep. "Those are standards."

"Is that the only difference between the three?"

Dixie nodded. "Yes. The breed standard or the guidelines are the same for all three. The only difference is the size. Some other breeds are differentiated by color or coat, but for poodles, it's the size."

"So, what are you going to do with her? It is a her, isn't it?" I held her up and looked underneath.

She nodded. "Yep. It's a female, and I'm looking for a good home for her." She narrowed her eyes and looked at me. "You wouldn't know anyone who is looking for a companion, by any chance?"

At that moment, the fluff ball sighed and laid her head on my shoulder. From that moment on, I knew this was my dog.

We spent the rest of the night talking and thinking up names for the new addition to my family. Dixie suggested I name her something that had meaning to me. I had always been a big mystery fan, so I settled on a registered name of Queen of the Cozy, call name Agatha. Although I intended to call her Aggie.

* * * *

The next morning, I woke up to barking, screaming, growling, and a few whimpers. I rushed downstairs and found Albert backed up against the front door. The whimpers were coming from him. The two standard poodles, which had seemed so docile and a bit ridiculous with their colored hair wrappings and ridiculous cuts, were lunging toward him with teeth bared. They emitted a rumbling growl that sounded ferocious. The barking came from Aggie, who had a hold on Albert's pants leg and was shaking it with all her might, as though she was going to rip him to shreds if he dared move.

Dixie had the standards' collars and was straining to keep them from taking Albert out and yelling at him to stop moving and stay still.

"What's going on here?" I hurried to Dixie's side.

"This lunatic just waltzed in the house, unannounced, and Chyna and Leia were protecting their territory."

"Their territory? This is *my* house!" Albert's voice had a bit of a tremor, but his eyes looked terrified. "Those ferocious beasts should be put down. They're dangerous."

"Keep talking like that, buttercup, and I might just lose my grip on their collars." Dixie relaxed her grip on Chyna, and she lunged to within inches of Albert, who tried to climb the wall.

I bent down and picked up Aggie. "Actually, you have no right to just waltz in here unannounced. You lost that right when you decided to move out."

Albert looked as though he wanted to argue, but with three dogs and two angry women glaring at him, he smartly kept his mouth shut.

"You want me to call the police or just let the poodles finish him off?" Dixie asked.

I thought about it for a moment and then decided he wasn't worth it. "We'd better not. I like these dogs too much and wouldn't want them to get sick eating rancid human flesh."

Albert scowled at me, and I held out Aggie, who barked and would have leapt out of my arms to attack him if I hadn't tightened my grip.

Albert held up his hands in surrender and whined, "Okay. Call off the attack."

Dixie looked at me for confirmation. Then she said. "Platz."

Both big dogs immediately stopped growling and lunging and lay down quietly. Despite their nonthreatening postures, they continued to stare at Albert.

Dixie connected the dogs' leashes and stood with her arms folded across her chest.

"Well?" I stroked my scrappy little ankle-biter and joined the staring contingency.

Albert looked wary. His gaze darted back and forth from Chyna to Leia and then to Dixie and me.

"What do you want, Albert?"

"I came by to remind you about the party?"

I frowned. "What party?"

"I knew you'd forget." He took a step forward.

Chyna and Leia remained in their sphinx-like positions, but their lips curled and both began a low, rumbling growl, which caused Albert to freeze, foot in midair. He looked at me helplessly.

I turned to Dixie. "Maybe you should take the dogs outside."

Dixie never turned her head or broke her stare. "You sure?"

"I'm sure."

She picked up the leashes. "Fuss." Which sounded like *Foos*.

The dogs stood up by her side.

Albert stepped aside and she opened the front door and they headed outside.

Before she left, she turned, walked over to Albert. and said in a low, steady voice, "I have a gun and I can shoot the hind legs off a possum in the dark at six hundred feet. So, you better watch yourself." She turned to me. "Holler if you need me."

I bit my lip to keep from laughing and nodded.

When she and the large poodles were gone, Albert breathed a sigh of relief. "That woman is crazy. She should be locked up, along with those vicious beasts she calls dogs."

"What do you want? Why are you here?"

"I told you. I came to remind you about the party. Clearly, you've forgotten." He rolled his eyes and gave a snide smile as if to say, *You poor little fool.*

In the past, I would have felt guilty for forgetting whatever it was I was being accused of forgetting and apologized. However, today I felt empowered. I held out Aggie, like Captain Kirk used the Tribbles to uncover the Klingon on *Star Trek*, and she didn't disappoint. She barked and snapped, and Albert backed up and removed the smug, self-satisfied look from his face.

I pulled her back to my chest. "What party?"

"Tonight's my grandmother's ninety-fifth birthday. We're hosting the party, remember?" He looked around the room. "Clearly, you forgot. There's not even one decoration up. No balloons. Did you even cook?"

"You have got to be kidding me. Did you forget? You walked out. That's not *my* grandmother. Why would you even think I'd host a birthday party for someone"—I held up a finger—"someone who isn't related to me, someone I don't like, and someone who can't stand me?" I stared into his blank eyes.

He stared and then blinked. "So, you're not planning to cook?"

"Ugh!" I marched into the kitchen. If I didn't get away from him, I might be tempted to take Dixie's gun and shoot him myself.

After a few moments, he followed me into the kitchen.

"If you have any sense of self-preservation, you'll go away and not talk to me until I've had some coffee." I filled the water basin on the fancy individual-cup coffeemaker Albert had given me for our last anniversary. At the time, I was so angry that he felt a coffeemaker was the perfect gift to give to a woman who rarely drank coffee, for a twenty-fifth wedding anniversary present. However, after he walked out, I found myself drinking more coffee and wine than I had in the past twenty-five years. So, I got it out of the box. Now, every time I made coffee, it reminded me what an insensitive louse I married.

Albert watched me make coffee. When it was done, I sat down and drank the entire cup, got up, and made another. At one point, he looked as though he was going to speak, but one look into my eyes and he quickly closed his mouth and remained silent.

By the time I'd downed my second cup of coffee, my nerves were less frazzled and I was able to formulate sentences that didn't question his parents' marital status when he was born.

"I can only assume, by your presence here, you haven't told your family we're getting divorced, nor have you bothered to cancel the birthday party for tonight."

He looked as though he was going to smirk, and I picked Aggie up and held her where he could see her. He promptly readjusted his countenance to a neutral state. He sighed. "No, I haven't told my family about the divorce. I thought we could tell them later."

I looked at my soon-to-be ex-husband, seeing him, perhaps for the first time, as the cowardly weasel that he was.

"We could tell them later? Why should *we* tell them anything? They aren't my family. They're your family. You should tell them yourself."

He looked startled. "But everyone is expecting us to have the party here, like always."

"Maybe you should let Bimbo host the party for you."

He sighed. "It's Bambi, and she's never hosted a party before. Plus, my family doesn't know about her."

"Oh, really?"

"Pleeease. I need your help. This will be the last time."

"What's in it for me?"

He tilted his head to the side. "What do you mean?"

"What's-in-it-for-me?" I moved my hands as if I were using sign language.

Albert merely stared.

I sighed. "Look, I'll host your party tonight, but it's going to cost you."

"How much?"

"First, you return your key. You do not enter this house without permission until the day when it is transferred over to you and I move out." I waited.

He nodded.

I held out my hand.

He looked for two seconds as though he wasn't going to give me the key.

"I can always have the locks changed."

He reached in his pocket and handed me his key.

"Second, you will return my access to our joint bank account." I squinted. "And don't even think about withdrawing the money from that account, because I was a CPA and I know how much should be in it."

He reluctantly nodded.

I folded my arms across my chest and waited.

"Now?"

I nodded.

He pulled out his cell phone and dialed the bank.

"And put it on speaker."

He glared but pressed the speaker button. When he finished, he ended the call and stared at me like a dog awaiting praise. He'd be waiting a long time.

"Thirdly, you agree to keep the children as your beneficiaries. You will *NOT* attempt to cut them out of their inheritance, even if you decide to marry that empty-headed nitwit."

He frowned and stared at me so long I thought this would be the deal breaker, but he eventually agreed and nodded his consent to my terms.

"Good. Now you can go. I'll take care of everything."

He stuttered, but eventually shrugged, turned, and walked out.

After he left, Dixie and the poodles returned. "Is everything okay?"

I nodded. "Yes, but we have a party to plan."

Dixie looked as though she thought I'd lost my mind.

"It's Stephanie's *bisnonna*'s birthday."

"What the heck is a *bisnonna*?"

I smiled. "It's Italian for great-grandmother. *Nonna* is grandmother, and *bisnonna* is great-grandmother."

We left the poodles in the RV and went to the store. Under normal circumstances, I would have spent all day slaving over a hot stove to make a home-cooked meal for Albert and his family. However, these weren't normal circumstances, and time wasn't on my side.

I picked up the telephone and ordered food from my favorite Italian restaurant, Café Roma's. Lasagna, chicken parmesan, Caesar salad, and garlic bread for a small army would be ready for pickup in three hours. I called Mama Adamo's Bakery and had a large sheet cake with strawberry filling and *Happy Birthday, Nonna* written on top. I went to the deli and got fruit trays, vegetable trays, wieners, and dip, and my last trip was to the liquor store for several nice bottles of wine and a few nonalcoholic beverages for the children. By the time we finished shopping and got home, we had just enough time to get everything set up and ready to go before the guests arrived.

Stephanie took the train home and arrived just before the first guest. She served as hostess, while I ran upstairs to shower and dress, and Dixie grabbed her toiletries from the RV and got prettied up.

When I had showered and refreshed, I came down to the party. I grabbed a glass of wine from a tray near the living room and took a sip as I looked around. The majority of those present were Albert's relatives. I was an only child, and my parents were both dead, so my family tree was pretty barren. Albert was one of three children. His parents were good Italian Catholics and had tried to do their part to procreate and replenish the earth, but his mother had been forced to stop after three children. At least that was what she said to me when I told her I had no intention of having more than two children after David was born.

Albert's mother, Camilia Conti, was a petite woman with unnaturally black hair. She had fallen in love with Albert's father, Darren Echosby, an American in the military, after World War II. He died mysteriously not long after they were married and was seldom spoken about. Her current husband, Lorenzo Conti, was a small, quiet man who seldom spoke but made up for it in drinking and smoking.

Dixie and Stephanie spotted me leaning against the wall and came and stood on either side of me. Stephanie put her arm around my waist and leaned close. "Mom, I don't want you to freak out or anything, but..."

She inclined her head slightly to a corner of the room.

I followed the direction of her head and nearly choked when I saw the bimbo, dressed in a skintight, body-hugging dress that left nothing to the imagination, wrapped around Albert. I nearly dropped my glass and came very close to letting out a shriek and lunging for her. Had it not been for

Dixie and Stephanie, I might have embarrassed myself by throttling the hussy in front of a room full of people.

"He brought that…floozy into our house?"

Dixie and Stephanie continued to whisper in my ear, all the while using their bodies to restrain me from murder.

"Honey, I know you have to be furious, but now is not the time to show it. That's what he wants you to do."

I downed the glass of wine my daughter handed me in one large gulp. Part of me wanted to cry, while another part wanted to beat the living daylights out of Albert and his tart, but I knew Stephanie and Dixie were right. Now wasn't the time. Instead, I took a deep breath, held it for as long as I could, and released it. I tried to remember the breathing exercises from Lamaze decades ago, but frankly, the deep breathing hadn't worked to distract me from the pain back then, and it wasn't working now.

"I'm okay."

I tried to put on a fake smile, but it must have come across as more of a grimace, because neither Dixie nor Stephanie looked convinced.

"Mom, there's more."

I tried to wrap my head around the idea of what could be worse than my husband bringing his girlfriend into the home where we had raised our children in the middle of a gathering of his relatives. "Am I dying?"

"No, but—" Dixie never got to finish that sentence, because my mother-in-law walked up.

"I always had a feeling something was a bit off with you." She shrugged. "When Alberto first told me, it took me a minute to adjust, but I say live and let live." She grabbed me by the shoulders, pulled me close, and kissed me on each cheek. "Love is love, right?"

I stood ramrod-straight in a state of shock. Albert and I had been married for more than twenty-five years, and this was only the third time my mother-in-law, a normally very demonstrative woman, had hugged me. The other two times were at the births of each of my children.

When the shock wore off, I was dazed. "What just happened?"

"That's what I was getting ready to tell you," Dixie whispered.

I waited, but her courage must have failed. She looked at Stephanie. "Maybe you should tell her."

"Tell me what?"

Stephanie grabbed another glass of wine and handed it to me. Then she took a deep breath. "Apparently Dad told everyone the reason you two are getting divorced is because you're a lesbian."

I stared at Stephanie and then Dixie.

"Don't look at me. Apparently, I'm your 'partner'." Her lips twitched, and I could tell by the way her eyes twinkled she was a few seconds away from bursting out in laughter.

"Excuse me." I waltzed around the large crowd of in-laws, neighbors, and friends, and cornered Albert. "Could I see you in the other room?" I didn't wait for his reply, but turned and walked out of the room, marched upstairs to the master bedroom, and waited. A few moments later, Albert came in behind me, and I slammed the door. "Can you please explain to me why your mother thinks I'm a lesbian?"

A flush of red went up his neck. "You told me I had to tell my family about the divorce."

I stared at him, waiting to hear how he planned to connect the dots to explain how *his* leaving *me* for another woman translated into *me* being *gay*.

He pulled at the neck of his shirt. "Well, I had to come up with a reason, and this seemed like a good way to explain things." He hemmed and hawed and stuttered. "I mean, what difference does it make to you what my family thinks? You weren't planning on seeing them again. Plus, you're the one who's all *equal rights for everyone*." He used air quotes. "I don't see why you're so upset."

I hadn't realized my mouth was open until I got a look at myself in the bureau mirror. "Do you really not get why I'm upset?" I took several deep breaths. "I'm not gay."

"So?" He sat down on the bed. "I don't get why it matters."

"It matters because you're not taking ownership for your adulterous relationship, and instead you're shifting blame for the dissolution of our marriage onto me. This is not about equality or gay rights, which, by the way, I support. This is about you not being man enough to tell your mother the truth. *You* cheated on me with that skinny bimbo. *You* broke your marriage vows. And *you* are shifting the responsibility for the divorce onto me." I was practically screaming.

"Shush. Keep your voice down."

"I will not be shushed in my own house." I picked up a bottle of perfume on the bureau and flung it as hard as I could at Albert's head. Unfortunately, he ducked and the bottle hit the wall and shattered.

"You're crazy. You could have killed me."

"You're right. I am crazy." There was a line of perfume bottles, jewelry boxes, and other objects atop the bureau, and I picked up each one and flung it at Albert, who was now standing against the bedroom wall, dodging flying objects. "I was crazy to have married you. I was crazy to have stayed married to you for twenty-five years. I was crazy to have believed you when you said you were working late at the office all of those nights." I flung the last object, which missed Albert but went flying through the window.

The bedroom door opened, and Stephanie and Dixie rushed inside.

"Mom, are you okay?"

The anger that had fueled my screaming, object-flinging tirade was spent, and I suddenly felt tired. I slumped down onto the bed. "Get out."

Albert didn't budge. He looked at me and then looked at Dixie. "This is all your fault. She was perfectly fine until you came up here with your killer poodles and your guns and started putting ideas in her head."

"Why, you lily-livered, bald-faced, two-timing sleazeball. I have half a mind to—"

We never found out what Dixie had half a mind to do, because, at that moment, the bimbo walked in.

"Al, are you going to be much longer? There's a weird man downstairs in a wheelchair who's giving me the creeps."

"That's Mr. Hurston. He lives next door," Stephanie said. "He doesn't get out much, so we always invite him over whenever we have parties." She looked from Bambi to me. "Why am I explaining this to her?"

Bambi walked into the bedroom and frowned at the smell from all of the broken perfume bottles. "We're going to have to redecorate. I hate all this. It looks like *old people* furniture. We're going to need new carpet in this room."

Stephanie looked as though she wanted to strangle Bambi, but I held up a hand to stop her.

"Get out." My words were steel. Firm, cold, and solid.

Whether it was the look in my eyes or the tone of my voice, I don't know. Whatever it was, Albert didn't argue. He grabbed Bambi by the arm and propelled her toward the door. He stopped only to reach into his jacket and pull out an envelope, which he placed in my purse, which was open and sitting on the dresser. Then they left.

Albert always thought money could buy him out of all of his problems, but I wasn't in the mood to fight. Miss Florrie was right. You had to pick your battles, and teaching my soon-to-be ex-husband that money couldn't buy everything was a lesson that would have to wait until another day. I was a limp dishcloth. I sat slumped over on the edge of the bed, all my energy spent.

I could feel the looks Dixie and Stephanie exchanged. Both of them sat down on either side of me and engulfed me in their arms. I felt their love and support surrounding and supporting me. I had no idea how long we sat like that—moments or hours, I couldn't say. I felt hollow inside.

Mentally, I drifted through the last twenty-five years. I acknowledged the good times, along with the not-so-good ones. Then I closed the door on that part of my life. No tears. Miss Florrie was right; those were too precious to waste on the likes of Albert.

My stomach growled, and I realized I hadn't eaten since the early morning.

Stephanie laughed. "You okay, Mom?"

I reached over and gave her a squeeze. "I'm going to be just fine." I stood up. "Now, let's go downstairs and get some food before those vultures devour everything."

We went downstairs. Most of the people were gone, along with the majority of the food. There were red stains on the carpet, which looked a lot like blood, but were most likely lasagna and red wine. For a brief moment, I was tempted to get the hydrogen peroxide and begin the process of treating the stains. Then I remembered Bambi's comments about redecorating and new carpet and stopped myself. No way was I cleaning the carpet for her.

Two of Albert's brothers, along with one nephew, were watching a baseball game on the television. Their wives were sitting in the kitchen, and children were running around everywhere.

I walked into the living room, picked up the remote, and turned off the television.

Their faces reflected confusion and thunderous clouds of rage. How dare I turn off the television in the middle of a game! Never mind the fact that it was my television, my remote, and my home, at least for a few more weeks anyway.

I held up a hand and announced loud enough for the wives in the other room to hear. "I have an announcement to make."

Gino, Albert's youngest brother, said, "Can it wait until after the game?" Gino was short but worked out, so he was very muscular. He liked to wear tight shirts, which emphasized his physique, and tight pants, to emphasize other areas of his anatomy. He had thick dark hair, dark eyes, and a dark complexion. He was a rogue. He enjoyed looking at himself and believed he was irresistible to women. Unfortunately, he also liked to wear a lot of cologne, which brought tears to my eyes.

"No, it cannot wait."

He rolled his eyes and waved his hand in a royal gesture. "Alright, get on with it. We're missing the game."

The wives came into the living room and stood by, looking at me, waiting for my announcement.

"Albert is having an affair with that twenty-year-old child he brought to the party. We're getting a divorce. I don't know what he's told you, and frankly, I don't really care. This party was a farce, and it's over." I walked to the front door and opened it. "So, I want all of you to leave now."

The room was silent, and no one moved for several seconds.

Eventually, Gino stood up. "Look, I'm real sorry things didn't work out between you and Albert, and if what you say is true, then that's really bad. But this is the playoffs. Why don't you go in the kitchen and take a load off?" He looked around for his wife, Angela. "Angela, take Lilly into the kitchen." He reached for the remote.

I snatched the remote from his hand. "I don't need to 'sit down and take a load off.' What I need is for you"—I looked around—"all of you, to leave my house right now." I marched back to the door. "Get out."

Gino stared for a few seconds, but then walked to the door. "Come on. We can watch the game at my house." He walked to the door, stopped in front of me, as if he was going to speak, but then apparently thought better of it and left.

The others followed and, within seconds, my house was empty, except for Dixie, Stephanie, and me. When the last guest left, I closed the door and heaved a heavy sigh of relief.

"Wow." Awe was reflected in Dixie's eyes. "That was amazing."

I chuckled, slightly embarrassed.

"That really was amazing, Mom." Stephanie kissed my cheek. "You're a lot stronger than I thought."

"I'm stronger than I thought I was too." I stared at the mess. "Now, let's eat."

Dixie went out to check on the dogs. She'd left them in the RV while we shopped and prepared for the party. I'd checked out her RV earlier, and it was actually nicer than my house. This was no ordinary RV. There was satellite television, granite countertops, air-conditioning, a shower, and every amenity known to man. Her RV was spacious and well-appointed. Aggie would be fine in that RV. My only question was if she'd want to lower her standards to living in whatever quarters I found for us.

I knew my in-laws well enough to realize there wouldn't be much food, if any left. Like buzzards, they'd picked clean everything that was placed out for public consumption. Not an olive or celery stick did they leave. While I hadn't seen them do it, I suspected they had wrapped up plates of food and taken it home with them. Twenty-five years had taught me to be prepared. I went downstairs and came back with a small tray of untouched food. I had held back lasagna, salad, chicken parmesan, and wine.

"You're a magician. Where were you hiding that?"

I smiled. "Stephanie's dorm refrigerator from when she was in college is downstairs."

Stephanie grabbed plates, glasses, and silverware. "Mom made this ingenious front that conceals the fridge. It looks like a wood file cabinet, but it's really hiding a fridge."

I smiled. "I found it on Pinterest."

We sat down and enjoyed a good meal with good food, good wine, and good company. The only spoiler came when my cell phone rang. I looked at the phone. "It's Albert."

"Don't answer it," Dixie said.

I was sure Albert had heard about the announcement I'd made to Gino and his other family members. He would be angry I didn't support his lies and hadn't allowed him to shift the responsibility for our divorce to me. However, that was something he'd have to deal with on his own. I let the call roll to voice mail and turned off my phone.

I went to bed and slept well. All of the tension and pent-up emotion of the past few months drifted away, like sand washed away by the tide.

I awoke refreshed and energized. After a shower, I felt ready to leave everything behind and start my new life. In fact, I even brought my suitcase upstairs from the basement. I was determined that when Dixie left at the end of the week, I would go with her.

I shared my thoughts with Dixie and Stephanie at breakfast, and they both agreed it sounded like a good plan.

"I have some boxes downstairs." I turned to Dixie.

"I'll bring them up." She hopped up and went downstairs.

Stephanie sat at the table for several minutes and stared into her cup of coffee.

"What's bothering you?"

Stephanie shook her head. "What makes you think..." She turned and stared at me.

The look on my face was one I'd honed over two decades of motherhood. It said, "*I'm your mother.*" It stopped her protest without me speaking a single word.

"Okay, something is bothering me, but I don't know what it means. It may not mean anything."

"Do you want to talk about it?"

She hesitated, but eventually took a deep breath. "It's just something that happened with Mr. Nelson." She looked down. "How well do you know him?"

I raised an eyebrow and tilted my head to the side. I had suspected her concern was related to her father bringing his girlfriend to her office, so this question took me by surprise. I wasn't expecting anything to do with Albert's attorney, Charles Nelson. I thought for a moment. "We've known Charles and his wife, Marilyn, for years. You know that."

She nodded. "I know they went to St. Adalbert's Parish and that he's been Dad's attorney for several years, but I mean, how well do you *know* him?"

I thought about the question. "We weren't what you would call '*close*' friends, if that's what you mean. We never hung in the same circles. They were way out of our league. Custom-made clothes, and they lived in that big house on Lake Michigan. They traveled to Monte Carlo, Paris, and the Riviera, and spent winters in south Florida. They were the jet-set crowd."

"That's what I remember too. They had one son."

"Charles Nelson the III."

"Chip." Stephanie smiled. "He used to drive a Porsche in high school and had pool parties I heard were alcohol and drug buffets."

"I had no idea. Why didn't you tell me?"

"Mom, I didn't go to those parties. He was out of my league too, but just because I didn't go to the parties didn't mean I was going to rat on him." She took a sip of her coffee. "Besides, I think the Nelsons knew about it." She hesitated for several seconds. "Doesn't it seem odd that Charles Nelson is now Dad's attorney?"

I hadn't given the matter much thought, but I didn't have any answers. I shrugged. "I guess. When your dad expanded his business to include imports, Chip started working at the dealership. Maybe he convinced his dad to represent your father." I thought for a few minutes. "I know Charles went through some difficult times for a while. Gossip around town said he had financial problems. He nearly lost everything a while back, but then he was okay again and back at the yacht club and country club and flying around the world."

"Do you remember when that was?"

I pondered. "About a year ago, I think." I stared closely at my daughter. "What's really going on?"

Stephanie looked thoughtful. "He's a big, well-known attorney. He graduated from Yale. It's just that he's made some rookie mistakes I wouldn't have expected of someone who's been a lawyer for as long as he has."

"Maybe it's old age."

"Maybe." Stephanie shrugged. "Come on. We have work to do."

* * * *

We sorted through the million items accumulated over the years. As far as I was concerned, Albert could have the furniture, appliances, and the *things*. Most of the items were his taste and not my own anyway. Stephanie argued it would be expensive to start over from scratch, but I didn't care. Paying to haul items across the country I didn't love was a price greater than any amount of money.

By lunchtime we had created pretty decent piles of items for charity, items for trash, and items that would remain with the house. The things that mattered most to me were pictures of the children, homemade cards, and other items given for Mother's Day, Christmas, and birthdays. I spent a great deal of time reading through those cards and reliving the moments that mattered most in my life. The doorbell pulled me away from memory lane.

When I opened the door and saw two policemen standing on my porch, my legs turned to Jell-O, and my heart raced. I gripped the doorknob to keep from falling.

"Mrs. Albert Echosby?" the uniformed officer with piercing blue eyes and a five-o'clock shadow asked.

"Oh God, please don't let it be David."

"Who's David?" The short, stout officer with curly red hair, light gray eyes, and freckles exchanged glances with the first officer.

"My son," I whispered.

"May we come in?" Blue Eyes asked.

I moved aside and they entered, but I couldn't walk and stayed rooted to the spot, my grip tight on the doorknob.

"Mrs. Echosby, we're sorry to inform you that your husband, Albert Echosby, is dead."

CHAPTER 3

Relief at not hearing my son's name come out of their mouths superseded all other emotions, common sense, and propriety. The pounding of my heart slowed, and the blood that rushed to my ears stopped. I released the breath I had been holding and slid down. I would have collapsed onto the floor if Blue Eyes hadn't rushed to my side and caught me before I hit the ground.

"Mom!" Stephanie chose that moment to walk into the living room and saw me supported by the police. She rushed to me. "Mom, what happened?"

Something rose inside me and erupted. Before I realized what was happening, I was laughing hysterically.

"I think we should call for an ambulance," the redheaded policeman said.

"Why? What have you done to my mom?"

"Nothing," Blue Eyes said. "I think she's in shock."

I shook my head but couldn't stop laughing, no matter how hard I tried. Nevertheless, I pointed at the sofa.

Blue Eyes helped me to the sofa and I sat down.

Stephanie, normally so cool, calm, and collected, looked frazzled. Her eyes darted, and her skin looked pale. There was a slight tremor in her voice when she spoke, and her voice was a couple of octaves higher than normal. She was scared, and why wouldn't she be? Two uniformed policemen were standing in the living room and her mom was hysterical. For an instant, she swayed as though she might fall, and Blue Eyes instinctively reached out for her. But Stephanie was tough. She waved off Blue Eyes and yelled, "Aunt Dixie!"

Dixie came into the room and, in pure Dixie-like fashion, quickly assessed the situation. After a moment, she walked to the sofa where

I sat, still laughing uncontrollably, reached back, and slapped me hard across the face.

Whether due to the shock of being hit or the pain of the blow, it worked, and I stopped laughing.

"Put your head down between your legs." Dixie didn't bother waiting for compliance but pushed my head down so the blood rushed to my head. She held the back of my head down.

After a few moments, I swatted away her hand and sat up. "I'm okay."

Stephanie collapsed onto the sofa next to me.

I wrapped my arms around my daughter and gave her a tight squeeze. "I'm sorry. I don't know what came over me."

The two officers stood awkwardly and watched for several seconds.

Dixie plopped down into a chair. "I wish someone would tell me what's going on."

Blue Eyes looked at her. "Are you a member of the fam—"

"Yes. This is my sister."

Despite the stony façade, which hid all emotions, Blue Eyes raised one eyebrow and stared.

I held my ground and refused to allow his uplifted eyebrow to force me to confess I was lying about Dixie's relationship.

Stephanie had recovered herself and put on her lawyer's cap. "What can we do for you, officers?"

The officers exchanged a brief glance.

Whether by mental telepathy or prior consent, Blue Eyes took the lead. "We're sorry to have to inform you that Albert Echosby was found dead this morning."

"Dead? He can't be dead. He was just here last night." In my mind, I knew the two facts had no correlation, but my logic didn't seem to be working very well at the moment.

Stephanie gasped and merely stared at the officers.

Dixie was the only one whose brain cells were firing on all cylinders. She asked the questions Stephanie and I were too stunned to ask. "How did it happen? Was it a heart attack?"

"Did he have a bad heart?" Redhead asked.

"Hell if I know." Dixie turned to me.

I shook my head. "I don't think so. He never mentioned it, but I suppose he could have." I looked at Stephanie.

She shook her head and whispered, "He never said."

"Did you ask his tart…ah, I mean, his girlfriend?" Dixie asked.

The officers hadn't missed her slip. I could tell by the quick glance they gave each other.

"How did he die?" Stephanie asked.

"He was shot," Blue Eyes said. "I have to ask if you know of anyone who wanted to see your husband dead?"

The irony of the question didn't escape me. "You mean, other than me?" I asked, with only the slightest bit of hysteria in my raised voice.

"Mom, don't say anything else." Stephanie stood up and squared her shoulders. "Officers, thank you for coming here to tell us about my father's death." She walked to the door. "However, unless you have a warrant, I'm going to ask you to leave and allow us to grieve in peace."

The officers exchanged looks but then walked toward the door. Before Blue Eyes got to the door, he stopped at a bureau and made a point of looking at one of the red marinara/red wine stains on the carpet. He turned and looked at me.

I started to explain about the party, but Stephanie held up a hand for silence and opened the door wider. The redheaded officer left and Blue Eyes followed.

Before Stephanie could close the door, Blue Eyes stepped back toward the door and handed her a card. "We will need a statement from each of you, eventually. In the meantime, if you think of anything that will aid in finding the person who murdered Mr. Echosby, please call."

Stephanie took the card but didn't say a word.

After a hesitation, Blue Eyes walked out and Stephanie closed the door.

We sat in stunned silence for so long the sun set and the dogs came in search of the kibble provider.

Dixie got up and flipped on the lamp. "I'm going to take the dogs out, and then I'll make something for you two to eat."

Stephanie and I started to protest, but Dixie held up a hand. "You're going to have to eat sooner or later, and cooking will give me something to do." She attached leashes to all three dogs and left.

Stephanie and I sat for a few moments.

"I can't believe he's dead." She shook her head.

I hugged her and she rested her head on my shoulder. "I know, dear. It's such a shock."

"I can't imagine what Nonna Conti must be going through." She turned to face me. "Do you think we should call?"

I thought for a few moments. "Maybe you should call. Find out if they need anything."

Stephanie pulled out her cell phone and dialed the number.

I only heard one side of the conversation, which was even more limited because she wasn't allowed to complete her sentences without interruption. After a few moments, she hung up and turned to me. The color had drained from her face. "She said, according to Bambi, they surprised a burglar and he shot Dad and took off."

"I wonder why the police didn't mention that."

She shrugged. "According to Aunt Angela, Nonna Conti is hysterical. The doctor had to sedate her. All of the uncles are at the house." Stephanie hesitated. "She wants *me* to come over."

I noted the emphasis on the singular word. "But not me?"

Stephanie blushed.

"It's okay, honey. It would be awkward if I was there, given the state of things," I reassured her. "I think you should go. They may need you."

Stephanie protested, but I convinced her that being confined in a house with my in-laws, whom I didn't like under the best of circumstances, was the last thing I wanted. Eventually, she agreed and left to console the family.

I called my son, David, and gave him the bad news. At twenty-three, David was two years younger than Stephanie. From the time he was a small child, he'd dreamed of being an actor. When he graduated from high school, he moved to New York and enrolled in the American Academy of Dramatic Arts. Albert was dead-set against it, and he and David had many battles. I found myself in the middle, trying to keep the peace. Albert quoted statistic after statistic about the odds of making it as an actor. Nothing swayed David's resolve and determination. In fact, I admired how determined he was to pursue his dream. In the end, Albert agreed to pay for college and two years' living expenses for him to break into the business. David wasn't really concerned about college or his father's feelings. He was determined to move to New York with or without his father's blessing or his money. As it turned out, David excelled in New York. He finished college, landed a role in a Broadway musical, and had been touring the world for close to a year. I wasn't sure what angered Albert most, the fact that David had proved him wrong or the fact that he was succeeding in his chosen career.

David was as shocked about the murder as the rest of us. He was going to make arrangements to fly home, but I suggested he wait until we knew more details about the funeral arrangements. I wasn't sure how long it would take the police to release the body, so there was no point in him coming back until we knew more. I promised to keep him informed as soon as I knew something.

Dixie made grilled cheese sandwiches. I didn't realize how hungry I was until I smelled them cooking. We sat and ate soup from a can and gooey grilled cheese after Stephanie left.

"You wanna talk?" Dixie asked.

I sighed. "I don't know. I don't know what I want to do."

The poodles had already eaten and were stretched out on the floor, all except Aggie, who was curled up in my lap.

I looked down at the sleeping dogs and wished I could lie down and sleep with the same type of careless abandon. They didn't worry where they would sleep tomorrow or pace the floor wondering if they would be able to afford any more kibble. "Why is their hair in those wrappers?"

"I do it to protect their coat." Dixie stared at the dogs. "Actually, I just finished their titles, so I could take the wrappers off and shave them down." She shrugged. "I hadn't decided whether I was going to go for their Grand Champion title or not, and there's another specialty show in Nashville next month."

"I have no idea what you just said."

Dixie smiled. "I show my dogs in conformation. That's where the dogs are judged on how well they measure up to the breed standard. It's basically to determine if they would make good breeding stock. So, all dogs entered must be intact, not spayed or neutered, and are shown in full coat."

I must have looked puzzled because she continued. "Have you ever watched the Westminster Dog Show on television?"

"Of course."

"That's conformation."

"Okay. What other types of shows are there?"

"Loads. There are performance events, like Obedience, where dogs demonstrate how well they can follow commands like heeling. There's Agility, which is the obstacle course where dogs have to perform various activities like jumping, going through tunnels, or climbing a dog walk. Agility measures speed and accuracy, and then there's Rally Obedience, which is kind of a combination of the two. Herding, Sled Dog Racing, Tracking…there are tons of other events I can't even remember. There's even Dancing."

"Dancing?" I raised an eyebrow. "You have got to be kidding me."

She laughed. "No, it's wonderful. They call it Canine Freestyle." She pulled her cell phone up. "You should Google it." She typed and then made a few swipes and handed me her phone.

I watched in stunned silence while a woman and her golden retriever performed to "You're the One That I Want" from *Grease*. It was amazing watching the woman spin and turn while her dog pranced alongside. "That was amazing. Do you do that?"

She smiled. "Honey, I can barely dance with Beau without stepping on his toes. I certainly couldn't do anything like that." She pointed to the phone. "But I am planning to try Obedience and possibly Agility when we're done with Conformation."

"Can you do more than one at a time?"

"Oh yes. Most of my friends at the East Tennessee Dog Club do lots of different things. It can take years to get a title, if at all."

I thought about what Dixie said and scratched Aggie behind the ears. "What do you think I should do with her?"

She shrugged. "Whatever you want. I will say that Conformation will be challenging. You don't have her AKC paperwork. There are other registries, like the United Kennel Club, that are a little easier to register with than the AKC, but I don't think you would enjoy Conformation. I would recommend Obedience and maybe Agility. Those are fun. You can also do Canine Good Citizen and Therapy Dog. That's a test you can take, and then your dog is certified and can go to nursing homes and hospitals."

"Sounds like something I'd like."

Dixie looked at me. "Now, are you ready to address the elephant in the room, or are we going to continue avoiding the subject of who shot your husband?" She tilted her head and looked at me.

I scratched Aggie behind her ear and avoided eye contact. "I don't know what to say."

"How are you feeling?" She reached across and grabbed one of my hands.

"I don't know. I feel cold. I don't feel anything inside. My mind has gone through so many emotions in the past two days that I don't know if I have anything left. I think I've depleted my supply."

She squeezed my hand. "You've had a lot of shock and gone through the gamut of emotions."

"I think I feel angry more than anything. He turned my life upside down and then he just dies and moves on, and now I have to figure out how to deal with this mess. When he was alive, I felt angry, but now I feel guilty for feeling angry, and then I feel bad."

"Honey, it's okay. There are no right or wrong emotions. You feel how you feel."

"It's like he drops a bomb and blows up everything and then dies and leaves me to figure out how to put the pieces back together. I don't even know if I should go to the funeral. Technically, we're still married. We were in the process of getting a divorce, but since it wasn't finalized yet, I don't know what my role is anymore."

"Your role is to take care of your children and yourself. Everything else will work itself out." She squeezed my hand again.

My cell phone rang. I took it out of my pocket and looked at the screen to read the name of the caller, then dropped the phone on the table when Albert's picture appeared. Why was my dead husband calling me from the grave?

CHAPTER 4

Dixie reached over and picked up the phone. "Hello."

She listened for a few seconds and then handed the phone to me and mouthed, "Bambi."

I took the phone and tried to regulate my breathing, which had become labored. "Hello."

"What am I supposed to do for money?"

"Excuse me?"

"I'm sure you had something to do with notifying the bank that Albert was dead. You couldn't even wait until the funeral? Now the bank has frozen his account and won't let me withdraw money. How am I supposed to live?"

I pulled the phone away from my ear and pushed the speaker button so Dixie could hear as Bambi rambled on about how she needed money and that it was my fault she couldn't withdraw anything from the bank. I looked up from the phone and saw a look of utter disgust on Dixie's face, which I suspected mirrored my own. After a few seconds, I pressed the button to disconnect the call.

"You have got to be kidding me!" Dixie said.

"I couldn't make this stuff up if I tried."

We stared at each other for several seconds and then burst into laughter.

"Do you think it was just a burglary gone bad?" Dixie asked.

I shrugged. "I have no idea. I mean, the police didn't really explain any details. All we know is what Stephanie found out, and I don't know how much faith we can place in that."

"Why not?"

"Albert's family is biased. He could do no wrong, as far as his family was concerned."

Dixie got up and headed to the cabinet. "Do you want coffee?"

I shook my head. "No, but I could use a glass of wine. You get the glasses, and I'll get a bottle."

Dixie smiled. "Sounds good to me." She returned the coffee mugs to the cabinet, got out two wineglasses, and placed them on the table.

I went downstairs and took a bottle of wine out of the refrigerator. I headed for the stairs but stopped and headed for the washer and dryer instead. I might as well do a load of laundry while I was down here. I made a mental note that my next house would have a washer and dryer on the same level as the bedrooms. As I transferred clothes to the dryer and loaded the washer, I thought about how long my list for changes to the new house had become. I wanted a garage attached to the house so I wasn't juggling my purse, an umbrella, and the groceries on rainy days. I wanted a fence for Aggie and a master bath that was large enough to move around in. Although, now that I was single, or a widow, or whatever I was, the size of the master bathroom wouldn't be an issue. I would be the only person using it. That thought put a smile on my face for a few seconds, but then I remembered what had happened to Albert and smiling seemed wrong, so I stopped.

I was on my way upstairs with my bottle of wine when I noticed that one of the basement windows was open. That was strange. We never opened the basement windows. I was too afraid mice would get inside. I went over to the window and closed it.

"Hey, did you get lost?" Dixie yelled from the top of the stairs.

"Coming." I hurried up the stairs.

"Your next-door neighbor came by."

Dixie pointed to a brownish mass in a round pie tin. I stared at the mass for several seconds and then looked up. "What is it?"

She shrugged. "She said it was rhubarb pie."

We both stared at the "pie." I took a fork and poked at the top, but the fork wasn't able to penetrate the hard outer shell. "Let me guess, small, petite woman with bright orange hair?"

Dixie nodded.

There was a blue willow plate under the pie tin, and when I picked it up, I nearly dropped the entire thing due to the unexpected weight. "Oh my God, that must weigh at least five pounds."

Dixie nodded. "You could use it as a boat anchor."

I put down the bottle of wine and used both hands to lift the pie tin, making sure to leave the plate on the counter. Carried the entire thing to the garbage can and dropped it in. I opened a cabinet and located an empty pie tin that matched the size of the one I trashed and placed it on the empty plate.

"You've done this before, I see."

"It's a wonder her brother has survived as long as he has."

"Maybe he doesn't eat it?"

I shrugged. "I take food over once a week, usually on Sundays. I think he also gets meals delivered from the Lighthouse Dunes Senior Citizens Center."

Dixie uncorked the wine and filled our glasses.

I pulled a bag from the freezer.

"Are those scones?" Dixie craned her neck to get a better look at the treats.

I nodded. "Yep. I made them myself."

"I never knew you could freeze them."

"I didn't either until I went to my favorite tea shop and bought a bag." I pulled a jar of Double Devon cream from the cabinet and ran the lid under the hot water to loosen it. It worked like a charm and when I twisted, I heard the seal pop and the lid came off easily. I put the cream and strawberry preserves on the table. In ninety seconds, the scones were ready. I put them on the table, and we sat down to scones and wine.

Dixie slathered Double Devon cream and strawberry preserves on her scone and took a large bite. She moaned as she chewed and closed her eyes. When she swallowed, she sighed.

We did a semester abroad in college and discovered the joys of real scones and clotted cream in a small tea shop on a back street in England. We'd been hooked on the delicacy from that point forward.

Dixie ate two scones before she spoke. "I can't tell you the last time I've had a scone with clotted cream." She licked the gooey cream from her fingers. "I can't believe you can get clotted cream in Lighthouse Dunes, Indiana."

"I found the recipe for the scones online. Then I found a little store by the lakeshore run by a British expat who orders it for me." I looked at the jar. "It's not the real stuff, but it's close enough for my taste." I finished my scone, then followed Dixie's example and licked my fingers. "It lasts for a long time if you don't open the jar. Once you open it, then you really need to finish it quickly."

Dixie looked at me with a sly grin. "Well, maybe we should finish this jar off. We wouldn't want it to go to waste."

I got up, pulled the rest of the scones out of the freezer, and nuked them in the microwave and we finished off four scones each and the jar of Double Devon cream.

Dixie stretched. "I'm stuffed like a turkey ready for Thanksgiving."

I smiled. I'd missed my friend and her quaint southern idioms.

"Now, back to your husband. Did you notice the way that police officer with the blue eyes stared at that marinara stain on your carpet?"

I nodded. "I wondered about that. He can't believe Albert was shot here and then dragged back to wherever he and the bimbo are staying."

"Not if it was a burglary."

I sipped my wine. "We don't know for sure it was a burglary. I mean, all we have is Bambi's word on that."

"Why would she lie?"

I shook my head. "No idea. It just seems odd that they surprised a burglar and he shoots Albert, and that's it. I mean, don't thieves usually stick to stealing? Besides, what was he trying to take? And why would the police come here asking questions?"

"Maybe the thieves thought they had a lot of money. I mean Albert owned a used car business."

I nodded. "Bambi mentioned waiting for him in the '*Vette* too." I tried to keep the bitterness out of my voice, but the wine had dissolved my filter. "He never let me drive anything as nice as a Corvette. I have a twelve-year-old Honda CRV with over two hundred thousand miles on it."

"The dirty dog."

I nodded. "Although I love my CRV. It's gotten me through many winter snowstorms without so much as a stutter. New tires and brakes are about the only things it's really needed."

Dixie patted my hand. "That's not the point."

I nodded. "I know." I looked up. "Oh my goodness, I just thought about the car lot. Somebody will need to make sure everything is taken care of there."

"Today is Sunday. We can go and check on things tomorrow."

Dixie and I stayed up late talking. We exhausted our brains about Albert's shooting and moved on to other topics. Neither of us spoke the reason for the late-night chat out loud, but the way we took turns looking at the time in between yawns spoke volumes. When Stephanie finally unlocked the door, we both breathed a sigh of relief.

"You didn't have to wait up." She flopped down next to me on the sofa.

"Who says I was waiting up?" I tried to smile, but my face wouldn't cooperate. Even without a mirror, I knew I had failed.

Stephanie raised her eyebrow and stared at me until I relented.

"Alright, I was waiting up, but I'm your mom and I'm entitled to worry."

Dixie nodded. "Yep. It's in the motherhood handbook."

Stephanie laughed. "There's a handbook?"

"Oh yes. It's like the president's book of secrets. You know, the one passed down from one president to the other that tells them what's really in Area Fifty-One and how to use the secret tunnels to sneak out without being seen by the Secret Service," I joked.

"Well, you can rest easy. I'm home now." Stephanie laughed but then quickly got serious. "But I'm actually very glad you're up."

I braced myself mentally. I had no idea what she might want to talk about, but I knew there would be some unpleasantness after she'd just spent so much time with my in-laws, especially given the circumstances.

She took a deep breath. "You already know Nonna Conti was so distraught she had to be sedated. Well, Bisnonna wasn't much better. She spoke in Italian the whole time." Stephanie rubbed the back of her neck and arched her back in a way I'd seen her do before when she was under stress. "My Italian isn't very good, but it sounded like she wanted Poppi to go to the head of the family to get revenge." She looked at me. "You don't think she really wants him to go to some mob boss, do you?"

I shook my head. "I doubt very seriously if your grandfather knows any mob bosses," I reassured her, but inside, I knew she was serious.

Stephanie shrugged. "Well, Gino and the other uncles just sat around drinking and talking about..." She looked down and pulled at a nonexistent bit of lint on her pants.

I lifted her chin and looked her in the eyes. "It's okay, honey. I'm sure your uncles and the rest of your father's family blames me. They always have. Albert was perfect in all of their eyes. Now he's dead, I figured they'd find some way to make it my fault."

"That's crazy. If he hadn't been prowling around like a common tomcat looking for a female in heat, he'd have been home where he belonged." Dixie huffed and immediately turned beet red from embarrassment. "I'm sorry. I shouldn't have said that."

"It's okay." I glanced at Stephanie.

"It's okay, Aunt Dixie." She sighed. "He's my dad, and I love him, but he's responsible for his own actions."

"I don't suppose Bambi was there?" I asked.

Stephanie shook her head. "No. Uncle Gino mentioned something about inviting her to come over to be with the family, and Bisnonna put her foot down." She smiled at the recollection. "Angela looked furious when he brought it up."

"Does Angela know her?" I asked.

Stephanie shrugged. "Beats me and, after the way she reacted when Gino mentioned her name, I was afraid to ask."

"Did they discuss funeral arrangements?" I asked.

"Briefly. Bisnonna talked about calling the priest and making arrangements, but I told her that wouldn't be necessary. I told her that was our responsibility. David, me…and you. We are his family and we would make the arrangements."

Stephanie's eyes were as cold as stone, and her chin was set in the rock-solid way that demonstrated her determination. I was certain there was a lot more she could have said, but her silence told me she'd given her arguments and was undeterred by the opposition.

I hugged my daughter tightly. "You're right. It is our responsibility, and we'll take care of it."

She nodded and then stretched. "I've already sent a message to my boss. They told me to take as much time as I need. What did David say?"

I filled her in on the conversation I'd had earlier.

"Tomorrow I'll call the police and find out what we need to do," she said.

"I'll call Father Dominick and make arrangements for the services."

"Look, I've never been politically correct. I'm just a straight shooter, so I need you to be honest. If you want me to leave, I can. I've got the RV and poodles and I can head back to Michigan for my workshop. I don't want to be in the way, but if you need me to stay, then I'll stay. You just tell me what you want."

"I know this isn't a fun trip, but I could use some moral support. I think, by the end of this week, I'll be in desperate need of a friend."

"Then I'll be right here." She smiled and reached over and squeezed my hand.

"Great. I was hoping you'd stay." Stephanie stood up and stretched. "Now I'm going to bed."

Dixie took the dogs outside for one last potty break before bed.

I tossed and turned, unable to get comfortable. After two hours, I got up. I tried not to wake Aggie, who had curled up in the bed next to me, but I had yet to master the skill of getting out of bed with stealth. She got up and stretched several times, her tail wagging a hundred miles a minute. She was a happy dog, and her energy and apparent cheerfulness made me smile. She yawned as though she'd worked a twelve-hour shift. I smiled again as I picked her up and cuddled her closely. I sat in a wingback chair near the window. Dixie had helped me board up the window yesterday, so I wasn't able to look outside. It was still dark outside and there wasn't much to look at anyway, so I didn't bother turning on the lights. Instead, I sat in the chair, cuddled up with my new companion, and tried to sort through my emotions. Part of me felt sad. Albert and I had been married over twenty-five years. He was the father of my children. We'd been through good times and bad. Unfortunately, the bad times outnumbered the good in recent years. I forced myself to think about the good times, the birth of our children and the early days of our marriage. I remembered tender moments, walking hand in hand on the beach, and the long days and nights at the car dealership when it first opened. We'd worked hard to start the business, and our hard work paid off. Albert was a good salesman. Tears flowed down my cheeks as I remembered the good times. I thought about the early years and allowed myself to grieve for what had once been.

Albert had never been exceptionally attractive, but as Dixie once said, he could charm the rattle off a rattlesnake. He was a born salesman; he could sell ice to Eskimos in the middle of a blizzard. Managing the business was where he struggled. Dealing with forms, taxes, legal concerns, and finances were Albert's weaknesses. Fortunately, business, accounting, and numbers were my strength. I used to think, between the two of us, we balanced out. Echosby Cars and Imports became successful. At least I thought it had been successful. If what Albert said in the divorce papers was true, though, business had taken a downturn. Stephanie didn't believe the numbers Albert's lawyer reported, and I hadn't believed them, either. How could business have been so bad? Bambi mentioned waiting for him in *the 'Vette.* Would he have given her a Corvette to drive if business was bad? Recently, he had taken to driving a BMW, but he often drove nicer vehicles on the premise that it was good advertising for his business. I wondered if perhaps the business really *wasn't* doing well. I hadn't done the books for the business for the last few years, but when I went by the dealership later today, I would make a mental note to get on the computer and take a look. I would also contact Father Dominick at the parish and talk about funeral arrangements, and then I would stop by Lighthouse Dunes Funeral Home.

Aggie was so tired she could barely keep her head up. I cuddled her warm little body and sat up watching her sleep until I fell asleep myself.

I awoke the next morning when I heard a light knock on the door.

"Come in."

Dixie opened the door and stuck her head inside. "I was going to take the dogs out and thought I'd take Aggie, too, if she's awake."

Aggie stretched. I didn't trust her to walk without relieving herself on the carpet yet, so I carried her to Dixie. When they left, I got in the shower. I had a headache from the lack of sleep and the strain from the emotional roller coaster of the past few days. Had it only been four days since I'd sat across the table from Albert in Stephanie's office? I sighed and allowed the warm water to massage away the stress of the past few days. I took several deep breaths. I'd need strength and a great deal of coffee to get through the next week.

After the shower, I needed something to boost my self-confidence, so I took extra care in dressing and applying makeup. Chances were good I'd run into Bambi or some member of Albert's family, and I was already vulnerable enough without feeling like an old, washed-up hag.

When I went downstairs, Stephanie was sitting at the kitchen table, drinking a cup of coffee. She'd brought up an old coffeemaker from the basement that brewed a pot rather than individual cups, and she'd replaced the high-tech individual coffeemaker with the old one. I held up the carafe and raised an eyebrow.

"It was easier than constantly getting up to make more."

I nodded and filled a mug. "Did you get any sleep?"

I could tell by her droopy eyelids and the puffy bags underneath her eyes that not only had she not slept well, but she had also been crying.

She shook her head. "No. I gave up trying around four o'clock and came downstairs." There was a pile of old photo albums on the table. She must have been looking through them and crying at what once had been, while I was upstairs doing the same.

I gave her a hug. "Are you hungry?"

She sniffed. "Surprisingly, yes." She smiled and then looked a bit sheepish. "I was just thinking how much I'd love some of your waffles."

"I haven't made waffles in years. I'm not sure where I put the waffle iron." I started to get up.

Stephanie reached down, picked up the large waffle iron, and placed it on the table. She gave me a sly grin. "When I was downstairs getting the old coffeemaker, I found this too."

I laughed. "Well, then I'd better get busy. Why don't you go and get a shower, and I'll have breakfast ready by the time you're done."

She left and I got busy. I fried a pound of bacon and mixed up the batter for waffles. By the time Stephanie came downstairs, Dixie and I were on a second pot of coffee and the bacon and waffles were ready.

We devoured the huge breakfast in silence. As she used her last forkful of waffle to sop up the remaining syrup, Stephanie released a satisfied sigh. "That was delicious."

I smiled. It had been a long time since I'd made breakfast for more than one person. Albert rarely ate at home, preferring to eat with business associates so he could claim them as tax deductions.

"Don't forget to call the police station and find out when they're going to release the..." I hesitated over the impersonal word *body.* Albert had been a living, breathing person, and regardless of his faults, he deserved to be remembered as more than simply a "body."

"It's okay, Mom. You can say it. You taught me to face things head-on." She sat up straight and pushed her shoulders back.

"Your father's remains."

"I already did. I called Officer Harrison earlier." I must have looked puzzled, because she added, "He's the officer who came by yesterday." She looked down and a flush came into her cheeks. She took a drink of coffee.

Dixie smiled. "Was that the one with the deep blue eyes?"

There was a moment of silence, and then Dixie and I burst out laughing.

Stephanie looked at us and then laughed herself. "Alright, that's enough of that." She smiled and then looked serious. "He wants us to come to the station to make a statement. He said the coroner would probably be able to release the body to the funeral home by Wednesday."

I nodded and picked up my cell phone. "I better call Father Dominick." The phone was still turned off from yesterday. Once the phone was on, I noticed I'd had fifteen missed calls and ten voice messages. For a moment, my heart raced. I'd turned off my phone to avoid talking to Albert. What if he'd left me a message? I took a deep breath, turned on the phone's speaker, and listened to each message. Most were from Bambi, continuing to rant about money. She sounded more frantic with each message. One message was from Father Dominick, offering his condolences and stating he would be at the parish later today if we needed anything.

There was a missed call from my mother in-law, with no message, and a call from Gino, asking me to call him first thing, but no messages from Albert. Part of me was relieved, while another part was curious why he'd called in the first place if he wasn't going to bother to leave a message. My brain wrestled with that for several minutes, but no answers came. Eventually, I had to shake it off and move forward.

I called Father Dominick and arranged to meet him at three this afternoon. I called my brother in-law but got his voice mail. I left a message, stating

I'd try him again later. I took a last swig of coffee and braced myself for the call to my mother in-law.

The phone was picked up on the first ring. "Good morn—"

It was clear, very early in the call, that this was not going to be a dialogue, but a monologue, in which my mother in-law screamed, shouted, cried, and then screamed some more. Thankfully, most of the rant was in Italian, so I didn't bother trying to figure out what she was saying. I had a pretty good idea it wasn't complimentary. After the first few seconds, I pressed the mute and the speaker buttons on the phone and placed it on the table.

Dixie, Stephanie, and I stared at each other and waited for the rant to wind down. It took about three minutes before her energy was spent and she ended with a wail and sobs.

I took a deep breath and turned off the mute button. "Camilia, we are going to the parish at three to discuss the arrangements." I hesitated a moment, then shut my eyes and hurried on. "Would you like to come with us? We can come by and pick you—"

She wailed louder and then the phone went silent.

"Camilia, are you there?"

After a few moments, I heard my father in-law's thick Italian accent. "Camilia is very upset. I think it would be best if she rested."

The wailing continued in the background.

He raised his voice to be heard over the noise. "Maybe you call us back a little later. Okay?"

"Okay." I hung up. "He sounds exhausted."

"I can only imagine how hard it must be to lose a child." Dixie shook her head.

Stephanie shook her head. "I hadn't thought about it like that."

"No parent is ever prepared for that." I patted her hand. "That's what keeps me from telling her off. I put myself in her place, and I'd be a basket case if I..." I choked down the tears.

Stephanie gave me a hug.

Dixie got up, grabbed a roll of paper towels, and placed it on the table. "We have to pull ourselves together. There's work to do."

I looked at my watch. "It's nine thirty. I think we should go to the dealership first and then swing by the police station and make our statements. We can grab lunch after that, and then head to St. Adalbert's to meet with Father Dominick."

Everyone agreed, and we headed out.

Highway 2 was the main highway that led into town. If you were traveling from the bigger town of South Bend, you would take Highway

2 west to Lighthouse Dunes. It was a straight shot. For the majority of the route, the two-lane highway was flanked by corn and wheat fields. As the highway led into Lighthouse Dunes, the speed limit decreased, and businesses begin to populate the landscape. Echosby Cars and Imports occupied a large lot just on the outskirts of the highway, which provided good visibility. I pulled my CRV into the back of the lot, behind the office. It was ten and the doors were still locked. I pulled in beside a bright yellow Corvette and then looked over at Dixie in the passenger seat of my Honda.

"Surely she wouldn't be dumb enough…" She shook her head. "Never mind. Apparently, she is."

Stephanie hopped out of the car and marched to the back of the building. Dixie and I hurried after her.

When we got inside, Bambi was in Albert's office at the back of the building. His desk had obviously been rifled through, and papers and drawers were all over the place. However, knowing my husband as I did, I couldn't necessarily blame all of that mess on Bambi. There was a metal lockbox on top of the desk, and Bambi was standing over it with a screwdriver to break the lock. When we flipped on the lights, she had just managed to get the lock open, and she stood there with her purse on the desk and a hand full of cash.

"Drop it," Stephanie yelled.

Bambi looked like a deer caught in the headlights for a split second but then quickly shoved the money into her purse and tried to run. Unfortunately for her, she was wearing a miniskirt and six-inch hooker heels. She tripped over a desk drawer that was on the floor. By the time she regained her footing, Stephanie had pounced on her. She grabbed Bambi's large purse, which left her slightly off balance. One shove and Bambi toppled over, landing on her butt. She scrambled to stand up.

"Sit tight, you dim-witted bimbo, or I'll deflate those weather balloons of yours." Dixie pulled out a large gun and pointed it directly at Bambi. "I've got me a whitetail in my sights, and I'll drop you so fast you won't know what hit you."

Bambi looked up with eyes as large as half dollars. Her mouth open, she sat back down and held up both hands.

Stephanie handed me the business card of the blue-eyed policeman. "Call this number." Stephanie grabbed Bambi's purse. "I'll hold on to the evidence."

I pulled out my cell phone and dialed.

By the time the police arrived, Bambi was a basket case. She had cried and blubbered so much she'd begun to hyperventilate. My fingers itched to slap her as Dixie had me when the police told me Albert was dead, but when I suggested it, she suddenly managed enough control to stop crying and breathe.

Our blue-eyed policeman walked in cautiously, with his hand on his holster. He dropped the cold-as-ice façade enough to permit a twinge to the corner of his lips before hardening his mask.

"They know perfectly well I wasn't stealing that money," Bambi whined.

I started to respond, but it was a lot more fun watching Stephanie and Officer Harrison pick her apart. Dixie and I sat down on the sofa and watched.

Stephanie stood over Bambi, who was now sitting on a chair. "We found you with a screwdriver in your hand, breaking the lock off of the petty cash box and shoving the bills in your purse."

"But I wasn't stealing it."

"What would you call it?"

"Al would have wanted me to have that money. When he was alive, he was always giving me money."

"Did he put that in writing?"

"Well, no, he didn't get a chance to write it down."

"So, in fact, you have no proof he wanted you to have the money, is that right?"

Bambi poked out her lip. "He would have written it down. We were going to be married. We lived together, and that's just like being married. I'm his wife in common."

"How long did you live with Mr. Echosby?" Blue Eyes asked innocently.

"Six months," she said triumphantly.

Blue Eyes said, "Wasn't Mr. Echosby already married?"

"Yeah, but he was getting a divorce." She shot me an angry glare.

"So, he was in no position to marry you because he was already married—and the term you're looking for is *common law wife*." Stephanie paced. "However, I doubt very seriously that any court in this country would consider you his common law wife." She held up her fingers and ticked off each argument. "He already had a wife. You only lived together for six months, when in most cases, couples would need to live together for years. He never referred to you as his wife in front of his friends or family. To the best of my knowledge, and having talked to his attorney just this morning, I know he did not provide any written documents indicating you were his wife, or anything more than his piece of—"

"Stephanie!" I yelled.

"Sorry, Mom."

Bambi's eyes got wider and filled with tears. "But he said he was going to change his insurance and make sure I was taken care of."

"Do you have any proof of that?" Stephanie asked.

Bambi hopped up and stared at me. "This is all your fault."

Officer Harrison had heard enough. He grabbed Bambi by the arm. "I don't think you understand your position."

Bambi looked at him. "Oh, I understand they're trying to cheat me out of the money Al wanted me to have."

Stephanie threw up her hands and walked away.

Officer Harrison spoke slowly, as though talking to a child. "Miss"—he flipped through his notes and hesitated a moment before continuing—"Love."

Dixie punched me in the arm. "You have got to be kidding me, Bambi Love?"

I shook my head in disbelief.

"Miss Love, regardless of what you *think* Mr. Echosby wanted, the bottom line is he's dead. So, unless you can produce some written proof showing you have a legal right to enter this property and take this money, I'm afraid, in the eyes of the law, you are stealing. So, if Mrs. Echosby wants you arrested, there's nothing I can do."

It took a few seconds for the words to sink in, but eventually Bambi realized things didn't look good for her. In a split second, she turned on the waterworks and burst into tears. She leaned against Officer Harrison's chest and cried.

Stephanie looked like she would like nothing better than to take Dixie's gun and shoot Bambi on the spot.

"We're not going to press charges." I suddenly felt tired and old.

"But, Mom, I can't believe you're going to let her go free?" Stephanie pleaded. "With the money."

Bambi stopped bawling and glanced in my direction.

"Let her have the money." I got up and faced her. "On a couple of conditions."

She looked at me. "What?"

"You take the money and go find yourself another meal ticket." I stood inches from her face and looked her dead in the eyes. "You don't come to the funeral. You don't call. You don't bother any members of our family, especially Albert's mother. You disappear, and I won't press charges."

"Miss Love, I think you should accept the offer. If you don't, you'll end up back in jail, and that would violate your parole," Officer Harrison said softly.

She paused. "What about the car?"

Dixie snorted, and Stephanie raised her hands in frustration.

"Take it," I said.

Bambi smiled and nodded. She snatched her bag from Officer Harrison and walked out of the office.

"The car? I can't believe you let her keep the car," Stephanie said.

"I'd never be able to look at that car without puking. It seemed a good way to get rid of it."

Dixie and Stephanie laughed. Even Officer Harrison cracked a quick smile.

Stephanie turned to him. "Parole? She's on parole?"

Officer Harrison nodded. He looked around to make sure no one else was nearby, then said, "Solicitation."

I shuddered. My husband had left me for a prostitute. I wasn't sure if that made me feel better or worse about the betrayal.

There were two other salesmen, a bookkeeper, and an office manager who worked for Albert. They waited in the front lobby while we dealt with Bambi. I considered closing the dealership, but I knew the salesmen depended on the commission they made from selling cars. Both men were married with families to support, so I was reluctant to close. Albert's brother, Vinnie, had worked at the used car lot for several years. I called and asked if he would help keep the car lot open while we figured out what to do. I was thankful he agreed. Vinnie was the middle brother, in between Albert and Gino. He was hardworking and quiet. I never learned what had happened between him and Albert. Whenever I asked, Albert simply said it was family business.

Officer Harrison helped me get the books and Albert's laptop into my SUV.

"Where's your partner?" I asked as I held the rear hatch of the SUV open so he could load the equipment in the back.

Officer Harrison looked puzzled for a brief moment, then nodded. "Oh, you mean Jim? Officer Kelly isn't my partner. I was just working overtime and got assigned to him. His regular partner had the flu." He pointed to his patrol car parked near the front door. The motor was running. Painted on the side was *Lighthouse Dunes K-9 Unit*. Inside the car, the entire backseat had been removed and there was a large, brownish-colored dog. "That's my partner."

The dog paced in the back of the car.

"Is that a plott hound?" Dixie asked.

Officer Harrison stared in awe. "You're the first person to correctly guess his breed."

Dixie had obviously risen in Officer Harrison's opinion.

"He's beautiful. Is he a purebred plott?" She craned her neck to get a better look.

He nodded. "Yep. I've got papers to prove it." He cracked the first smile we'd seen. "We got our first plott about three years ago and fell in love with the breed. They were bred to hunt bears, and they have a keen sense of smell, an amazing work ethic, and drive."

"You sound like a teacher," Stephanie said.

"Sorry, I do a lot of presentations at local schools." He smiled. "I guess I get excited talking about dogs. They're my passion."

"Mine too." Dixie asked, "Can we see him?"

"Sure. I need to take him out anyway." Officer Harrison went to his patrol car, which was exceptionally nice as far as patrol cars went. The Chevy Charger had been retrofitted to accommodate the dog.

We stayed well back from the vehicle while he got the dog out of the car. He took the dog for a quick potty break and then brought him over. "This is Turbo."

Turbo paced anxiously around Officer Harrison.

"He's beautiful. I show dogs, but I've only seen a handful of plott hounds. Are they common in police work?" Dixie asked.

"Not really, although they are getting more recognition. They're hounds that were bred to track bear and wild boar. So, they're not only good for tracking and nose work, but they are fearless. We used to use bloodhounds for tracking, but they're not great for bite work and protection. We have German shepherds and Czech shepherds, but plotts originated in the States, and we have a good breeder in North Carolina who donates some of his dogs every year to police departments."

"That's great. How are they with people?" I squinted at the dog. My only experience of what police K-9 dogs were capable of came from watching television, which I admit wasn't the best source for accurate information.

However, even dog lover, trainer, and competitor Dixie kept her distance. She cautioned us, "I've done some Schutzen training, and tracking, and I would recommend that you don't make sudden aggressive moves."

"Really?" I racked my brain, trying to figure out what an eighty-pound dog would consider sudden or aggressive. I then had an overwhelming desire to sneeze, which I focused all of my mental ability to squelch.

"Turbo is three years old, and I've had him since he was six weeks old." He petted the dog affectionately.

"Does he live with you?" Stephanie asked.

"Yeah. He's with me almost twenty-four-seven."

He walked Turbo by us. We stood perfectly still and allowed him to sniff. For some reason, Turbo stuck his nose in my crotch and refused to move on.

I nearly wet my pants but tried to lighten the mood. "I'll bet he smells our poodles."

Turbo's attention to me had me extremely uncomfortable. At one point, he began licking my thighs.

Officer Harrison pulled him off. "That's odd. He's never acted like that."

Dixie laughed. "I've seen that behavior before."

"Well, I wish you'd tell me what I've done to attract such attention so I'll be sure not to do it again."

"You had Aggie on your lap this morning."

"So what?"

"She hasn't been spayed and she may be in heat."

My mouth dropped open and I stared. "You have got to be kidding me."

Officer Harrison cracked a brief smile. "That explains a lot. We train them to ignore just about every possible distraction you can imagine. But a bitch in heat is one thing that is hard for a male to ignore."

"Apparently," I said as Turbo tried to leap up my leg.

Officer Harrison yanked him off. "I better put him back in the car."

I breathed a heavy sigh of relief when Turbo was removed. I tried to ignore the snickering I heard on either side of me and didn't bother looking at them. "Shut up."

They laughed out loud.

We got in our vehicle. I checked both ways, put the car in reverse, and backed out. From the corner of my eye, I saw a red flash. A car pulled into the lot from the wrong direction and nearly collided with us. I slammed on the brakes and screeched to a halt as a cherry-red convertible barely missed taking off the rear of my car.

The driver laid on the horn and screamed profanities that would have made a sailor blush as he swung into a parking space next to the building.

I sat for several seconds and recovered my composure. My heart raced and my hands shook. I took a deep breath and turned to make sure Dixie and Stephanie were okay.

As soon as the car stopped, Dixie hopped out. She hurried to within inches of the rude driver, pulled her nearly six-foot frame up to its full height, and launched into a series of profanities that included hand gestures and southern idioms, which I'd need to look up later.

I climbed out of the car more slowly and gave my legs a minute to stiffen from their loose noodle state, then walked over to the shouting fest.

Officer Harrison saw the entire incident and pulled back into the lot and parked his vehicle. He quickly got out of his car and hurried to settle things.

"If these senile old ladies would stick to the nursing home circuit, our streets would be a lot safer," the arrogant young man yelled.

"I'll show you a senile old lady." Dixie reached into her purse.

I grabbed her arm to prevent her from pulling out a gun, especially in front of a policeman.

"Chip?" Stephanie came up behind me.

The young man stopped screaming and stared.

"You know this person?" Officer Harrison asked.

On closer inspection, I realized Stephanie was correct. Our foul-mouthed, arrogant drag racer was none other than Charles Nelson III, aka Chip, the only child of Charles and Marilyn Nelson.

Chip stared. "Stephanie?" His eyes roved up and down her body and looked at her like a dog with a new bone. "Little Stephanie Echosby." He grinned.

Dixie made a retching noise, which reminded Chip there were others present.

He turned to me. "And the beautiful Mrs. Echosby." He had the good sense to blush at the realization that not only had he nearly collided with his boss's wife and daughter, but he had been swearing at them in front of a police officer, no less. "Well, I guess it's too late to say I'm sorry." He turned on the charm and smiled broadly.

"It's never too late to use good manners," Dixie said.

Chip bowed low with a sweeping gesture and then held up both hands in a pleading gesture. "Then I humbly apologize. I have no excuse for my bad behavior, other than to say I was overwrought with grief at the horrible news that Mr. Echosby was burglarized and shot." He turned and bowed to each of us. "Please, please, please forgive me."

Dixie looked like she was two seconds away from putting him over her knee.

"May I see your license and registration?" Officer Harrison asked.

Chip plastered on a fake smile. "Look, we had a near-fender-bender." He placed both hands on his chest. "It was totally my fault, and I take full responsibility, but there was no collision. No damage was done. No harm, no foul."

Officer Harrison stared unblinking. "You were traveling above the speed limit. You went the wrong way on a one-way street, *and* were it not for Mrs. Echosby's quick reflexes, you would have hit a car carrying three people. You were reckless and failed to use your turn signal." Still, Officer Harrison hadn't blinked, but a vein on the side of his forehead had begun to pulse. "Your license and registration."

Chip's smile faded. He sighed and pulled his license from his wallet. Then he reached down and retrieved his registration from the glove compartment of his car and handed them over.

Officer Harrison took them back to his vehicle.

Chip looked annoyed. "I have a ton of unpaid parking and speeding tickets, and one more moving violation is going to mean points on my license." He stared at us. "Unless you have some pull with the officer. Or..." He reached for his wallet and pulled out a wad of bills.

Officer Harrison walked back in time to see the wallet and Chip with a handful of bills. The policeman's normal icy demeanor hardened to one of pure granite. He stared unblinking. "I certainly hope you aren't planning to offer me a bribe," he said slowly and deliberately. He flicked back his jacket so his holster, holding his gun, and handcuffs were exposed. He kept his hand on the holster and his eyes fixed on Chip.

Chip gave a half-hearted laugh, returned the money to his wallet, and put the wallet back in his pocket.

Officer Harrison gave him the death stare for several more uncomfortable seconds.

"Sorry," Chip said reluctantly and raked his hand through his hair.

Office Harrison still hadn't blinked, but he handed him the ticket.

He accepted the ticket. "Thanks."

Officer Harrison turned and walked back to his patrol car.

We got back in our car and buckled up.

"I like that Officer Harrison. I wonder how they train them not to blink," Dixie said.

I wondered the same thing as I looked both ways at least six times before inching out of the parking space. In my rearview mirror, Chip Nelson was having an animated conversation on his cell phone. Chalk one up for *senile old ladies*.

The Lighthouse Dunes' one and only police station was a small, single-story brick building situated on prime lakefront real estate. The building had been around since the early twentieth century and had the charm and nautical aesthetic that contributed to the quaint feeling of the city. The building had a lot of character, but was low on twenty-first-century functionality. The facility was small, overcrowded, and wasn't ADA compliant. The city was building a new thirteen-million-dollar high-tech facility on the outskirts of town, but it was behind schedule, so the police had yet to move.

The lobby area was small. We gave our names to the desk sergeant and sat down in metal folding chairs until Officer Harrison came to get us. Our wait wasn't long, but Blue Eyes was out of breath when he came into the lobby.

"Sorry for your wait," he explained as he led us down a narrow hallway. "I needed to take care of Turbo."

Officer Harrison already rated pretty highly on my maternal scale of *Men I'd Like to Date My Daughter* list based solely on the way he'd handled Bambi and how he'd brought Chip Nelson down from his throne. "No problem." Anyone who recognized the importance of caring for his canine companion instantly gained twenty bonus points.

I slowed down so I was several paces behind Officer Harrison. Dixie must have gotten the same idea, because she, too, was walking slower than her normally fast pace. I glanced at Dixie, and she smiled and gave a slight nod. She obviously approved.

Stephanie was now walking side by side with Blue Eyes, and they made a nice couple.

Officer Harrison hurried ahead to open a door, and Stephanie smiled as she sidled past him. Dixie and I hurried through the doorway and then lingered back, while he moved to the front and led us past a series of cubicles. He stopped at one of the cubicles and quickly dragged nearby chairs so we each had a place to sit. Once we were settled, he sat down and started typing.

"I just need to get your statements and then you'll be free to go." He typed on a computer that looked older than my children.

"That thing is just one step above a typewriter," Dixie said.

He grinned. "Some days I think a typewriter would be faster." He typed. "We're getting new systems in the new building."

"Why don't I go first, since my statement will be really short," Dixie volunteered.

Officer Harrison nodded.

"I arrived on Friday. I barely knew Albert. I didn't like him, but I didn't kill him, nor do I know who did," she said.

Officer Harrison asked clarifying questions and typed quickly, albeit with only two fingers. He asked about her whereabouts during the time frame when the burglary must have taken place. When he was done, he printed out the document and asked Dixie to sign and date it. He went through the process with me next. My statement was longer, since I obviously knew Albert the best. However, when he was done, he followed the same procedure.

He was just about to start the process with Stephanie when Dixie nudged me in the ribs.

"Don't you have an appointment?" She winked at me and then tilted her head toward the door. "You know, that *appointment*."

I grabbed my purse and stood. "Oh dear, look at the time. I do have an appointment and I need to go." I stared innocently at Officer Harrison. "I hate to be a bother, but could you see that Stephanie gets home safely?"

Stephanie bowed her head in shame. "Oh Mother."

I detected the slightest glimmer of a smile in Officer Harrison's eyes. "Of course. I'll be happy to make sure she gets home safely. And the name is Joe."

"Joe, thank you so much." I smiled broadly and ignored the daggers Stephanie was now sending with her eyes.

"Mom, I'm sure Officer Harrison—"

"Joe. He asked us to call him Joe," I said with a smile.

Stephanie grimaced. "I'm sure *JOE* has more important things to do than to drive me around town. I can call a taxi."

"*No*," Joe said eagerly. "I'll be more than happy to make sure you get home safely."

Stephanie knew when she was outnumbered. She sighed and accepted her fate. "Thank you."

Dixie and I hurried out of the precinct. I took off driving, with no real destination in mind. After going a few blocks, I stopped at a stoplight and looked at her. "Where to?"

"I'm starving. Let's grab some grub."

My stomach growled at the mention of food, and I headed to a local restaurant near the beach, which was popular with the locals for its onion rings and milk shakes.

Our timing was good, and we were able to get a seat quickly. Burgers, onion rings, and shakes were ordered and consumed quickly. With full stomachs, we then headed for St. Adalbert's and our meeting with Father Dominick.

St. Adalbert's was one of the oldest churches in Lighthouse Dunes. The redbrick building had been built in the early twentieth century. Designed in the Romanesque architectural style, the building was complete with beautiful stained-glass windows and Italianate chandeliers. Arcades ran along both sides of the nave, with a large arch framing the main altar.

Images of Saint Casimir, Christ the King, and Saint Stanislaus Kostka were painted on the apse above the main altar.

Father Dominick met us at the back of the church. He was a round, jolly older priest. He had fat, rosy cheeks, a round belly, and soft eyes. He had a bald, egg-shaped head and a quick wit. He came late to his calling as a priest and had spent his early days driving a truck.

I introduced Dixie, who was Southern Baptist and awed by the statues, relics, and traditions of the church. She had confided at lunch she was also afraid of offending our priest. However, I reassured her there was probably very little he hadn't seen or done in the days prior to his joining the priesthood, or heard in the confessional.

We followed Father Dominick around the side of the building to the rectory. He had an office that was full of books. He sat in a chair behind an old desk covered in books and papers, and I sat in the guest chair in front of the desk. Dixie was drawn to the books that lined the walls from floor to ceiling and lay strewn on every available surface.

"Please feel free." Father Dominick smiled and waved his hand in a magnanimous gesture.

Dixie nearly ran over to the bookshelves.

"Please accept my condolences on the loss of your husband," Father Dominick said softly.

We'd talked many times in the months since Albert moved out, so he was well aware of our situation, but I thanked him.

"Now, what can I do to help you?"

I thought about that question for a second and then explained what I knew of Albert's wishes. We hadn't spoken much about this over the years. Albert always said we had plenty of time. However, having lost both of my parents at a fairly young age, I preferred to be prepared. Toward that end, I'd purchased funeral plots and gravestones. Everything was already selected and paid for. Father Dominick and I went through the program for a traditional mass, and I selected hymns and scriptures I thought Albert might have liked. Stephanie sent a text message while we were at the rectory that the coroner had released the body and Lighthouse Dunes Funeral Home would be picking it up later today.

Dixie and I left the church, swung by a local florist's shop, and purchased floral sprays for the coffin, as well as grave markers and candles.

I was worn out by the time I got home. I wasn't surprised to see the K-9 Patrol car in the driveway, parked next to Dixie's RV, but there was another car behind it, which I didn't recognize.

I went into the house and smiled at Joe and Stephanie sitting in the living room. As a well-trained gentleman, Joe rose when we entered. However, he looked serious and official. Stephanie hopped up from her seat too.

"Mom, this is Detective Wilson."

I extended my hand toward the detective. Detective Wilson was an African American woman of medium height, with silky-smooth skin the color of an espresso coffee. She had light gray eyes and a bright smile.

"It's a pleasure to meet you. Please call me Olivia," she said with a clipped British accent. "I'm sorry to bother you at home, but I was only assigned to this case a couple of hours ago." She smiled.

I looked from Joe to Detective Wilson. I must have looked as puzzled as I felt, because she quickly added, "I'm a homicide detective. Officer Harrison is a member of the K-9 squad and has been graciously helping us out with our caseload."

I smiled. "Please have a seat."

Everyone sat down, and I waited patiently for Detective Wilson to explain why she was here.

"Now, I have read your statements and I have a few other questions I'd like to ask you."

I nodded. "Of course."

She flashed a friendly smile and then pulled out a notepad. "I'm sure you know the circumstances of your husband's death."

"I know what my in-laws told my daughter."

"You and your husband were estranged?"

"If by 'estranged' you mean separated and preparing to get divorced, then yes. We were estranged."

She smiled. "Was it an amicable separation?"

"Depends on what you mean by amicable."

"Mrs. Echosby, maybe it would be easier if you just tell me about your separation in your own words."

I looked at Stephanie, who gave me a slight nod. "My husband left me for another woman, a younger woman."

"A much younger woman," Dixie mumbled.

"Her name, or what she calls herself, because I can't believe any mother would name their daughter that, is Bambi Love. She's about twenty years old—"

"And dumb as a box of rocks," Dixie added.

"He moved out about six months ago."

"That had to be very difficult for you," Detective Wilson sympathized. "How long had you been married?"

"Twenty-five years. It was difficult at first." I sighed. "I don't suppose any woman wants to feel like she's been replaced with a younger model, just because she's gotten old."

"Were you still in love with your husband?"

"I honestly don't know." I pondered the question for a long time. Finally, I shrugged. "I suppose I'd gotten accustomed to my husband and my marriage. It was a comfortable habit, but if I'm completely honest, I don't think I did love him…not anymore." I took a deep breath. "I didn't know it at the time, but I've had a lot of time to think lately."

"I understand," she added. "So, before you had time to think about your true feelings, you didn't want the divorce?"

"No. I didn't. I'd become a creature of habit, and I didn't want to change. At first, I thought he'd come back, but then when it was clear he wasn't coming back, I had to accept it."

"When did you come to the realization that he wasn't coming back?"

"Just a few days ago, when we were in Chicago."

"You went to Chicago with your husband?"

"We didn't go together. We met there, in my daughter's office." I pointed to Stephanie. "She's an attorney."

"I see."

Stephanie had begun to pace while we were talking. She stopped. "I think I see now too. Detective Wilson, you think my mother had something to do with my father's death."

I stared at Stephanie. Surely she was wrong, but Detective Wilson didn't deny it, and Joe looked as though he wanted to sink through the floor.

"That's ridiculous. You can't possibly believe I had anything to do with Albert's death. Regardless of what was happening to our marriage, he was still my husband."

"Lilly is the least violent person I know." Dixie jumped to my defense.

"My mother wouldn't hurt anyone, especially not my dad."

"So, you didn't leap across a conference table and attempt to strangle your husband's girlfriend? Or hurl objects at your husband's head and have a screaming match the day before he was killed?" she asked innocently.

I stared openmouthed. "Touché."

"That's enough. You can leave. My mother won't be answering any more questions without a lawyer."

Detective Wilson sighed. "Look, I'm just doing my job. I need to ask these questions and investigate everyone who could possibly have had a reason to harm your husband. Hopefully, I'll be able to eliminate you as a suspect and move on, but that won't happen unless you're honest and cooperative."

I had to hand it to Detective Wilson. She was good at gaining confidence. I'd read a lot of mysteries in my day, and I knew the spouse was always the number-one suspect. I also knew that talking to the police without a criminal attorney was a bad idea. Detectives had a way of twisting your words. Nevertheless, there was something about this detective's nature that made me want to trust her. I wasn't sure if it was her sympathetic eyes, British accent, or calm demeanor, but I liked her and she came across as sincere. "I don't have anything to hide. I didn't kill my...Albert. I'll answer your questions."

Stephanie looked as though she thought I'd lost my mind. "Mom, I really don't think this is a good idea...?"

"You're probably right, dear, but what could possibly go wrong?"

CHAPTER 5

What could possibly go wrong? Well, I learned the answer to that question very quickly. What could go wrong was that after three hours of rehashing not only the circumstances of my marriage, my love life, my divorce, the fact that I stood to inherit his car dealership, and the million dollars they'd discovered he had in an offshore bank account, I had no confirmable alibi for the time of the murder.

Detective Wilson returned with a search warrant, which allowed detectives to search every nook and cranny of my house. Apparently the police found boxes and packed suitcases suspicious, especially after a murder. If having police detectives go through my underwear wasn't bad enough, they removed samples of the carpet, because the red wine– and marinara-stained carpet was suspicious too.

Tuesday afternoon, I realized antagonizing my husband's girlfriend had been a bad idea, since she apparently took pleasure in not only bad-mouthing me to the police, but enjoyed bad-mouthing me to reporters as well.

I watched openmouthed as she primped, smacked her gum, and cried, all in less than two minutes, then displayed the marks on her throat where I tried to strangle her.

"I can't believe you're watching that." Stephanie paced in front of the television.

Dixie picked up the remote. "It's like a train wreck. You know you shouldn't look, but you can't help yourself."

"Don't you dare turn that off. I need to know what I'm fighting against." I steeled myself and watched as Bambi batted false eyelashes at the reporter. When the segment ended, I turned to Dixie. "Okay, now you can turn it off."

"Well, that was pathetic." Dixie petted one of the poodles lounging by her chair.

"What time is the lawyer coming?" Did I have time to vacuum? One look at the holes in the carpet made the entire idea ridiculous.

"Should be any minute." Stephanie paced.

As if on cue, the doorbell rang. The poodles might not have looked fierce, but they barked like killer attack dogs. We'd taken to keeping all of them in the house since reporters and curiosity seekers started showing up on the doorstep.

Stephanie was already up, so she looked out of the peephole and then opened the door.

Dixie held tight to the big poodles, while I scooped up Aggie, who reminded me of Scrappy Doo as she yapped and lunged at the door, confident as long as there was 150 pounds of poodles backing her up. She looked utterly ridiculous with her pink halter dress that I couldn't resist buying and a little pink diaper. After the amorous attentions of Turbo, we checked and detected slight drops of blood on the carpet, or rather the police found the blood drops. Dixie went to the pet store and procured a small doggy diaper to protect the furniture, since nothing her standard poodles had would fit little Aggie. She did, however, have spray to reduce the scent since her females were also still intact. Aggie wasn't thrilled about wearing the pink diaper, but she hadn't yet figured out a way to remove it.

Christopher Williams entered. "Steph, it's good to see you again." He hugged her and kissed her on the cheek. Their embrace lasted longer than casual friends tended to hug, but then, he and Stephanie had dated for a while in law school.

When the embrace ended, he smiled at me and extended his hand. "How are you holding up, Mrs. Echosby?"

I shook his hand and responded appropriately.

Stephanie introduced him to Dixie, and he won big points with her by extending a hand so the poodles could sniff. When they had determined he wasn't a serial killer or carrying concealed hot dogs anywhere on his person, they signaled he was okay with profuse tail wagging.

Christopher got down on one knee and scratched both dogs behind their ears, finding the spot that made their eyes roll up into their heads and their back legs jiggle. He was definitely a charmer.

After a few moments, he stood up and we all sat down.

Christopher was taller than Dixie, so that made him more than six feet tall. He was thin but fit and handsome in an unassuming way. Even in college he had been impeccably well dressed. Today was no exception. He had on a tailored suit that, even to my inexperienced eye, looked expensive and shoes that looked like Italian leather.

Stephanie had obviously prepped Christopher ahead of time, but he asked to hear my version of events anyway. It took forty-five minutes for me to go through everything, even though I could see he had copies of the statements I'd made to the police. He took notes and sat quietly and listened.

When I finished, he asked a few clarifying questions, but at no point during our talk did he ask if I'd murdered my husband. I hoped he believed me incapable of murder, but knew it was more likely he didn't want to know the answer to that question. Having a daughter as a lawyer, I'd learned a lot about ethics as they related to attorneys. It wasn't always pretty when you looked at it from the outside, but when looking at things purely from a legal standpoint, it made sense. Everyone, no matter who they were or what they'd done, was entitled to legal representation. Lawyers were tasked to provide the best defense on behalf of their client. So even serial killers were entitled to legal representation.

"First, you're not to talk to the police again without me." He stared at me in a way that made me feel guilty for ignoring Stephanie's advice.

I nodded.

"Good. I don't think I need to tell you this, but no interviews with the media."

I nodded again.

Christopher looked down, as if he needed to collect his thoughts and find the right words.

Stephanie must have recognized the look. "Whatever it is, just say it. Stop trying to spare our feelings. We need the truth, whatever it is."

I nodded. "Whatever it is, just give it to me straight."

He nodded and took a deep breath. "It's possible that you could be arrested."

I gasped, and Dixie came over and gave my hand a squeeze of support. Stephanie bit her lip, hopped up, and paced.

"I hope that doesn't happen, but you had motive and opportunity and..."

"What?" I squeezed Dixie's hand tighter.

"Do you own a gun?" he asked.

"No. I don't like guns, but Albert had one."

"Do you know where it is?" he asked.

"I have no idea. I assume he took it with him. I haven't looked for it." I stared. "You don't mean to tell me Albert was shot with his own gun?"

"The police don't know. They know he had a..." He rifled through one of the folders on his lap and pulled out a document. He scanned through the folder and stopped when he found what he was looking for. "He had a nine-millimeter semiautomatic pistol, a Glock 17. That's the same caliber of bullet used by the assailant, and the police have yet to find Mr. Echosby's gun."

"Is that what they were searching for?" I asked.

He shrugged. "Probably. They didn't find the gun at his apartment or the car dealership. So they're thinking maybe he left it here."

"What?" Stephanie stared. "I can tell by your face something's wrong."

I shook my head. "I just remembered the downstairs window was open."

"When was this?" Christopher asked.

"Saturday night. The night of the party." I shook myself. "They think I took my husband's gun, snuck out in the middle of the night, and shot him with it—with his own gun."

"Lends a new meaning to '*hoist with his own petard*'," Dixie mumbled. "I'm sorry." She looked up. "I repeat stupid quotes when I'm nervous."

I patted her hand. "It's okay, so do I, although I don't usually quote Shakespeare." I tried to lighten the mood.

Christopher smiled briefly but then got serious again. "If the police find that gun, here or someplace where you could have accessed it, then they'll definitely arrest you. There's a chance they'll try to arrest you even if they don't find the gun, but let's hope not."

I digested this and nodded.

"Now, I want to hire a private investigator to look into a few things."

"What things?" Stephanie asked.

Christopher sighed. "There are some things with his car dealership that seem sketchy."

Stephanie looked as though she was going to ask another question, but Christopher held up a hand to forestall interruption. "Look, you asked for it straight, so I'm giving it to you straight."

Stephanie nodded.

"I'm not saying he did anything wrong, but how did a small used car dealer in Lighthouse Dunes get a million dollars in an offshore bank account?"

We shook our heads. In the midst of all of the struggles in dealing with the police, planning a funeral, and all of the emotional baggage I'd accumulated in the past six months, I had catalogued that piece of information into a mental file cabinet I'd been too afraid to open. However, I realized I'd better open that file—and quickly—before I found myself locked up for a murder I hadn't committed.

CHAPTER 6

After Christopher left, we sat in stunned silence for a few moments, and I tried to process everything he'd told me. I had no idea how to mentally, emotionally, or physically prepare myself to be arrested.

"Should I pack?" I asked Stephanie.

She shook her head. "I pray it doesn't come to that, but you won't be allowed to take anything with you." She then explained I'd have a bond hearing and would hopefully be released after posting bond.

"On television, they list bonds in the tens of thousands of dollars." I thought about the last episode of *Matlock* I'd seen where someone had to post bond.

"The amount will be determined by the judge. The prosecution will want it to be a high number, but Christopher will argue that you aren't a flight risk and will ask for the bond to be waived," Stephanie explained.

"They can do that?" I asked.

She nodded. "It may not happen, but he'll ask. The judge will set the amount, and then we pay ten percent of that amount. So, if bail is set at ten thousand dollars, then you'd only have to pay one thousand."

I breathed a sigh of relief. "That's doable."

Dixie nodded. "I can help," she said. I protested, but she interrupted. "It's only money and we have plenty of it. I'd like to help."

I looked in her eyes and recognized the helplessness I saw reflected back at me. She wanted to be helpful, and here was one way she could contribute. So I hugged her. "Thank you. It's good to know I have good friends."

We ordered pizza and Stephanie went to pick it up. While we waited for her to return, we sat at the kitchen table.

"*Well, Stanley, this is certainly a fine mess.*" Dixie quoted Laurel and Hardy.

I laughed.

"I told you I repeat stupid quotes when I'm nervous." She shrugged.

"I'm the one about to be arrested. Why are you so nervous?"

"I feel about as useful as a bartender at a Southern Baptist camp meeting." She fidgeted but then cocked her head to the side and stared at me. "So, why are you so calm? You've got an idea. I can see the little wheels turning."

"Well, I was just thinking about what Miss Florrie would say."

"Who's Miss Florrie?"

I smiled. "Just a lady I met on the train the other day." I told Dixie about my conversation with Miss Florrie and how she inspired me to find my "happy place."

"So, what do you think Miss Florrie would say?"

I pondered for a moment. "Well, I think she'd say some of the same things she said the other night. 'You been done wrong. Now, what you gonna do 'bout it?'"

"Well, what are you going to do?"

"I'm going to have to figure out who killed Albert. The police don't seem to be interested in anyone but me. Unless I can figure out who killed him, I'm going to either end up in jail or with a black cloud over my head because everyone is going to *think* I killed him and got away with it."

Dixie looked at me for several seconds, but then slapped her hand down on the table. "Well, count me in, Sherlock. I been itching for something to do, and helping you figure out who killed that weasel of a husband of yours will be just the ticket. Forget the dog agility workshop I was supposed to attend. Deal me in."

The poodles had been lying down fast asleep, but they suddenly jumped up and started barking and pawing the back door. Dixie and I had been so intent on our conversation, we jumped at the abrupt change.

Dixie grabbed her purse, pulled her gun out, and pointed it at the back door.

I grabbed a large rolling pin from the drawer, and we both braced ourselves to attack whoever came through that door.

The knob turned and the door squeaked as it was slowly pushed open. A curly dark head with a baseball cap appeared in the opening. "Mom?"

"David?"

Dixie lowered her weapon and quickly yelled, "Fuss." The dogs hurried to her side.

I ran the short distance and hugged my son. "When did you get here? I thought you weren't going to make it until tomorrow?" I fired questions at the speed of light and hugged him tighter with each one.

"The airline got me on a different flight at the last minute. I've been flying all night." He yawned.

"But how did you get from the airport?"

The closest big airport to Lighthouse Dunes was in South Bend, but the airport didn't have international flights.

"I flew into Midway and rented a car." He held out a hand to Dixie. "You must be my mom's friend Dixie."

They shook hands.

"And who are these guys?" He eyed the poodles.

"Chyna"—she pointed to the dog on her right. "Leia"—she pointed to the left. Then she held up the still-yapping fluff ball she was holding. "And Aggie."

David extended his hand to each dog so they could sniff. The standards sniffed and then gave the hand a lick, apparently approving. Aggie took more convincing. She continued yapping, and when David stretched out his hand, she snapped at him.

"Aggie," I reprimanded her. "I've never seen her bite anyone. Are you okay? Did she break the skin?"

"No. I'm fine."

Aggie continued to bark and lunged at David even more aggressively. I turned to Dixie, who tightened her hold on Aggie but was also carefully observing David.

"What's wrong with her?" I asked Dixie.

"I'm not sure, but she's definitely taken a dislike to you for some reason. Do you have dogs?" she asked.

David shook his head.

"Maybe she doesn't like men. She tried to bite your father."

"She was fine around the attorney." She continued to stare at David. "Would you humor me and remove your cap?"

David shrugged and took off his baseball cap.

As if a switch had been pressed, Aggie stopped barking and her tail wagged a hundred miles per minute.

I looked in stunned amazement.

Dixie nodded. "Now, let's try this again. Let her sniff your hand."

David tentatively brought his open hand to her nose. She sniffed and then licked his hand.

"What in the world?" I asked.

Dixie shrugged. "Obviously someone wearing a baseball cap wasn't very kind to her." She set Aggie on the floor.

We watched as she sniffed David's pants and then got on her back legs and pawed his pants to be picked up.

He reached down and picked her up, and she snuggled into his chest, as if she hadn't just tried to take off his fingers.

We sat down and let David fill us in on his travel adventures in getting in from New York. We talked until Stephanie came home with the pizza and a bottle of wine. She hadn't seen her brother for months and was excited, and I think a bit relieved, to have him here.

We ate and drank wine and filled David in on everything we knew about the murder, the police investigation, and expectations for my impending arrest. He listened in silent shock. After David was up to speed, I filled both him and Stephanie in on my plan to catch the killer.

Neither one of them was excited about the idea of their mother playing detective and they voiced their concerns repeatedly. However, neither could argue with the fact that, unless we figured out who murdered their father, I'd most likely be arrested and placed on trial for murder. In the early hours of the morning, David's yawns increased in frequency and his eyes drooped.

"You better get some sleep. You look like you're going to fall over." I kissed his cheek.

He was too tired to resist and went upstairs.

We sat and talked a little longer, but then Stephanie said, "We better get some sleep. We've got a hectic day tomorrow."

"What do you mean?" I panicked at the thought that maybe Christopher had warned her tomorrow was the day the police would arrest me.

"You're going to need all of your strength to deal with the funeral and Dad's family."

In all of the excitement and worry, I had forgotten the funeral was tomorrow. Stephanie was right. Tomorrow would be a challenging day, and I'd need all of my wits about me to get through it. So, we all headed to bed.

* * * *

The sound of a car engine woke me early. I got up and looked out the window. The spare car was gone. One of the children must have gone out to pick something up. I got back in bed and tried to go to sleep. I tossed and turned for what felt like hours. I dozed off for a bit but awoke shortly afterward. Technically, I probably didn't sleep more than a couple of hours, so I'm not sure that counted as actual sleep. I struggled to get my mind to shut down. The idea of being arrested made my heart race. Even if the real killer was discovered, how did you live down being arrested? How could I show my face at the supermarket, at church, or even in my neighborhood? Who hated Albert enough to want him dead? Who went to his apartment with hatred in their heart and a gun in their hand, prepared for murder? Lots of people might have wanted him out of the way, but who would have had a gun and truly wanted him dead? To actually take someone's life was a completely different matter altogether. I struggled to think of anyone who hated him that much. I tossed and turned for what felt like hours, trying to think of someone who wanted Albert dead. Every mystery novel I'd ever read showed me there were basic reasons people resorted to murder as a resolution for their problems.

I sat up in bed and turned on the lamp on the nightstand. I scavenged in the nightstand drawer until I found a notepad and then repeated the search until I found a pen that wrote. I sat poised to write for several moments. Then I wrote Albert's name across the top of the paper, followed by *reasons for murder.* After a few moments, I followed with a list, which included: Money, Jealousy, Revenge. There were probably a lot of other reasons, but those seemed the most likely. "I wonder where Albert had money?" I looked at Aggie, but she seemed intent on trying to chew the pearls off the fancy, blinged-out collar I'd bought her. The collar was a little too big, and I didn't want her to ingest any of the pearls or rhinestones, so I removed it and placed it in the nightstand before I returned to my list.

Next to money, I wrote *car dealership*, *insurance*, and *pension.* As far as I knew, those were Albert's only sources of money. The last statement I'd seen from our 401k wasn't enough to inspire murder, at least not in my opinion. We'd taken loans against the money over the years to pay for things like college tuition, taxes, a new roof, and damage to the basement after two days of torrential rains left the basement flooded, something the insurance company viewed as *an act of God* and refused to cover in our standard home owner's policy. Insurance would only provide a motive if you were the beneficiary on the account. If Albert had done as I asked, then the children were his beneficiaries. I made a note to contact the insurance company when things settled down to verify. Because we'd prepaid our burial plot and funeral services, I hadn't bothered to reach out to the insurance company earlier. However, this would need to be done eventually.

The car dealership was the only other source of income, and I couldn't believe it was generating enough money to merit killing for. Albert sold enough cars to provide a comfortable living, but nothing extravagant. We certainly couldn't afford one of those big houses on Lake Michigan, like Albert's attorney, Charles Nelson, had. Lighthouse Dunes wasn't like those wealthy Chicago suburbs with foreign luxury car dealerships on every corner. Besides, someone would have to believe they could access the money with Albert gone. Bambi's face crossed my mind, but I might still have been bitter. I needed to be objective to figure this out. Nevertheless, I'd have to take a closer look through those books at some point. Somehow, he'd managed to sock away a million dollars, so either the car dealership was doing much better than I thought, or…there was something else going on here. The last thing I wrote was *illegal activity*. Could Albert have been involved in some type of illegal activity that led to him getting killed? It seemed highly unlikely that the man I'd been married to for more than two decades could have been involved in illegal activities without my knowledge. But then, I hadn't known about his girlfriend either, so obviously Albert was better at hiding things than I'd given him credit for. But a girlfriend was very different from the type of illegal activities that generated the kind of money people killed for. Wasn't it? I racked my brain to think of what those types of activities might be and wrote down each that I thought of—*drugs, weapons, money laundering for the mob*. Did Lighthouse Dunes even have a mob? I wasn't sure, but I had to consider they were everywhere. The thought made me shiver.

I stared at the paper. If I was serious about figuring out who killed Albert, I'd need to investigate each of these things. How did someone even begin to investigate the mob? Or drugs or illegal weapons either, for that matter? I looked over at Aggie, who had fallen asleep with her head on my leg. "Agatha Christie made investigating seem so easy." I scratched Aggie behind her ear. "Miss Marple did it and rarely left her village of St. Mary Mead, but how on earth can I do it in Lighthouse Dunes?" Eventually, I gave up. I needed to think. I got up, dressed, and went downstairs.

I didn't want to wake the house by brewing coffee at four in the morning, so I decided to leave. My car was in the garage and most likely blocked by David's rental. So I grabbed the spare keys from the hook by the back door. I'd take the car Stephanie drove whenever she was in town. Multiple vehicles were one of the perks when your husband owned a used car dealership.

Outside, I remembered the spare car had been gone earlier. I almost turned around to go back inside and get my own car keys but noticed all of the cars were back. No point in going back for my car keys now. Besides, the garage door was loud and would wake the house. So, I kept walking to the spare car. When I walked by the RV, I noticed the light was on. So I tapped lightly on the door.

Dixie opened the door. "Where do you think you're going?"

"I couldn't sleep. I'm going out for coffee. What's your excuse?"

"Wait for me." She stuck her head back inside and grabbed her purse. Then she came out and locked the door behind her. "I'm going with you."

"I don't need a babysitter."

"I know, but you're going out for coffee, and I may need a gallon before the day's out."

We hopped in the older model Volvo we used to drive around town or for one of the kids when they were in town. The car was close to fifteen years old and had over two hundred thousand miles on it. It was easier for my mother-in-law to get in and out of if I had to transport her or her mother to the doctor's office or on other errands. Albert often found himself too busy to do so. I tried not to get bitter at the thought of all the times I'd dropped what I was doing to play taxi service for people who barely tolerated me.

"You might want to slow down a tad." Dixie looked at me from the corner of her eye.

I glanced at the speedometer. I was going eighty-five miles per hour down the moonlit streets of Lighthouse Dunes. "Sorry." I eased off the gas.

"It would be perfectly normal if you were feeling stressed," she said in that quiet, sympathetic voice people always used at funerals. "Your husband's funeral service is in a few hours and, regardless of what happened in the last year or so, he was still your husband, your lover, and the father of your children."

I drove past the grocery store and past Albert's car dealership to the interstate. I got on the interstate and drove west toward Chicago, putting the pedal to the floor. It took a bit for my old beater to get revved up. She was great around town for city driving but needed a bit of coaxing for interstates. However, once she got up to speed, she flew down the highway. The old girl didn't look like much, but she had it where it counted. We drove in silence for twenty miles. I didn't even realize I was crying until the tears made it hard to see. When my nose started to run, I took the next exit and pulled off the interstate. There was a casino, and I pulled into the parking lot and cried.

Dixie took off her seat belt and reached over and hugged me. I cried on her shoulder in the parking lot of the casino until I didn't have any more tears left.

"I'm done." I pulled away and used my sleeve to wipe my face dry. "Can you get me a tissue from the glove box?"

Dixie opened the glove box and reached in. She felt around in the deep compartment and then froze.

"What?" I looked concerned. "Don't tell me I left something gross in there." I laughed.

She shook her head and then slowly lifted her hand up. At the end of her hand was a gun.

"Where did you get that?" I asked.

"From your glove compartment," she said.

I stared at the gun. "Whose is it?"

She shrugged. "I have no idea. Isn't it yours?"

"I've never seen that before in my life."

We sat staring at each other for what felt like an hour but, in reality, was more like thirty seconds.

"Well, what's it doing in there?" I asked.

"It's framing you for murder is what it's doing."

I pulled a handkerchief from my purse, reached over, and picked up the gun from the handle, careful to keep the business end pointed away from Dixie and me. Never having handled a gun before, I was not only cautious but just short of terrified.

"We should get rid of it," Dixie said.

"We can't do that. It's evidence. We need to get this to the police. Maybe they can find out who owns it and trace it to the killer." I stared at the gun and then shoved it into my purse.

"We need to tie a rock to it and toss it into Lake Michigan, if you ask me," Dixie said. "The killer would be a fool to use his own gun to commit murder. Besides, why leave it in your glove box if it can be traced back to him?"

I stared. When my brain finally grasped what she was saying, I started to shake. My hands shook and I started to hyperventilate.

Dixie closed the glove box and got out of the car. She came around to the driver's side and helped me out of the car. "You need a drink."

She looked around and then hurried me toward the casino.

We went inside. It was early in the morning and it wasn't crowded, although there were still a good number of people. The air was thick with smoke. Casinos and bars were two of the few places where smokers were allowed to smoke unfettered in the state, and they took advantage of it. We spotted a bar over to the right and headed for it.

Seated at a table near the back of the bar, we ordered two glasses of wine and waited until our waitress brought them.

My hand shook so bad when I tried to take a drink, I spilled most of it down the front of my blouse. Eventually, I managed to get the glass to my mouth and took a long sip. I looked around to make sure no one was close enough to overhear our conversation, then leaned close and whispered, "How do you think that got in there?"

Dixie shook her head. "I have no idea. Who had access to your car?"

I thought. "Well, anyone could have done it. The car's been on the street for nearly a week."

"Was it locked?"

I shook my head. "We don't keep anything valuable in it, and frankly, if someone wanted to steal it, I'd be happy to give them fifty dollars to take it away." I paused and took another drink. "It never occurred to me someone would put something in it." Something else occurred to me, and I nearly spilled my glass.

"What is it? You just went as white as a sheet." Dixie reached across and touched my hand. "And your hand is ice cold."

"It just dawned on me. Whoever murdered Albert knows me. He—"

"Or she."

I nodded. "Or she, knows where I live. They know what kind of car I drive. They came to my house and entered my vehicle and planted a gun—"

"Shhh." She looked around at the waitress, who had just come up to the table.

"Can I get you another drink?" A thin girl dressed in a green Robin Hood costume, with green hair to match, asked.

"Yes, can you please bring us two more glasses of wine?" Dixie ordered.

I was still too shaken to speak. I watched the girl walk away, although she glanced back at us twice. "Do you think she heard me?"

Dixie shrugged. "I don't know."

We sat quietly until she brought our drinks.

She placed the glasses on the table and then looked at me again. "Do I know you?" She paused. "You look really familiar, but I can't place where I've seen you before."

I shrugged. "I guess I just have one of those faces," I said vaguely.

She stood and tilted her head to the side. "No, I know I've seen your face before. I just can't remember where."

I grabbed the glass of wine and downed it in one gulp. "Well, I think we're ready for our check now."

She walked away to ring up our bill. When she returned, she placed the bill on the table and continued to stare.

I wanted to tell her it was rude to stare at people but didn't want to draw any more attention to myself than I already had. I fumbled in my purse for the money to pay the bill and found twenty dollars. I put it on the table, grabbed my purse, and rose from the table.

"I'll get your change."

"No. Just keep the change." I hurried to get around her.

She stood openmouthed. "That's ten dollars."

"Merry Christmas." I walked toward the door to leave.

Right before we walked out of the bar, I heard the waitress say, "Now I know where I've seen you before. You're the lady who shot your husband."

CHAPTER 7

My heart raced and heat rose up my neck. I hurried to the car, eager to get away as quickly as possible. I jumped behind the wheel and sped out of the parking lot, almost before Dixie's door was closed. I got on the interstate and headed back toward Lighthouse Dunes. The blood rushed to my head, and my heart pulsated so my ears sounded like I was hearing the ocean in my head. It was nearly impossible to hear anything as I sped along the interstate.

"Lilly, you need to slow down. You're going too fast."

I glanced at the speedometer. My adrenaline had manifested in another pedal-to-the-metal mad dash down the freeway. I eased off the gas and pressed the brake, but not before I passed a patrol car, waiting in the median with his radar detection gun pointed right at my vehicle.

I was almost to my exit for Lighthouse Dunes. I looked over to apologize to Dixie for my crazy driving, when I noticed the lights on at the dealership. I was just about to mention the lights when I heard the sirens. "That's for me, isn't it?"

"Ask not for whom the sirens blare. They blare for you."

"Gobble-darn, blast-dab-nab-bit."

"Keep that up and you'll need to wash your mouth out with soap."

I pulled over to the side of the road. "Can you look in the glove box for the registration?"

Dixie opened the glove box and rummaged around, pulling out paper after paper. She held each of them up and squinted to read what they were.

I rooted through my purse in search of my driver's license and froze when my hand hit the gun. "Oh my God."

"What?"

I pulled the gun, still wrapped in the handkerchief, out of my purse.

Dixie reached for it. "Give me that." She took the gun and shoved it into the glove box and slammed the door shut, just as the officer approached the window.

I rolled down the window. "Hello, Officer, I'm so sorry. I didn't realize how rapidly I was going. I think my foot must have gotten stuck." I laughed.

"Can I see your driver's license, vehicle registration, and proof of insurance?" the square-jawed, buzz-cut, just-the-facts-ma'am patrolman demanded.

I fumbled in my purse for my driver's license, but Officer Prune Face stared at me as though he was waiting for me to offer to sell him drugs or illegal weapons. Eventually, I found my driver's license and insurance card and handed them over.

"Vehicle registration?"

I looked at Dixie, and she opened the glove box wide enough to get her hand inside and then reached in and fumbled around for what felt like hours. I tried to lighten the mood. "Have you been doing this long?"

Officer Stony Face grunted. "It might help if you opened the glove box and turned on the car's interior light."

Dixie looked stricken.

"The hinge is broken. Unless you hold it properly, it falls off," I said quickly.

He stared at me as though he was reading my mind. I tried desperately to empty all of my thoughts and look as innocent as I possibly could while, at the same time, mentally willing Dixie to hurry up and find the vehicle registration.

I must have done too good of a job at emptying my mind, because my vacant expression caused the officer to lean close. "Have you been drinking?"

I paused. "I had a glass of wine."

He sniffed the air like a hound dog and then stood up and patted his gun. "Would you mind getting out of the car?"

I huffed, probably not a good idea when your breath smells like red wine and you've got a supersensitive bloodhound-nosed policeman sniffing around you. I opened the car door and put one leg out. Unfortunately, I got the strap of my purse, which I'd placed on the floor behind my legs, wrapped around my right leg. So when I tried to stand up, I tripped and would have fallen flat on the asphalt had gun-patting Officer Go-Ahead-And-Make-My-Day not broken my fall.

Once I was upright, Officer Granite Jaw did what I didn't think possible and became even more serious and uptight. "Stand over there and don't move," he said without the slightest crack of a smile.

Dixie looked as shocked as I felt. "Come on, officer. Is that really necessary?" She opened her car door.

Officer Quick-Draw-McGraw pulled his gun from his hip, pointed it at her, and shouted at the top of his voice, "Stay in the car. Get back in the car *now*!"

Talk about a buzzkill. I stood by the car as straight as a rod, with both hands raised. When Dixie was back in the car, he lowered his weapon and walked back to his patrol car. He got on the radio and stayed there for about fifteen minutes, while I stood outside my car and Dixie sat inside.

"Do you think he's going to search the car?" Dixie whispered.

"I don't know. Can you look for that registration while he's in his patrol car?" I whispered like a ventriloquist, trying not to move my lips or alter my facial expression.

"We need to get rid of this gun," Dixie said, while she tackled the glove box. Eventually, she announced, "Found it."

I breathed a sigh of relief and glanced over to the patrol car. Just when I thought we might be able to get out of this without any further humiliation, I heard sirens and three other patrol cars arrived. Obviously, Officer Lock-'Em-Up had called for backup.

I stood on the interstate, shivering, but not from the cold. What was going on here? Why were there five policemen standing together like a solid wall of blue steel looking at me? Had Officer Get-Out-Of-The-Car seen the gun in the glove box? Did the rocket scientist/waitress at the bar call the police and tell them to be on the lookout for me? Or, when he got on his radio, did he discover I was a wanted criminal? Was there a warrant out for my arrest? A million questions tumbled through my head at the speed of light. I'd been standing outside for a long time, and all the uncertainty and a good amount of fear had turned my legs into jelly. Every newspaper headline or media clip of negative encounters with the police flashed through my head, and I was so terrified I had an overwhelming desire to laugh hysterically. In my mind, I knew the vast majority of police officers were nice, hardworking men and women who got paid a pittance for putting their lives on the line, and up until Albert was shot, I had never run afoul of the law. Police officers were my friends. That was what I had been taught in school. That was what I believed. I repeated that mantra over and over in my head. *Police officers are my friend. Police officers are my friend.*

Officer I-Feel-Tough-With-My-Posse-Backing-Me-Up strutted over to me and stood almost toe to toe. "Look in my eyes," he ordered.

I was tempted to step back. He was violating my personal space, but I decided to do exactly what was asked and stared him in the eyes. It was uncomfortable to be that close to someone and have to look directly in their eyes, but I did. After what felt like an hour, he backed up.

"I want you to walk a straight line. Take nine steps, heel to toe, along a straight line, turn on one foot, and then do it in the opposite direction, heel to toe."

I'd seen this on television, so I felt pretty comfortable. Again, I made sure to do exactly what the officer asked and took nine and only nine steps, turned, and then took nine steps in the opposite direction. Thankfully, years of ballet as a child and yoga recently had left me with a modicum of grace. I didn't wobble. If Dixie was outside of the car, I would have been tempted to high-five her when I finished, but instead, I merely stopped and waited.

"Now lift one leg about six inches off the ground and stand that way for thirty seconds."

"Does it matter which leg?"

He shook his head.

I took a deep breath, found my center, then lifted one leg and stood that way until he told me it was okay to put my leg down.

When I'd successfully completed all three tasks, I thought the ordeal was over, until he whipped out a Breathalyzer.

I knew I wasn't drunk. In fact, if I had been previously, the reality of this situation had certainly scared me sober. Nevertheless, with a lawyer for a daughter, I knew that refusing to take a Breathalyzer would violate something called *implied consent*. My take-the-world-by-storm daughter was a big proponent of civil liberties and the individual's rights to due process and a lot of other lawyerly mumbo-jumbo that sounded great when you were watching *Perry Mason* or watching hearings on television. In reality, refusing to take a Breathalyzer in Indiana meant immediate arrest and having your license suspended. Stephanie was the fight-for-your-rights, stand-up-to-the-establishment, and change-the-system person in our family. Funny, at the time, I remember saying to her, "You should never drink and drive, and if you have nothing to hide, why not take the Breathalyzer?" My words had come back to bite me.

I said a brief prayer and blew into the device.

Officer Keep-My-Cards-Close-to-My-Chest looked at the results but didn't say anything to me. Instead, he walked over to the wall of policemen and conferred.

As they huddled, a car pulled alongside the officers and then parked in front of my car. The officers went on high alert. Each of them automatically moved their hands to their hips to their weapons.

Suddenly, the air felt tense and static filled.

The car doors opened. Stephanie and David got out.

"Get back in your vehicle."

"Don't move."

"Stay where you are!"

The officers yelled and moved toward my children, their weapons drawn and pointed.

"Stop! Those are my kids," I yelled and started to move forward.

"Stay where you are," someone shouted.

I froze.

Suddenly, a Dodge Charger pulled up with lights flashing and skidded to a stop in between Stephanie and David and the ready-to-fire policemen. Officer Joseph Harrison leapt out of the car. He motioned for David and Stephanie to stay put, then walked over to the patrolmen and spoke to them.

I couldn't hear what was said, but the result was that the officers visibly relaxed. They all put their weapons back in their holsters. Their shoulders eased, and eventually they all walked back to their vehicles.

I hadn't realized I was holding my breath until I exhaled.

Officer Harrison walked over to me. "Stephanie called me. You okay?"

I was so thankful to see him, I hugged him. "Yes, and thank you for coming." I might have clung to him for an uncomfortably long time because he motioned that Stephanie and David could come over.

"Is it okay for me to get out of the car now?" Dixie yelled.

I laughed and pulled away in time to see the last of the police cars roll away.

Stephanie ran and threw her arms around my neck and hugged me close. When David arrived, I pulled him into a group hug and clung to my two children as tears streamed down my face.

Officer Harrison walked over to his vehicle and let Turbo out of the back of the car and walked him to the side of the road, where he sniffed and then relieved himself. When they were done, they took a slow walk back to us. I suspected he wanted to give me time to gather my emotions.

"Thank you so much, Officer Harrison," I said.

He nodded. "Glad I could help, and it's Joe."

Stephanie walked over, reached up, and kissed him on the cheek. "Yes, thank you so much. I don't know what I would have done if you hadn't come." She choked up, and seeing my daughter so emotional made me emotional. I started crying all over again.

Dixie ran back around to the passenger side of the car, reached inside, and pulled out a box of tissues. Obviously, she'd found the box of tissues in the glove box as she had been digging for the vehicle registration. She brought the box around, and Stephanie and I both made good use of them.

I stared from Stephanie to Joseph Harrison. "You say Stephanie called you?"

He nodded.

I turned to Stephanie. "How did you know?"

A semi sped past us so rapidly, the ground shook. It sounded like a freight train, and it generated a huge gust of wind that nearly tore David's cap off of his head.

Detective Harrison started to speak, but stopped when two more semis passed with double the effect of the last truck. He mouthed the words, *Follow me.*

We nodded our understanding and then got into our respective vehicles.

When I opened the car door, David hurried over and whispered, "Mom, maybe I should drive."

I nodded and got in the backseat.

Detective Harrison drove to the next exit and got off. There was a twenty-four-hour truck stop restaurant right off the interstate and he pulled into the parking lot.

Inside, the tiny restaurant was practically empty, which worked out well, considering there were five of us and a dog. I thought the staff would have balked at the idea of a dog in the restaurant, but apparently Turbo was well-known there. When the skinny-as-a-rail waitress spotted us, she hurried to the back. When she came out, she put a bowl of water on the floor and a huge bone in front of Turbo before she even greeted us. Turbo lapped up nearly half the bowl of water and then lay down and gnawed on his bone.

Once the important guest was taken care of, the waitress diverted her attention to the rest of us. "Hi, Joe, you brought company this time." She smiled broadly.

Officer Harrison nodded but didn't elaborate.

The short, perky waitress had big blue eyes and long, thick, dark curly hair. She'd braided her hair and pinned it to her head. "Coffee?"

We all nodded and she hurried to the back and came back with a pot and five cups. She put a non-sugar sweetener in a blue wrapper in front of Officer Harrison and then filled each of our cups. When she was done, she asked. "You want menus?"

We shook our heads, and Officer Harrison said, "We'll just have the coffee for now, Carla."

Carla nodded and went back to wiping down the already-clean counters.

We sipped our coffee and sat in an awkward silence for a few minutes.

"You must come here often," Stephanie said. "The waitress knows you and Turbo so well."

The question seemed nonchalant, as though she was merely making casual conversation. However, when Stephanie graduated the bar and had her first court case, I went to Chicago to see her. I was impressed at the way she questioned witnesses. She started out as though she was merely making casual conversation, but with each answer, she drew her noose tighter and tighter around the person's neck, and before they knew what hit them, she had blindsided them into revealing their darkest secrets.

Officer Harrison smiled. "I've known her for twenty years." He took a sip of coffee. "She's my sister."

I doubted Officer Harrison noticed the tips of Stephanie's ears. They turned red when she was embarrassed.

"How wonderful," I said. "She's so cute."

Officer Harrison looked toward his sister and his eyes softened. "She's a good kid. She works here at night to pay for school. She's taking classes during the daytime." He took another sip of coffee. "I worry about her, so Turbo and I come by whenever we can to keep an eye on things."

I was already viewing Officer Harrison quite fondly, and hearing this just made him rise a bit higher in my estimation. I suspected Stephanie was looking at Officer Harrison quite fondly too. "So, you said Stephanie called you?"

He nodded.

I turned to stare at my daughter. "But why?"

Stephanie put down her coffee and started to explain. "Joe…I mean, Officer Harrison…gave me his card. I got—"

"No, I mean how did you know anything was wrong?" I paused. "Don't get me wrong, I totally appreciate the help, but how did you know?" I turned to Stephanie. "How could you possibly have known what was going on and where we were?"

Dixie piped in. "That was me. I texted her."

I should have known, but in my own defense, a lot had happened in the past few hours, and I was completely rattled. I had nearly been arrested and the very thought of it made my stomach quiver. Drinking those glasses of wine was stupid, and I should never have gotten behind the wheel of the car. While I didn't feel the wine had impaired my reflexes, I was old enough to know better. I was already an emotional basket case. The last thing I needed to do was mix my emotional muck with alcohol and a nearly two-ton weapon. It was stupid, and I was thankful I hadn't injured myself or anyone else. I stared into my coffee cup at the ripples the liquid made when anyone jolted the table. One small bump by anyone transferred through the table into my cup. The results varied from small ripples to what amounted to waves that caused my coffee to slosh outside of the cup onto the table. I could see how one bump in the always-under-construction interstate, an errant piece of debris, or a deer could have led to a serious accident in which an innocent person could have been injured…or worse. Something tugged at the back of my mind, but, for the life of me, I couldn't remember what it was.

"Earth to Lilly." Dixie touched my arm.

The unexpected touch jolted me back from the precipice of despair but caused me to jump, spilling most of my coffee onto the table.

Carla hurried over with a towel and the coffeepot. She quickly wiped up my mess and refilled my cup without missing a beat.

"I'm sorry."

"It's okay, Mom." Stephanie reached across the table and squeezed my hand.

"Accidents happen." David yawned.

I shook my head and took one of the extra napkins Carla had left before she hurried away. "I'm not talking about the coffee." I dabbed at my eyes. "I am sorry I spilled the coffee, but I'm sorrier I did something so stupid. I should never have had those two glasses of wine. I shouldn't have gotten behind the wheel of the car. Thankfully, no one was injured, but that situation could have turned out so much worse." I stared at my children. "I'm really sorry."

Stephanie squeezed my hand again.

David nodded and took a drink of coffee.

They say confession is good for the soul. So, I decided, in for a penny, in for a pound. I took a deep breath. "I've been debating whether or not I should do this, but…I raised my children to be truthful and to trust that justice will prevail. There's no right way to do a wrong thing." I took another deep breath. I then proceeded to tell Officer Harrison about the gun we'd found in the glove box of the car.

"Where's the gun now?" he asked.

I nodded to Dixie and she put her purse on the table.

Officer Harrison looked around the restaurant. The only other person there was a trucker sitting at the counter with his back to us. He nodded and Dixie reached into her bag, pulled out the weapon, and placed it on the table in front of him.

He looked at the weapon. "I'm guessing you've both handled this?"

We both nodded.

"I'm afraid we didn't even think about fingerprints," I said.

He picked it up. "I doubt if the killer would be stupid enough to leave his fingerprints on the weapon." He examined it and then put it inside his jacket. "Have you ever seen this gun before?"

I shook my head. "I'm not fond of guns. That's the gun that killed him, isn't it?"

He shrugged. "We won't know for sure until we get a ballistics report, but it fires the same type of bullets, nine millimeter, which is what killed him. I'd say it's almost certainly the murder weapon."

"It's obvious someone is trying to frame her. Why would she leave the gun in the glove box?" Stephanie asked.

Officer Harrison's facial expression hadn't changed, but something in his tone told me he wasn't happy. "The district attorney will say she hadn't had time to dispose of the gun yet."

"Time? She could have driven to Lake Michigan any number of times and tossed that gun into the lake," David argued.

"Maybe." Officer Harrison shrugged.

"If she was guilty, would she have confessed she had the gun and given it to you? You didn't know she had it. She could have kept her mouth shut and driven to the lake or found the nearest sewer grate and gotten rid of it. You would never have known," Stephanie argued.

Officer Harrison stared into his coffee. He was silent, but his silence spoke volumes. The air was electric and tense. When he eventually looked at Stephanie, there was something in his eyes that told me where his allegiances lay. He was a cop, first and foremost; he was a cop who had a duty to fulfill, and he intended to perform his duty, no matter who got hurt.

Stephanie must have seen the same thing I did, because she nodded briefly and closed her eyes for several seconds. When she opened them, it was as though a veil had dropped, shading her inner self. "Alright then, I guess we know where we stand."

When she spoke, I felt as though the temperature had dropped ten degrees, and I shivered.

For one brief instant, there was a flicker in the back of Officer Harrison's eyes, a pleading, hungry look that flashed for a nanosecond, but as quickly as it came, it passed. "I'd better get this gun to the station." He stood. Turbo rose slowly and stretched with the bone still in his mouth. Officer Harrison waved to his sister and walked out into the sunrise.

CHAPTER 8

The limousine was scheduled to arrive in just a few hours, so we paid for our coffees and left a generous tip for Carla. Then we hurried home to dress for the funeral. As I showered, I tried not to think about the fact this might be the last time I got to take a shower alone for many years. On television, the shower situation in prison was never ideal. I briefly wondered how long I could go without showering before my own body odor would knock me out. I reined my thoughts away from that rabbit trail. It was best not to stroll down that path.

I dressed in a black sheath dress, with black stockings, and looked at myself in the mirror. Mourning didn't suit me. I felt like such a fraud. I was sorry Albert was dead. I didn't wish death on anyone, but I was far from the grieving widow. I looked in my closet and found a black suit. I donned the skirt and a charcoal gray blouse. I replaced the black panty hose with nude and put on sensible black ballet flats. One last look in the mirror assured me I looked appropriate, without being overly somber. I grabbed my Bible and rosary from the dresser and headed downstairs.

David was downstairs in a black suit, with a new white shirt that still bore the wrinkles from where it had been folded before he took it out of the bag. He must have picked it up at the airport on his way home. The mother in me was tempted to tell him to take the shirt off so I could iron the wrinkles out. However, the mom in me also realized my son was grieving the loss of his father. Regardless of their relationship, Albert was still his father. The fact the two of them weren't close probably made this even harder. There had to be a part of my son that wished things had been different, yet knew now they could never reconcile and have a better relationship. Someone had taken that option away. As a mom, I needed to provide whatever love and emotional support I could to my children. His father was dead, and it didn't matter if his shirt was wrinkled or not. I walked up to my son and gave him a hug.

He seemed startled at first but hugged me back in a perfunctory manner.

When I felt him pull away, I held on to him tighter and refused to let go. Initially, his body was a bow, drawn tight and ready to fire. After the hug continued, his shoulders relaxed and his body slumped. When I felt his sobs and the dampness of tears on my neck, I knew he would be okay. He needed to grieve, to cry and to release the emotions I knew he wouldn't allow himself to show at the funeral. My son, the actor, would put on the performance of a lifetime. He would push his emotions down deep within himself and put on the stoic exterior mask he'd learned to wear after years of hiding his emotions.

I don't know how long we stood that way, but when he'd cried himself out and the sobs ceased, only then did I slacken my hold and release him. When he stood up, I took his face in my hands, kissed him on the cheek, and whispered, "I love you."

He looked in my eyes for confirmation. He must have found it, because after a brief pause, he nodded.

David and I had always understood each other. He was a strong, independent spirit, and I was thankful to have him in my life.

When I stood back and looked around, I saw that Dixie and Stephanie were wiping away tears. I looked at Stephanie. She was a different animal than her brother. She wouldn't keep her feelings bottled up. Stephanie was more likely to join a kickboxing class to kick some butt rather than bury her feelings and let them fester. She smiled, and I knew she was okay. I held out my hands to hug her anyway and engulfed my daughter in a warm embrace. However, from the first moment, I could tell the difference between the two.

When the doorbell rang, we separated. Dixie went to open the door, while Stephanie and I shoved tissues into our purses.

We walked outside, and when the driver opened the door, I was surprised to see that the vehicle was already full. Inside were Albert's mother and father, grandmother, two brothers, and their wives. In fact, the limo was completely full, and there was no room for me or the children.

Mrs. Conti refused to look in my direction but stared straight ahead. "I told him not to stop. There's no room, but he wouldn't listen."

Part of me wanted to reach in and pull them all out of the car one at a time. I sensed the frustration and anger rumbling inside of Stephanie—like the winds of a hurricane. Perhaps it was that sense of right and wrong—

and of justice—that lived in both of us that wanted to shout, *This isn't right!* There was another part of me that felt weary. I had been up all night and was tired. I was facing the likelihood of being arrested for a crime I hadn't committed. Part of my brain wondered if there was even such a thing as justice. There were certainly a lot of people who had been tried, convicted, and executed for crimes they hadn't committed. Would I be one of them? Before I allowed those dark, melancholy thoughts to engulf me, I shook myself.

"Fine." I slammed the limo door shut. I marched toward my SUV and dug my keys out of my purse. "We'll take my car."

David hurried to catch up to me. "Perhaps I should drive." He took the keys out of my hand.

"I'm not drunk."

"I know you're not, but I could use something to do." He walked over to the passenger door and held it open for Stephanie, Dixie, and me.

We got into the car, and he closed our doors and then hurried to the driver's side and got in.

"This is crazy," Stephanie huffed.

I shrugged. "I don't care."

Stephanie stared at me. "Why are you so calm?"

"Yeah, why aren't you yelling and screaming? I would be, if my mother-in-law tried that crap with me!" Dixie said.

"I'm rather surprised myself." David glanced at me as he backed out of the driveway. "Don't get me wrong, I'm glad I didn't have to separate my mom and my grandmother from a physical fight." He smiled. "But I can't help wondering—"

"Who are you, and what have you done with our mother?" Stephanie poked the back of my neck.

"Ouch! What are you doing?" I yelped.

"Checking for pods. You must have been taken over by alien spores and become one of those *pod people*," Stephanie said.

We all laughed at the reference. I remembered going to a drive-in movie with the children to watch *Invasion of the Body Snatchers*. Albert and I had argued over whether the film would frighten them. I thought it might cause nightmares. Fortunately, they found the 1956 film hilarious, rather than scary.

"I'm not an alien." I sighed. "I'm just tired." The emotional burden of the divorce and the stress of waiting to be arrested had weighed me down. "Besides, this will be over in a few hours, and I will never have to deal with any of these people again—unless Nonna Conti or Bisnonna get put in jail." I attempted to lighten the mood.

No one laughed.

"Oh, come on. My joke wasn't that bad," I quipped.

I looked from face to face, but no one would make eye contact with me. "What's wrong?"

After a pause, Dixie reached underneath the seat and pulled out a newspaper. On the front page, my own face stared back at me. The headline read "Lighthouse Dunes' Merry Widow Visits Casino Night before Husband's Funeral."

I didn't bother reading the article. I had already lived through the ordeal once. The last thing I needed was a reminder. The picture of the waitress from the casino bar assured me that the story wasn't written in my favor. "Good grief, that picture of me was from a community fund-raiser ten years ago." I tossed the paper back to Dixie. "I was having a bad hair day."

Dixie's smile never made it to her eyes.

I sighed. "I almost wish they'd just lock me up already and get it over with."

Dixie gasped, and from the rearview mirror, I saw Stephanie and David exchange looks that reminded me I needed to be strong for them. I wasn't deliberately trying to be morbid. I wasn't enthused about the idea of getting arrested, but the anticipation of waiting for it to happen was worse. I hated walking around under a cloud of guilt and suspicion. I glanced out the window and couldn't help wondering if every car I saw was an unmarked police car waiting to pick me up. I had to remind myself, *I'm not that important*, several times before I developed a twitch.

We arrived at the church, and David pulled up to the front door. One of the funeral home attendants scrambled to open the doors and provide a hand for us as we dispersed. As we lined up, the funeral director, a short, balding man whose name I couldn't remember for the life of me, and Father Dominick were waiting in the vestibule. After paying respects to Bisnonna and Nonna and Lorenzo Conti, he motioned for Stephanie, David, and me to come closer.

I walked around the Conti family, rather than waiting for them to part and permit me to move forward.

Father Dominick spoke in the soft "Holy Father" voice he used at times like this—gentle yet firm. "I will lead the processional into the church. The immediate family will be behind me and will sit on the first row. Spouses, children, and close friends of immediate family members will sit in the rows directly behind them."

Mrs. Conti looked as though she wanted to say something, but Father Dominick gave her a "Holy Father" look, which managed to silence her.

Frankly, I was impressed. I'd never seen anyone who was adept at silencing my mother-in-law, and certainly not with a mere look.

Dixie whispered into my ear, "Do you think they teach them how to do that in seminary?"

I shook my head. "I have no idea, but if they ever decide to market the secret, it would be worth a fortune."

Dixie gave my hand a squeeze and then stepped to the back of the line.

Father Dominick asked if everyone would bow their heads for a brief prayer. He prayed for peace and comfort for the grieving family, and then reminded us of the love of our heavenly Father, which he freely gave to us all. It wasn't a long prayer, but it was effective. In a very few words, he prayed for compassion and forgiveness. He reminded us of God's commandment to love. When he was done, he turned and led us into the sanctuary.

The funeral mass was beautiful in its simplicity and ritual. The time-honored hymns spoke comfort to my soul. Father Dominick chose scriptures to read that provided reassurance and hope, rather than remorse. As I sat on the front row and listened to the mass, I watched the light filter through the stained-glass windows onto the altar. Something about the light through those windows left me feeling loved as I'd scarcely felt before. Apart from Mrs. Conti's tears and an occasional wail from his grandmother, the mass proceeded without incident. Thankfully, David sat on one side of me and Stephanie on the other, so I felt surrounded by the love of my children, despite the frost coming my way from the rest of the Conti family.

When the mass was over, there was a brief ceremony to take place at the gravesite. Father Dominick led a prayer and blessed the grave and coffin with holy water that had been sanctified by the archbishop of the diocese. Dixie skipped the graveside ceremony and bummed a ride back to the house with one of the parishioners to help with the repast, which would follow the graveside ceremony.

Two obstacles down and one to go. I released a heavy sigh as David helped me back into the car. I wasn't sure if Albert's family would come back to the house or not. None of them had spoken one word to me since the limousine had left for the church and the strain of trying to maintain an appearance of companionship was draining, especially without a good night's sleep.

Unfortunately, when David pulled up to the house, it appeared that Albert's family had not decided to skip the repast and were already at the house. I sighed and got out of the car, reminding myself it would be over in just a few more hours. Well, mostly over.

I went in through the front door. The majority of people inside were Albert's family members. Brothers, sisters-in-law, nieces, and nephews filled the living room. Mrs. Conti sat in a position of prominence on the sofa, flanked by her husband and sons. When I stepped inside, the atmosphere altered. From the front porch, I heard the hum of conversation. Once I stepped inside, the hum ceased. Nearly everyone in the room turned to stare at me. I felt their judgment in the silence that followed and in the cold stares they bestowed on me. Thankfully, Stephanie came over and hugged me tightly. That hug froze the silence, and the masses returned to their whispered conversations.

"Thank you." I hugged Stephanie in return.

Stephanie handed me a small plate of food and a glass of wine. "I thought you might need this."

"Thank you." I took a sip and placed the glass on a nearby console table. The ham, macaroni and cheese, and green bean casserole, along with all of the other comfort foods Stephanie had given me, smelled delicious. I was hungry and prepared to take a few bites. Before I had ingested my first forkful, however, I looked around and noticed my neighbor watching me as though she was trying to memorize my every movement.

Bradley Hurston was sitting in a wheelchair near the front door, with a plate of food on his lap and his binoculars around his neck. Unfortunately, I made eye contact with Marianne Carpenter, and she took that as an invitation to come over.

She grabbed the handles of her brother's wheelchair and pushed him in my direction so suddenly, his plate of food slid to the floor. Unnoticed by Marianne, she rolled the wheels of his chair right over the plate, compacting the food into the carpet as efficiently as those large asphalt rollers flattened hot tar.

"I wanted to be the first to give my condolences." She grabbed my shoulders and pulled me into an embrace that nearly spilled my own plate onto the front of my shirt.

I pulled away and placed the plate behind me onto the console table. "Thank you, Marianne."

"I've been meaning to come over sooner, but with all of the police and the reporters roaming all over the place day and night, it's been hard to find a time when you were alone," she said anxiously.

"What do you mean?" I asked.

She looked positively elated. "Well, I mean, those men who keep coming around the house looking for things." She leaned close and whispered, "You know…evidence."

"I know what you did. I saw you," Bradley Hurston said from his wheelchair.

I smiled at him. "You dropped your plate. Let me get you another one."

I turned, and instead of one plate on the console table, I saw there were two. I hadn't remembered anyone else leaving a plate there, but then, there was a lot going on. Both plates looked untouched and contained virtually the same items. I looked around and didn't see the other plate's owner. *It must have been Stephanie.* I took one of the two plates and handed it to Bradley Hurston.

When I looked up, I saw my brother in-law Gino in an animated conversation with Albert's attorney, Charles Nelson.

"I saw what you did." Bradley Hurston took a bite of chicken.

I heard a crash and turned back around. On the console table, the plate of food that had been there moments ago was now covered with glass shards and wine from a shattered wineglass.

"I'm thirsty," Bradley Hurston said to his sister.

Marianne looked as though she would have liked to throttle her brother for a brief second, until she glanced over and saw David near the drink table. She smiled at me and then wheeled Bradley over toward David.

Gino's face was red with rage. He glared at me and then stomped away, leaving me wondering what had gotten him so upset.

While Gino was red with fury, Chip looked as white as a ghost. Charles Nelson in his tailor-made suits always looked as though butter wouldn't melt in his mouth, and today was no exception. If he was angry, upset, or furious, he had apparently trained himself not to show any emotion. His wife, Marilyn, on the other hand, was nothing but emotion.

If Marilyn Nelson's eyes were a measure of alcohol consumption, she was well on her way to inebriation. The police wouldn't need a breathalyzer to tell she was in no shape to walk, let alone drive.

"Lilly, please accept our condo…console…condolences." Marilyn kissed the air next to my cheek and sloshed her glass of wine down the front of my blouse.

Marilyn Nelson was a thin, well-preserved woman in her late forties. However, the years and bouts of alcoholism hadn't been kind, and up close, she looked older. Despite a ton of makeup, her skin looked horrible. Her eyes were almost as red as her lipstick, and her bobbed hair looked dull and lifeless. Her dress was expensive and bore the unmistakable signs of one of the most expensive designers, but she'd lost a lot of weight and it hung loosely off her frame. She had removed her three-inch heels, and they were now sticking out of her purse. The red-soled Louboutin shoes made me drool for a few seconds, until her thin, bony fingers, adorned with diamonds, grabbed my arm. "Lilly, I'm so sorry," she whispered in a voice that carried so that anyone standing nearby couldn't help but overhear. "I'm terribly sorry."

"Thank you." I tried to steady the tottering woman.

Charles's eyes narrowed, and a vein on the side of his head pulsed. He removed the wineglass from his wife's hand and took her around the waist. "That's enough."

Marilyn placed her head on his shoulder. "Yes, Charles," she said meekly.

"As you can see, my wife isn't well." He grimaced. "I wanted to talk to you about the will, but I really need to get her home."

"Of course. Why don't you call me tomorrow?"

Charles nodded. "Chip, help me get your mother to the car."

Before he left, Charles Nelson took out a handkerchief and wiped up the broken glass and wine. Albert used to refer to Charles Nelson as the "Cleanup Man." He had always been there to clean up after Chip, and apparently Marilyn. Now I understood what he meant.

Chip Nelson, slightly bleary-eyed and nervous, snapped out of his trance. The blood drained back into his face, and he got on the other side of his mother. Between the two of them, they helped Marilyn outside.

"One thing you have to say about Charles Nelson, he is one fine dresser." I took a deep breath and looked.

Christopher Williams, my own lawyer, was standing nearby. "How're you holding up?"

I shrugged. "I'm tired, but I haven't been arrested yet, so I guess that's good news." I looked around. "Unless you're here to tell me the 'thing which I greatly feared is come upon me.'"

"Job, right?"

I nodded. "Job three twenty-five."

He smiled. "I guess I do remember some things from Sunday school." He took a sip of his wine and then shook his head. "Not yet. They've agreed to give you until tomorrow to turn yourself in, but if you don't turn yourself in by noon tomorrow, then they'll issue a warrant and you'll be arrested."

I nodded, grateful I wouldn't be dragged out of my house in handcuffs in front of my husband's family. Something told me that was the main reason my mother in-law had even bothered to come to the house after the service. She would have taken pleasure in seeing me humiliated.

I received condolences from friends and Albert's business associates for close to an hour. When the funeral director thanked me for entrusting my husband's remains with his company and announced they would be leaving, I breathed a sigh of relief. The end was in sight.

Stephanie shared the news of the limousine's impending departure with Albert's family, and they made their way outside to load into the vehicles.

Albert's grandmother had to be helped outside. Mrs. Conti started to wail. It took her husband and both daughters-in-law to help her out. She made an elaborate production of *not* looking at me as she left. Just when I thought her performance couldn't get any better, she stopped at the door, turned toward me, and uttered what sounded like a curse in Italian, then she spat on the ground and finally allowed herself to be dragged outside into the limo.

I hadn't heard Dixie's approach until she whispered in my ear, "And the Oscar for best performance at a funeral goes to Camilia Conti."

* * * *

I honestly didn't expect to sleep. Between finding the gun that was most likely used to murder my husband, getting stopped by the police and almost being arrested for DUI, my husband's funeral, complete with crazy in-laws, oh, and having to turn myself in for arrest, I thought my mind would be running 90 miles per hour and sleep would be the furthest thing from my mind. Fortunately, exhaustion and fatigue won out, and I slept like a toddler. In fact, I was out as soon as my head hit the pillow. No dreams, at least none I remembered, haunted me. I woke up refreshed and invigorated.

I showered and dressed while Aggie waited anxiously in the small, pink pet carrier Dixie had bought after the funeral yesterday. She'd said she was in need of retail therapy. I spent extra time cuddling Aggie, partly because she'd been neglected a bit with all of the chaos I'd been through lately. However, if I was honest with myself, I snuggled with her more because I wasn't sure when I'd be able to do it again. Between Christopher and Stephanie's help, I realized it was unlikely that I'd immediately be taken to prison. In fact, they assured me chances were good I'd be home this afternoon. Yet, as I scratched Aggie's belly and cooed at her, I wondered if I was doing her a disservice. She deserved a stable home where she didn't have to wonder where her next bowl of dog food was going to come from. Aggie took that moment to lay her head on my chest and looked up at me with her trusting brown eyes.

Before Christopher had left the previous night, we'd arranged for him to meet me here today at ten. That would give us plenty of time to get to the police station before the noon deadline. I smelled coffee and suddenly realized I was famished.

Downstairs, Dixie, Stephanie, and David sat at the kitchen table. If the dark circles under Stephanie's eyes, the red, bleary-eyed gaze from David, or the makeup-streaked tissues next to Dixie were used to measure sleep, it didn't appear any of them had gotten much.

"Good morning." I poured myself a cup of coffee. "I'm starving. How about breakfast?"

They each looked at me as though I'd just asked for arsenic or a cyanide tablet.

After a few seconds, Dixie hopped up and rushed around the kitchen. "Good idea. Why don't I make you something? What would you like?"

"Why don't I make breakfast?" I took a sip of coffee and placed my mug on the counter. I could tell Dixie was about to protest, so I forestalled it by adding, "It'll give me something to do." I smiled at my friend. "Would you mind taking Aggie outside? I think she could use a little exercise."

Dixie nodded. "Of course not. I'm sure Chyna and Leia could use a brisk walk around the block too."

David stood up. "Can I help? Three dogs is a lot to manage. Do you think either of the big girls would be up for a run?"

"Actually, that sounds like a great idea. I'm sure either Chyna or Leia would love a romp around the block. My husband usually takes them for six-mile runs before the weather gets too hot."

"I could use a job myself." Stephanie stretched. "I haven't gotten any exercise since...well, in quite a few days."

"Great. Why don't you all get out of my way and let me cook? Then, when you come back, I'll have breakfast ready." I put a carton of eggs and a loaf of bread on the counter and hoisted a bag of potatoes up next to them. I didn't see any looks exchanged, but I felt them anyway. "I feel like hash browns."

Dixie put retractable leashes on each of the larger dogs and handed one to each of the kids, along with a couple of plastic bags for waste cleanup. She took the tiny pink leash she'd bought for Aggie and headed outside.

David stood for several seconds after Stephanie and Dixie left. He looked as though he wanted to say something, but instead, he turned and walked out with the standard poodle on the leash.

I took a deep breath, grateful for a few moments of peace. Something had been bothering me ever since the incident with the police, but I couldn't remember what it was. When I tried to focus and make myself remember, it flitted away, just out of reach. Focusing on something else, like cooking, would allow me to think about other things, and hopefully, the thing I wanted to remember would come out of the shadows and into the light. I picked up a sharp knife and started peeling potatoes. I had barely started when the back door slammed. I yelled, "Did you forget something?"

David stood in the back door with Chyna and Leia and a stricken look on his face.

"What's happened?"

He took a deep breath. "There are police cars and an ambulance next door. I think something might have happened to Mr. Hurston."

I wiped my hands on a dishcloth and hurried to the door.

David reached out to stop me. "Stephanie said to wait here until she can have a quick talk with the detective."

"Detective? I thought you said there was an ambulance? He must have had a stroke or a heart attack or something."

Something in David's eyes told me there was more to this than met the eye.

"What is it? What aren't you telling me?"

He swallowed. "Mrs. Carpenter was outside. I heard her say he was murdered. He'd been stabbed."

CHAPTER 9

The idea of eating made me want to gag. However, cooking was different. Cooking provided my hands with something to do. If the item I chose to cook was something I'd made many times before, then my mind could disengage and wander while my hands went on autopilot and did all of the work. Cooking was comforting, and I indulged by making a breakfast casserole. In fact, I sent David to the store to buy more eggs, and I made two of them: one for us and one for Marianne. That was what good neighbors did, right? When your next-door neighbor was stabbed, you made a casserole. I forced myself not to laugh hysterically and fried the sausage for the casseroles.

In addition to breakfast casseroles, I made hash browns. Normally, my least favorite part about making hash browns was squeezing the water out of the potatoes. The key to getting crispy hash brown potatoes was to get as much of the water out of the potatoes as possible. I was always amazed at how much water there was in just a few potatoes. So, after I peeled and shredded the potatoes, I put them in cheesecloth and squeezed, wrung, wrung, and squeezed until I couldn't squeeze or wring anymore.

I hadn't realized David was watching me until he walked up behind me and removed the dripping, potato-stained cloth from my hands. I was drenched in water from the potatoes. My hands were dripping wet, but the water that dripped from my face had nothing to do with the hash browns.

Today was my turn for support, and David provided the comfort and love I needed. He wrapped his arms around me and held me. I put my head on his shoulder and cried. I cried for all the loss. I cried for the loss of trust when my husband violated our marriage vows. I cried for the loss of life when someone decided to murder him. I cried for Bradley Hurston, who had dedicated years to serving his community, and for the disease that stole his memories and crippled him, putting him in a wheelchair. Finally, I cried for the life next door that was taken so violently. When I was cried out, I stood back and accepted the paper towel he provided.

I wiped my eyes and blew my nose. “It’s not fair.”

He nodded. “I know.”

“Bradley Hurston deserved so much better than to die like that.”

I could smell the casseroles and knew they were done. I washed my face, turned off the oven, and then removed the bubbling goodness from the oven. I wrapped one in foil and walked it across the yard.

The police had taped a boundary around the perimeter of the house, and there was what appeared to be an army of policemen walking, photographing, and scanning the ground.

I walked up to a policeman who was standing at the tape boundary. “I’m Lilly Echosby. I live next door. Could I leave this for Marianne?”

His head was tilted down in my direction, but he wore mirrored sunglasses that prevented anyone from seeing his eyes. His face didn’t relax, and nothing resembling a smile penetrated his façade. He had a wire bungee cord coming out of his ear and a radio secured to his shoulder. He pushed a button and spoke into the radio. I heard static and muffled sounds but couldn’t make out words. Apparently the border patrol was better at deciphering garbled messages than me.

“I’m sorry, but no one is allowed to enter. This is an active crime scene.”

“Can you take this and just leave it inside then?” I tried to hand him the casserole.

“No, ma’am.”

I huffed and turned to walk away. I’d just have to put the breakfast casserole in the fridge and bring it over later. I took a few steps and then heard my name.

“Lilly, oh God, Lilly.” Marianne Carpenter ran from the side of the house. She nearly collided with me, which would have meant second- and possibly third-degree burns from the still-hot casserole.

Fortunately, I managed to turn so the casserole wasn’t between us as she put her arms around my neck. Both of my arms were out to one side in an effort to prevent casserole calamity, and Marianne hung from my neck. I felt the casserole slip and was about to adjust my position when Dixie hurried up and relieved me of the dish.

The strain must have been too much, because Marianne’s legs gave out and she would have fallen and taken me down with her, had David not rushed over at that moment. He scooped Marianne up in his arms.

Dixie rushed into the house. She reappeared moments later, minus the casserole, and held the back door open. As David got Marianne inside, I saw Stephanie, out of the side of my eye, hurrying to the ambulance in the front of the house, which had yet to leave.

David put Marianne on the sofa. Stephanie returned with one of the emergency medical technicians who checked her pulse and blood pressure, and then diagnosed her as having fainted. I hadn't studied medicine, but I already knew that much.

Marianne came around a few moments later. "I'm so sorry. I just suddenly felt lightheaded."

"It's okay. You've had a terrible shock," I reassured her.

The EMTs took Marianne to the hospital, just to make sure she was okay. As they were leaving, the coroner arrived to remove Bradley Hurston.

After all of the excitement died down, I finished cooking the hash browns. When they were done, my attorney, Christopher Williams, arrived. Christopher was wearing what appeared, to my inexperienced eyes, to be an extremely expensive, hand-tailored dark brown suit. His shoes were a dark caramel color that looked like truffles.

"You're just in time for breakfast," I said as he came in and petted the poodles.

Dogs fed and lying on the floor, we ate almost an entire breakfast casserole. The hash browns were all that hash browns should be: crispy and well-seasoned, with bits of onions and red and green peppers.

"This is delicious." Christopher washed down the last of his hash browns with coffee.

There was nothing like preparing food for people you cared about and watching them enjoy it. Almost everyone seemed to have enjoyed the breakfast, and I smiled. David had barely touched his food.

"Is everything okay?" I asked.

David looked up and it took a few moments for his eyes to focus. It was as though he'd been miles away. However, when he focused, he looked at me with a softness and tenderness that made me weepy.

I patted his hand. "I'm going to be fine. I know you're worried about me, but I'm okay. I didn't kill your father, and I believe that, with my excellent attorney here"—I stared at Christopher—"the police, and my friends, we're going to find the person who did."

David nodded. "I know you didn't kill him. But there's something you need to know."

I waited expectantly.

David took a deep breath. "I think I know how the gun got in the glove box of the car."

I gasped. Of all the things I'd expected, that wasn't in the top two hundred. "How?" I whispered.

He took another deep breath. "The night I got home, I went up to bed. I was tired, but I couldn't sleep. I kept wondering...wondering about her."

I tilted my head and stared. "Who?"

He swallowed. "Her? That Bambi person. I couldn't get her out of my mind. How could he do that? How could he just throw away over a quarter of a century of marriage and give up our family for some...some...b—"

"I believe the politically correct term is *home-wrecking harlot*," Dixie said.

David smiled. "Yeah, I guess that's as good as anything."

"So, what did you do?" I asked.

"Hold on," Christopher interrupted. "I need to caution you. I'm representing your mother, not you. If what you're about to say has any bearing on the case, I might be compelled to reveal it in the course of her defense."

"Perhaps you should step outside," Stephanie suggested.

Christopher rose, but David waved him back to his seat.

"Don't bother. I'm going to make a statement to the police later."

Christopher sat back down, and we all waited patiently.

"I went to see her," David said.

"Bambi? You went to the apartment?" Stephanie asked.

David shook his head. "No. I went to the Purple Panther."

"The strip club?" I tried to keep my voice neutral. My son was old enough to frequent such establishments, and I wasn't naïve enough to believe that at twenty-three, he'd never been to a strip club before, but the Purple Panther was a sleazy dive that made me want to spray the entire house down with Lysol.

He nodded.

"How did you know she'd be there?" Christopher asked.

"Before I came back, I reached out to Chip Nelson. I knew he worked at the dealership with Dad." He paced in the small kitchen. "Besides, Chip was the sleaziest person I knew. If anyone knew where Bambi worked, it'd be Chip."

"Seems logical." Stephanie took a sip of coffee.

"Okay, so you went to the Purple Panther. Did you see her?" I asked.

"Oh, yeah. I saw her. I saw *all* of her."

I smiled.

"Did you talk to her?" Christopher asked.

David hung his head. "Not at first. It's such a disgusting place. The floor was sticky. The place reeked of smoke and weed and vomit. The women were…well, let's just say none of them were the type of talent one would find dancing on Broadway or at Radio City Music Hall."

I smiled. "I doubt the clientele of the Purple Panther actually cares how well the women dance."

"I just meant it was incredibly sleazy, and the thought of my dad in a place like that made me feel sick." He paced. "How could he seriously believe that any woman who worked there would be interested in anything other than his money?"

"Did you talk to her?" I asked.

David nodded. "Yeah. I couldn't help myself. I had to know."

"So, how'd that go?" I asked as casually as I could.

He shook his head. "Not good. I bought her a drink, and she came to the table. The first words out of her mouth were, 'Twenty dollars for a lap dance, and the price goes up depending on what else you want.'" He shuddered.

"Did she know who you were?" Christopher asked.

He nodded. "I told her. I thought it would make a difference."

"Did it?" I asked.

"No. She just said she didn't do family and friend discounts."

Dixie spit out her coffee. "Sorry." She took a napkin and wiped up the mess.

"I'm sorry, but I still don't get it. I may be dense, but I still don't see how the gun got in the glove box." I swallowed and tried hard to steady my voice. "You didn't take her anywhere in the car, did you?"

David stared at me. "You must be kidding. Of course not."

Dixie, Stephanie, and I all released breaths at the same time. We looked at each other and laughed.

"I guess we're all relieved about that, but still…" I looked at David.

"I was there. I was at the Purple Panther. She must have put the gun in the glove box while I was there."

"You think Bambi put the gun in the glove box?" I asked.

David paced. "It's the only thing that makes sense. She knew Dad. She wanted his money and thought she could get it if she killed him. So, she shot him and then hid the gun while I was at the Purple Panther." He paced quickly. "God knows, there must be tons of illegal things going on in that place." He paused. "When she saw me, she must have either put the gun in the glove box or had someone do it for her."

I pondered what he said.

"I'm so sorry, Mom. I never should have gone there. I just felt like I needed to see her for myself."

I patted his hand. "It's okay, dear. Curiosity is normal. If I hadn't seen her for myself at Stephanie's office, I might have been tempted to do the same thing."

David turned to Christopher. "Can't the police check to see if her fingerprints are on the gun?"

Christopher shook his head. "I've already checked the police report. The only fingerprints on the gun were your mother's, Mrs. Jefferson's, and Detective Harrison's. The gun was reported stolen over a year ago by a very prominent member of society, Dr. Andrew Price."

"It wasn't dad's gun?" Stephanie asked.

He shook his head.

"Dr. Price? That name sounds familiar," I said.

"It should. Dr. Price is a prominent member of the Lighthouse Dunes community. He is a world-renowned psychologist. He's—"

"Oh my God, not *the* Dr. Price?" Dixie smacked her hand down on the table, shaking our mugs and spilling coffee on the table. "He's famous."

I stared and shook my head.

"You have got to be kidding? How can you *not* know Dr. Price?" Dixie stared at me as though I was dense. "He's a genius with helping people with addictions." She leaned close. "They say all of the big celebrities go to him. He's been on *Oprah* and *Dr. Phil* and all of those talk shows."

"*Oprah*?"

She nodded. "When she had her talk show, she had him on whenever she had someone who was suffering from alcohol or drug addiction. Now Dr. Phil uses him all the time. I had no idea he lived here."

"Me, either," I said. "Could he be involved in this somehow? I mean, it was his gun."

Christopher shook his head. "He reported the gun missing, and he's been in Hollywood ...filming."

Something in the way he added the last word caused us to stare at him.

Dixie bounced in her chair with excitement. "Oh my God. He's getting his own show, isn't he? Please tell me he's getting his own show!"

Christopher took a sip of coffee and nodded. "You didn't hear it from me, but I did hear it from a very reliable source."

"He is so handsome. I just knew they'd give him his own show sooner or later!" Dixie stared at me. "He has the bluest eyes you've ever seen, and his jaw...it's like Rock Hudson."

"Well, that surely warrants getting your own television show." I took a sip of coffee.

Stephanie smiled. "Unfortunately, he's not just handsome, he's smart too."

"Don't tell me you watch those types of shows too?" I stared at my daughter.

She chuckled. "I wish I had time to watch, but it's usually playing whenever I go to get a manicure." She held out her hands. "From what I've seen, he's actually very well-known and extremely sought after. His track record is pretty good too."

"So, the gun that shot Albert was stolen from this Rock Hudson–looking psychologist and just now shows up in the glove box of our spare car," I summarized.

"Unfortunately, it could have been in that glove box a long time." Christopher looked at his watch. "We'd better get down to the precinct."

Before I could get up, there was a knock at the door.

Stephanie answered the door and came back after a few moments, followed by Detective Olivia Wilson.

"We were just leaving for the precinct," I said.

She waved me back to my seat. "In light of the murder next door, we've decided to expedite things a bit."

I stared. "Expedite? What do you mean?"

Detective Wilson came around the table and pulled out a set of handcuffs. "I am arresting you for the murder of your husband, Albert Echosby, and for suspicion for the murder of your neighbor, Bradley Hurston."

CHAPTER 10

The next five hours were a nightmare I wouldn't want to relive if my life depended on it. I couldn't believe a few days ago I thought my husband leaving me for an exotic dancer named Bambi was the most humiliating thing that could ever happen in my life. But feeling tossed aside like an old car being exchanged for a newer model was nothing in comparison to being accused of murdering your husband. Being handcuffed in the kitchen of my house in front of my children was awful. I don't think I'll ever be able to forget the looks on their faces as they stood by helplessly watching their mother be marched out of the house and put into the back of a police car.

Even though I knew I'd be charged with murder, I wasn't prepared for the reality of having my fingerprints and a mugshot taken. I was placed in a jail cell, where I was, thankfully, left alone for over an hour. Even though the Lighthouse Dunes police hadn't moved into their new facilities yet, I was pleasantly surprised to find the cinder-block cell clean, despite the concrete floor and graffiti-covered walls. There was a rusted bed with a threadbare blanket and sheets that might have been white at one time but were closer to beige now. I pondered why establishments like this didn't switch to some other color for their linens that wouldn't be quite so obvious when they lost their color. However, after further thought, I realized that white allowed for the use of bleach, which was probably more important, all things considered.

After an hour in my cell, I was brought out into an interrogation room, where Christopher waited with Detective Wilson. The clock on the wall told me it had only been a couple of hours since Olivia Wilson walked into my kitchen, but I felt like I'd lived a lifetime in that time frame.

Christopher started by reassuring me Stephanie, David, and Dixie were outside waiting.

I nodded, grateful he had recognized my family would be my number-one priority.

I sat, and he explained that Detective Wilson was going to ask me some questions and I just needed to answer them truthfully. He also explained that he was there to prevent her from asking any questions that would violate my rights and to prevent the police from browbeating me into a confession.

Detective Wilson frowned at that but didn't say anything.

Once I understood the procedure, he nodded, and the grilling began. I should say that it didn't start out as a grilling, but felt more like a friendly chat between friends. Detective Wilson was very good at lulling people into a false sense of security, even friendship. As the questioning continued, the questions repeated and repeated and repeated, and Detective Wilson's displeasure increased. I must have answered the question of whether I'd killed my husband at least twelve different ways. No, I hadn't shot my husband. No, I didn't know who shot my husband. And no, I had no idea how the gun that shot my husband happened to get in the glove box of our spare car. I hadn't paid anyone to shoot Albert, nor did I know who killed him.

After three hours of questions about Albert, she began to ask questions about Bradley Hurston. I didn't feel like her heart was in it, though, because she certainly didn't linger over those questions nearly as long as she had the questions about my husband. I had been home all night and hadn't left the house. She seemed as surprised as I was that I had managed to sleep through the night and hadn't heard my neighbor being stabbed to death.

"I didn't leave the house. You can ask my kids. Stephanie or David. Or Dixie. She was there too."

"Your daughter left the house to meet Officer Harrison. So she can't confirm your alibi." Detective Wilson was reading from a statement.

I hadn't realized Stephanie had gone out with Officer Harrison. I'm sure it wasn't the first time the two had met up, and I couldn't stop myself from smiling. I liked the police officer. "What about David or Dixie? Surely they can confirm that I never left the house."

"Your son went to a bar with a friend, and your friend Dixie says she wasn't able to sleep and left the house once to take the dogs outside." She looked at me skeptically. "Seems strange you didn't hear her or the dogs leave?"

"Not really. The dogs are well behaved, and she's a dog trainer. Besides, I was *asleep*."

Detective Wilson sat back and looked at me. "None of them are exactly unbiased, and yet not one of the people who were in your house that night can corroborate that you never left."

I huffed. "Well, my timing would have had to have been impeccable to have managed to sneak out at the exact time when everyone was gone *and* Bradley Hurston was alone."

"Have you heard of Henry Poole?" she asked.

Christopher looked puzzled, but said nothing.

I shook my head. "No. Who is he?"

Detective Wilson didn't respond. Instead, she changed the subject and asked about my sleeping habits again. The questions continued. Eventually, I grew tired and my responses became curt and snarky.

Detective Wilson nearly lost her cool when I replied, "If Marianne Carpenter managed to sleep through the murder of her brother when she was in the same house with him, why are you so surprised I was able to sleep through it next door?"

Christopher hid a snicker, and my stomach growled.

"I'm hungry."

Detective Wilson's nostrils flared. When she was frustrated, she drummed her fingers on the table. The rhythm of the finger drumming increased. She was obviously frustrated, but so was I. Not only was I frustrated, but I was hungry too, and that wasn't a good combination.

Christopher's cell phone vibrated, and he looked at the message, then stood up. "That's enough. We're done here."

I stared up at him. "Seriously?"

"Yes." He walked to the door and held it open.

I stared from him to Detective Wilson. "Seriously, I can go?"

She nodded at the policeman, who was standing guard at the door. He escorted us down the hall and then into another sterile room. Stephanie and David ran to me and hugged me. I was so excited, I could have wept. Dixie wept quietly in her chair and then eventually came up and joined us in a group hug.

Christopher had been on his phone from the time he walked out of the interrogation room, until I'd finished hugging my family. When he finally hung up, he cleared his throat. "I hate to be a party pooper, but we've got about fifteen minutes to get over to court for your bond hearing."

We left Stephanie, David, and Dixie at the police station, and Christopher and I went back through the doors we had come through initially. I hurried after Christopher and the policeman, who escorted me at a trot, while we walked down corridors, through an underground tunnel, and went up an elevator. When we finally emerged, we were in the Lighthouse Dunes Courthouse. The building was across a parklike square from the police station.

"I didn't even know there was a tunnel that led from the jail to the courthouse." I stared in amazement at the high ceilings, marble floors, and paneled walls of the courthouse. I'd only been inside the building once for jury duty over a decade ago.

"Most law-abiding citizens never get a chance to use the tunnels, but it's easier to transport prisoners underneath the square than to risk taking them outside." The policeman spoke for the first time.

He led Christopher and me to a small waiting room where we stayed until an armed guard called my name. I followed the guard through a door to the courtroom. I walked to the seat and waited for Christopher to tell me what to do. We sat and waited for the judge to call my name. When my name was called, I stood. The judge was a surprisingly young man, with a receding hairline and a wiry mane of red hair forming a U around the back and sides of his head. He wore reading glasses perched atop his dome, where the hair should have been. He slid the glasses down and read the charges. "Felony murder." Then he asked me a series of questions. "Do you understand the charges against you?"

"Yes, sir."

"Are you represented by legal counsel?"

"Yes, sir."

"How do you plead?"

"Not guilty."

At this point, Christopher stepped forward. He explained I was a wife, a mother, and a fine upstanding citizen of Lighthouse Dunes. He mentioned all of the volunteer work I did in the community. If my life hadn't actually been in jeopardy, I might have blushed from all of the accolades. He finished by stating that not only was I *not* a flight risk, but how anxious I was to begin my defense to clear my good name. Christopher sounded confident and sure. His voice rang true with honesty, and he looked successful, without seeming cocky or arrogant. He asked that the judge release me to my own recognizance.

In contrast, the prosecuting attorney was a nervous young man in a cheap polyester suit, which was wrinkled and stained. He barely made eye contact with the judge when he spoke and had a nervous habit of saying, "Uhm" after every two or three words. It was so noticeable, I started counting them. When he finally stopped, I had counted forty-seven *Uhms*. He asked that bail be denied.

I held my breath for several seconds while the judge considered the matter. I tried my best to look innocent.

The judge declared that bond be set at fifty thousand dollars and banged his gavel.

Christopher hurried me out the same door we had come in as the next case was called. As I left, that was the first time I saw the rest of the courtroom. I saw Stephanie, David, and Dixie seated together near the front. They must have come across the square and entered through the main doors.

Back in the waiting room, Christopher introduced me to a tall, thin African American woman with thick, natural hair and the most amazingly smooth skin I'd ever seen. She looked like a model, and I couldn't help wondering if there was something going on between her and Christopher.

"Hello, gorgeous. I'm so glad you were able to make it."

She grunted, but the corners of her lips twitched with the effort to keep from smiling. "Skip the sweet talk. How much?"

"Five thousand."

She nodded, sat down at a table, and started filling out paperwork.

I beckoned to Christopher, and we stepped away. "Five thousand? I thought the judge said fifty thousand?" I whispered.

"He did. However, you only have to post ten percent, which is five thousand dollars."

"That's right. I remember Stephanie told me that, but I'd forgotten." I breathed a sigh of relief. "I was grateful he didn't listen to that other attorney and deny giving me bail, but I was so nervous! I will still have to sell everything I own, have a bake sale at church, and wash cars to come up with that kind of money."

Christopher laughed. "Thankfully, you won't have to go to those extremes yet, although I do expect some baked goods from you when this is all over."

I hugged him. "Anything you want."

It took another hour before I was able to leave. I stared at the sunlight as though I'd been locked up for years. I didn't know how people who were incarcerated for long periods of time were able to stand it, but I knew I would never take my freedom for granted again.

When we left, I asked David to drive us to Lighthouse Beach Pizza, a small restaurant on the sand dunes overlooking Lake Michigan. We sat outside and ate a pizza called "Everything but the Kitchen Sink." It was the best pizza I'd ever eaten. I wasn't sure if it was the crust, the toppings, or the sauce that tasted so good, but the entire thing piled together tasted like freedom, and that was delicious. We sat and watched the sunset, and I tried not to cry as the huge fiery orb descended and piles of red, orange, and yellow melted atop the crisp blue waters of Lake Michigan. The peace and serenity of the sunset touched something deep in my soul. I didn't know what the future held, but in that moment, I set my heart, mind, and soul to finding the person who killed my husband and threatened to steal my freedom. I turned to my family. "Let's put our heads together and figure out who killed Albert."

CHAPTER 11

From the patio of Lighthouse Beach Pizza, we discussed my predicament.

"The police think I killed Albert." I ticked each item off one by one. "I had a motive, I had the opportunity, and I had the means."

"Yeah, with the gun the killer so thoughtfully left in the glove box of your car," Dixie said sarcastically.

David avoided eye contact with me, and I held his chin and forced him to look me in the eyes. "And you can stop blaming yourself. None of this is your fault."

He gave me the poor, deluded child smile. "If I hadn't gone to that strip club, the killer wouldn't have been able to put the gun in your glove box."

We were so engrossed in our own conversation, we didn't notice Officer Harrison's arrival until he spoke. "Actually that was probably a plus, if you ask me."

We turned around in surprise, and I shot a sideways glance toward Stephanie. "Officer Harrison, fancy meeting you here."

"Is this a private party, or can anyone join?" He made the comment jokingly, but his eyes looked at Stephanie.

She shrugged and took a sip of her wine.

"Please, pull up a chair," I said.

We slid our chairs together to make a spot, and Officer Harrison pulled a chair from a nearby table. Once he was seated, the conversation stalled. The waitress came, and he ordered a beer.

The silence was awkward. I attempted to lighten the mood. "Nice weather we're having, isn't it?"

Officer Harrison leaned close. "I know you don't really trust me, but I do want to help."

Dixie cleared her throat. "I hate to look a gift horse in the mouth, but aren't you pitching for the other team?"

He gave a half shrug and looked toward me. "I like to think we're on the same side. We both want to find out who killed your husband and who killed your neighbor Bradley Hurston."

"I don't trust him," Stephanie said.

Officer Harrison leaned back, but the only indication he gave that he was bothered was a red blotch that rose up the side of his neck and made his ears turn red.

Stephanie leaned forward with more passion. "I think he's a spy, a double agent. He's been sent to find out what we know and to get information he can report back. Policemen aren't like normal people. They don't work nine-to-five jobs like the rest of us. They're sworn to uphold the law at all times" She turned to me. "Anything you say can and will be used against you." She glared at Officer Harrison. "Isn't that right, Detective?"

For a full minute, he didn't say anything while a vein pulsed on the side of his head and Stephanie glared at him. The rest of us were too dazed to speak. Besides, I think we all knew this conversation was about more than just my case.

Eventually, Officer Harrison took a deep breath. "I am sworn to uphold the law at all times, but I believe that helping your mother prove her innocence and catching a killer don't have to be mutually exclusive." He shook his head. "Look, it's obvious I'm not welcome here, so I'll just leave." He stood up, pulled out his wallet, and flung a ten-dollar bill on the table, then turned to leave.

"Stop." I used my mom voice, which halted him in his tracks, along with a nearby waiter who was about to put a pizza on a nearby table.

"Sit down."

He looked as though he wasn't going to comply for a split second, but the look in my eyes must have convinced him I meant business.

"Now, obviously something's going on between the two of you."

Stephanie started to object, but I shot her a look that silenced her.

"Whatever it is, work it out or don't work it out. I don't really care. That's between the two of you."

Neither one looked at the other, but their body language relaxed, so I knew they both accepted my assessment.

"The important thing is figuring out who killed your father and who tried to frame me for it. Now, I don't trust every member of the police force, but I was raised to believe that police officers are my friends." I repeated the mantra from the night on the interstate. "So, I'm willing to trust Officer Harrison"—I pointed to him—"to a point, at least until he proves he can't be trusted." I turned to stare at Stephanie and David. "I tried to raise you both to believe that same thing, and I think, if you're honest, you'll acknowledge Officer Harrison hasn't really violated any trust"—I looked at him—"yet."

I turned to Stephanie. She reluctantly shrugged.

"Good. Also, while I've read a lot of mysteries in my time, I don't know the first thing about finding a murderer, and I feel sure Officer Harrison can help us." I turned to stare at him.

He nodded.

"Glad that's settled."

Dixie raised her glass. "Let's get this party started. Where do we begin?"

We turned to Officer Harrison.

He leaned forward. "I think we should go someplace more private and come up with a game plan."

We agreed and so we made our way back to the house. Once we were assembled at the kitchen table—five adults and four dogs—we started.

I'd used the ride in the car to come up with my idea of a game plan. I pulled out my laptop. "Now, we need to figure out who had a motive for killing Albert." I paused and typed. "Who other than me, that is."

"Bambi might have done it?" Dixie offered.

"Why?" I typed.

"Maybe she thought she was going to get his money?" she said.

I typed. "That reminds me, I need to talk to Charles Nelson and find out what exactly was stipulated in Albert's will." I stopped typing for a minute. A thought fluttered in my mind, but as quickly as it came, it was gone. "He tried to tell me something about the will after the funeral, but then Marilyn was…unwell, and so he left."

"Bambi was there when Dad was shot," Stephanie said.

"We only have her word that someone came in and shot him. Maybe she made the whole thing up," Dixie said. "I saw an episode on one of those crime programs where a woman killed her boyfriend for his money. She told the police two masked men came in to rob him. She claimed they tied her to a chair and blindfolded her so she couldn't see anything and then shot him."

"What about it? Could she have made the whole thing up?" David asked Officer Harrison.

He was silent for a minute. "It's possible. There wasn't any evidence in the apartment that confirmed or contradicted her story. She claimed she was in bed asleep and heard the shot. When she went to the living room, she found him dead."

David looked excited. "She could have put the gun in the glove box of the car when I went to the Purple Panther."

"When was this?" Officer Harrison looked at David.

He related the story about how he went to the Purple Panther the night before the funeral. Officer Harrison asked a few questions about who else knew David was going there. Who else had he seen? Was there ever a time when Bambi was out of his sight?

"What's with the grilling?" Stephanie asked.

"Sorry. I was just trying to figure out who else knew he'd be there and who had the opportunity to put the gun in the car. That's all." He raised his hands in a gesture of surrender.

Stephanie looked contrite but didn't apologize.

I finished typing. "Who else?"

We couldn't think of anyone else, but something in Officer Harrison's eyes told me he had a suggestion.

"You know something?" I asked.

He rubbed the back of his neck. "I was wondering if there could be anything connected to the car dealership?"

"Something like what?" Stephanie asked.

He shrugged. "I don't know, but something doesn't feel right about that place. That guy, Chip Nelson, he just seems shady to me."

I smiled, remembering how Officer Harrison had shut Chip down when he nearly ran into me at the dealership.

I turned to Stephanie. "I think you should tell him what you know about Chip."

She nodded and shared the story she told me many moons ago about Chip's drug problem.

Officer Harrison listened attentively, then nodded. "I suspected he was involved in drugs. I can ask around at the precinct and see if anyone knows anything more."

"You won't get in trouble?" Stephanie asked.

He shrugged. "Not if I'm careful."

I typed *Chip's history* into the spreadsheet I'd made. I loved spreadsheets. They were great at keeping numbers organized and would work equally well for keeping murder suspects organized. "Marilyn also has a problem, although her drug of choice is alcohol."

"That's obvious from her behavior the other day. Can you believe she actually got sloshed at a funeral?" Dixie added.

"I haven't seen Marilyn for a number of years. I knew she had a problem back then, but I thought she went to some clinic and got cleaned up."

"It wouldn't happen to have been Lighthouse Dunes Therapy and Rehabilitation?" Officer Harrison asked.

A light bulb went off in my head. "That's why Dr. Andrew Price's name sounded so familiar. That's his clinic!"

"So, the murder weapon was stolen from Dr. Price six months ago, and Dr. Price treated Marilyn Nelson for alcohol addiction," Dixie said.

"Not just Marilyn Nelson." Stephanie stared. "He also treated Chip Nelson."

"Now we're getting somewhere." I typed.

"I'll look into it," Officer Harrison said. "I need you all to let me handle this. If Chip Nelson is responsible for stealing the gun, then he's a dangerous man who may have killed twice already."

David sat up straighter. "I almost forgot. Chip's also the one who told me Bambi worked at the Purple Panther. He could have put the gun in the car."

"I'll look into it." Officer Harrison's eyes held a sparkle that hadn't been there before. "This is a great lead."

We were all excited that there was at least one other person on our list who might have killed Albert. However, Stephanie didn't seem as excited as the rest of us.

"What's wrong?" I asked.

She shook her head. "Chip had the opportunity and the means—but why? Why kill Dad?"

That put a bit of a wet blanket over our celebration.

"Maybe Officer Harrison was right," Dixie said. "Maybe there was something going on with the business. Maybe Albert was going to fire him." She looked around, but no one looked excited about that theory.

"Or maybe he was stealing money from the company and Dad found out," David added.

"I have the accounts. I'll take a look at the financial statements and the business accounts and see if anything suspicious was going on." I kept typing.

"Okay, but if you find anything, you let me know immediately. Don't go off and confront anyone by yourself," Detective Harrison cautioned.

I crossed my heart and held up three fingers in what I remembered to be the Girl Scout oath. He nodded his acceptance of my promise.

"Something's been bothering me too." I looked at Officer Harrison. "I know why the police believe I killed Albert, but why do they think I killed Bradley Hurston?"

Officer Harrison paused. "Someone heard him saying he saw what you did after the funeral."

I looked at Stephanie and David, and the three of us burst into laughter.

"I wish someone would share the joke. I could use a good laugh." Dixie looked from me to Stephanie and David.

"I'd like in on the joke too," Officer Harrison said.

"Bradley Hurston is a sweet old man who had dementia," I said. "He says that to literally everyone."

"He sits in his living room looking out the window with his binoculars, and that's the first thing he says to everyone he meets," Stephanie said.

"He's been saying the same thing for at least the last ten years." David laughed.

"That explains a lot." Officer Harrison smiled. "Unfortunately, no one bothered to tell the police about that."

"Marianne would have told you, but she fainted after he was found shot and was taken to the hospital. I suspect she's still there." I made a mental note to send flowers.

We talked for a bit, and then Officer Harrison stood up. Turbo had gotten comfortable and wasn't enthusiastic about leaving, but after a few stretches, he trotted alongside his master. "I'll let you know what I find out, but promise me that you won't do anything stupid and will leave the actual investigating to the professionals."

We all held up three fingers. "Scouts' honor."

He shook his head with the first glimmer of a smile I'd seen, then left.

"My fingers were crossed behind my back." Dixie held up her left hand and showed her crossed fingers.

We all lifted our hands with crossed fingers.

Dixie smiled. "Good. So, what's the plan?"

I turned to my daughter. "Stephanie, maybe you could reach out to Charles Nelson, you know, lawyer to lawyer, and find out about your father's will." I shared the agreement I'd made with Albert to host his grandmother's birthday bash as long as he promised to keep the children as his beneficiaries.

"I wondered why you agreed to do that," Dixie said.

"It's sad you had to resort to that. He was our father, after all." David sounded bitter.

I shrugged. "Maybe he would have done it anyway. I just wanted to make sure. Anyway, I'm hoping if you're a beneficiary, then he'll share the contents of the will with you."

Stephanie nodded.

I turned to David. “I can’t believe I’m doing this, but could you stomach another trip back to the Purple Panther?”

He raised an eyebrow. “I can’t believe my mom is sending me to a strip club.” He grinned. “Sure, what do you want me to do?”

“Bambi didn’t strike me as the sharpest tack in the box.”

“You can say that again.” Dixie rolled her eyes.

“I was hoping you could ask her a few questions. Find out if she had any expectations of receiving money.”

“She certainly seemed to have expectations when she was rifling through his things at the car dealership.”

I nodded. “Do you think you could do that?”

“I’m an actor. I shall put on the performance of a lifetime.” He made a sweeping gesture with his arm and then a low bow.

“What about me?” Dixie scooted to the edge of her seat.

I stared at the dogs lying on the floor. “Did you tell me your dogs are registered therapy assistant dogs?”

She looked at the lounging poodles and nodded. “Yep. Both of them are registered with Therapy Dogs International.”

“So, they can go into hospitals, right?”

She nodded.

“What’s a registered therapy dog?” David asked.

Dixie’s voice took on the teacher tone she always got when talking about the work she did with dogs. “A registered therapy dog means the dogs have been trained to provide affection and comfort for people in hospitals or nursing homes. Sometimes they also go into schools or disaster areas. They’ve even been used to help people with autism. The dogs must pass a test, certifying they have the right temperament for the work.”

“Are they service dogs like Joe’s dog, Turbo?”

Dixie shook her head. “Not necessarily. Service dogs go through a lot more rigorous training than a therapy dog. A service dog *could* be a therapy dog, but the two things are not necessarily the same thing. Turbo is a trained police dog, so his skill set is vastly different from a service or assist dog.” She smiled. “I suspect he wouldn’t make the best therapy dog, but I might be wrong.”

David looked at the poodles with a new respect.

Dixie looked at me. “Now, why do you want to know about Chyna and Leia?”

“I was hoping you could take them to the hospital to visit Marianne. Maybe you could ask her some questions. I’m hoping she heard or saw something without knowing she saw it.”

Dixie nodded. "Sure thing. Now, what are you going to do?"

"I'm going to go through Albert's books with a fine-tooth comb. If there's anything amiss in his books, I'm going to find it."

We talked awhile longer and then went to bed. It had been a long day, and I was tired.

I lay in bed and cuddled with Aggie, thankful to be back in my comfortable room and out of that cell. Something kept flittering around in my head, but I couldn't remember what it was. Every time I tried to catch it, it floated out of reach. I decided to focus on other things and hoped it would come to me later.

I had just drifted off to sleep when the telephone rang. I looked over at the clock on my nightstand. It was two in the morning. No good phone calls happened at two in the morning. I took a deep breath and braced myself for bad news.

Before I could get the greeting out of my mouth, I heard Bambi's screeching voice. "Someone stole my car. Was it you?"

"What are you talking about?"

"It was you, wasn't it? You stole my car. You told me I could have the Corvette and then you came and took it back. I should have known you wouldn't keep your word."

"Bambi, I don't have the slightest idea what you're talking about."

"Oh, don't give me that. I always park the car outside the Purple Panther, and it's never been a problem, but now, all of a sudden, it gets broken into one day and then stolen. I know it was you, and you can't get away with it. I'll call Albert's attorney, and he'll make you give the car back. You promised and—"

"I don't have the car. If someone stole it, I suggest you file a report with the police."

I hung up, turned off my phone, and went back to sleep.

CHAPTER 12

I woke up with a headache. My sheets were in knots, and Aggie, who normally slept curled up beside me, was asleep on the bench at the foot of the bed. Apparently, I'd kicked too much during the night and she sought shelter a little farther away. I had a vague recollection of being chased by a large yellow steam roller. At some point, the steam roller turned into purple poodles that growled and snarled and chased me through the Louvre Museum. Fortunately, or unfortunately, I couldn't remember much more.

A long, hot shower, two aspirin, and a hot cup of coffee helped. Stephanie and David came down when I was on my second cup.

"Would you two like breakfast?"

"I think Aunt Dixie went to pick up some pastries to go with the breakfast casserole you made for Marianne yesterday." Stephanie took the casserole out of the refrigerator and placed it on the counter.

"I can always make her another one," I said.

"Our thoughts exactly." Stephanie set the timer on the oven, sat down, and poured herself a cup of coffee.

We drank in silence until the preheat timer went off.

David got up. "Allow me." He opened the oven door and put the casserole inside.

By the time the breakfast casserole was ready, Dixie returned, juggling two white boxes and a grocery bag. David and Stephanie jumped up to relieve her of her bags and she slumped into one of the vacant kitchen chairs. She had a large Styrofoam cup, which bore the same *French Pastry* logo as that of the boxes.

"I thought you were just going to pick up a few pastries." I stared at the strawberry tarts, bear claws, lemon squares, and apple turnovers Stephanie displayed on the table.

"I did, but I guess I got a little carried away. Everything looked so tasty. I couldn't decide what to get."

"So, you got one of everything?" Stephanie moaned as she bit into a lemon square and the yellow filling oozed out of the side of her mouth.

I handed her a napkin to wipe away the powdered sugar that now coated her mouth.

"Besides, it's the least I could do, considering the racket the girls kept up last night." Dixie picked up an apple turnover and bit into it.

"What racket?" I asked around a mouth full of strawberry tart.

"Are you joking?" She stared at me as though I'd suddenly grown another appendage. "They heard something outside and nearly lost their minds."

"Really?" David added.

She looked from one of us to the other. "None of you heard it?"

We each shook our heads.

"Well, I'll be jiggered," Dixie said.

At some point, I'd have to find out what that meant, but at the moment, I was consumed by strawberries with a bright glaze that reflected the sugar crystals and melted in my mouth.

We made short work of the breakfast casserole and pastries. I looked at the box that had been filled with delicious treats and now lay barren, with one sole chocolate éclair left behind.

"I can't believe we ate that entire box of pastries." I looked at the counter, where two other boxes sat. "How many boxes did you buy?"

Dixie held up three fingers. "Actually, I got one box to take to the hospital. Marianne might be more willing to chat with me if she has some delicious sweets to tempt her."

Stephanie laughed, and David nearly choked as he swallowed the last éclair.

"Marianne Carpenter won't need any inducement to talk," Stephanie said.

"The trouble will be getting her to stop talking." David gulped down the last of his coffee.

"Well, what she doesn't eat, the nurses and doctors will appreciate," Dixie said.

"That's a great idea. Why don't you take my car?" I got up and grabbed my purse from the counter and rummaged around for the keys. "No sense in driving that big RV around town. Parking at the hospital will be scarce anyway."

I felt around in my purse, which felt like the bottomless pit. Eventually, I dumped the contents on the table. The keys were hiding in my wallet. I gave them to Dixie and started putting things back when I noticed an envelope. "What's this?" I stared at the envelope.

"One way to find out?" David handed me a letter opener.

I slit the envelope open and gasped when I read the single sheet of paper folded inside.

"Lilly Anne, you're as white as a sheet. What is it?" Dixie asked.

Stephanie and David looked concerned.

"I feel lightheaded and dizzy."

"Put your head down." Dixie stood up and shoved my head down between my legs.

The blood rushed to my head and, in seconds, I felt better. "I'm fine." I sat up and shoved the letter at Stephanie.

She took the letter and nearly stumbled.

"Not you too?" Dixie made a move toward Stephanie.

Stephanie recovered herself better than me and held up a hand to fend off assistance. She had been leaning against the sink and turned, got a glass of water, and drank half of the glass. Then she turned. "It's from Daddy."

"Oh my." Dixie sank into her chair.

David looked flushed and got up and stood, looking over Stephanie's shoulder.

"He's made a new will." Stephanie scanned the document. "He's leaving everything to Mom." She looked up.

I leaned back down and put my head through my legs. When I had gotten enough blood to my brain, I sat up. Someone had gotten me a glass of water. My hands shook while I drank, so I only took a few gulps and set the glass on the table. "When? How?"

"Why?" Dixie asked.

Stephanie stared at the letter again. "It's dated the day of Bisnonna's birthday party."

I groaned. "I told him to make you two the beneficiaries, not me."

"Is it legal?" Dixie asked.

Stephanie shrugged. "It looks to be in order. This looks like his handwriting." She looked at me and I nodded. "It's signed, dated and witnessed."

"Who are the witnesses?" I asked.

"Uncle Gino and Uncle Vinnie," she said.

I groaned. "I guess that explains why the entire Conti family thinks I killed Albert."

"But why did he put it in your purse? Why not give it to his attorney?" David asked.

I shrugged.

Dixie whistled. "Can you imagine what would happen if the police knew about this?"

I put my head between my knees again. When I sat up this time, I felt more at ease. "Well, nothing we can do about it now." I looked at Stephanie. "You'll need to hand that over to Charles Nelson when you talk to him and also make sure you tell Officer Harrison about it."

David rubbed the back of his neck and paced. "But, Mom, I—"

I looked across at Stephanie. She was wearing a T-shirt and the words leapt out at me. It was from my alma mater, Northwestern University, and read *Quaecumque Sunt Vera.* I pointed to her shirt. "'Whatsoever things are true.' We have to do the right thing. We have to trust that *the truth will make you free*."

Dixie sighed. "John eight, thirty-two."

David stopped pacing and looked as though he wanted to argue but took a deep breath and then nodded.

Stephanie hugged me.

I was getting teary and this wasn't the time. Once the police got that will, things might get more challenging. Albert had, perhaps unwittingly, made my position even more precarious. We needed to get busy and figure out who killed Albert, and quickly. I took a long drink of water and steadied my nerves.

Dixie squeezed my hand in a show of support.

"Thank you for the pastries and for thinking about Marianne and the nurses. I'm sure they will appreciate them. Please tell Marianne I'll swing by to see her later."

Dixie nodded. "I thought you might want to take the third box to the car dealership."

"I can drop them off for you," David said. "Maybe I'll nose around the place and see if I hear anything that might be useful. I should have plenty of time on my hands today. My assignment won't start until later. Places like the Purple Panther aren't exactly morning hangouts." He winked at me.

"Good idea. When you're at the dealership, maybe you can check into the dealership registration for the yellow Corvette your father gave Bambi. She called last night and said it was stolen."

"She called you?" Dixie nearly choked on her coffee. "That little tart sure has nerve. You gotta hand her that."

I nodded. "Well, she was upset and accused me of taking it."

Stephanie loaded the dishes into the dishwasher. "The nerve of that little gold digger. You gave her a car, and she had the audacity to accuse you of stealing a car that rightfully belongs to you." She slammed the door and pushed the button to start the cycle.

"I'm going to chalk it up to stress, but she also mentioned the car had been broken into." I looked at Stephanie. "Do you think you could check with Officer Harrison and find out if she actually filed a police report like I told her to. Also, if she reported the previous break in."

Stephanie colored slightly but nodded.

"Great. I'm going to tackle Albert's books and see if there's anything in them that someone would want to kill over."

It had been years since I'd done any serious accounting work, but I read accounting journals and attended the required educational classes needed to maintain my license. Similar to teachers and lawyers, CPAs were required to take a certain number of educational classes every year or so to keep their licenses. I was thankful Albert's software wasn't complicated. I'd actually set the system up when he first opened the business and was grateful to see he hadn't changed much, including the password.

Albert's laptop on the kitchen table and Aggie curled up in a dog bed nearby was reassuring. Once I successfully logged in to the system and started navigating around, it was like riding a bicycle. Before I knew it, it was lunchtime. My stomach growled. I scanned the cabinets and found the options left much to be desired. For months I'd shopped for one. Now there were four of us again, and I needed to readjust my shopping routine and cooking habits. However, deep down inside, I knew this wouldn't last long. Before long, David and Stephanie would have to leave, and Dixie would need to get back to her husband and her life in Chattanooga.

I pulled a few cans of tuna out of the cabinet and made myself a tuna fish sandwich and a cup of tea and got back to work. Two hours later, Aggie's whimpering alerted me to trouble. I looked up in time to see her walking in a circle and sniffing in a way which meant danger ahead.

"Eh," I said in the loud, authoritative manner Dixie taught me.

It always surprised me when she stopped whatever bad behavior she was up to and looked at me with her large, innocent brown eyes.

I picked her up, grabbed a leash, and hurried outside. I snapped the leash onto her pink and white plaid harness designed to look like a dress and put her down on the grass. She immediate squatted and took care of business. I praised her as if she'd just unearthed buried treasure, which caused her to prance around as though she'd just won the top prize at Westminster.

When our celebrations were completed, I looked around. The tape the police had used to surround Bradley Hurston's house and protect whatever evidence the killer left had been removed. The grass which I'd mowed a week ago—*had it only been a week?*—looked long and unkempt. In fact, my own lawn wasn't looking so great either. I looked at my watch and decided cutting the grass would be one less thing Marianne or Bradley's son, Mike, would have to worry about. Having just gone through funeral preparations myself, I was anxious to do something helpful.

When Aggie seemed more concerned with pouncing on a twig she found in the grass than anything else, I figured it was safe to take her inside. As a further measure of safety, I secured her in her crate with a yummy treat that smelled like rotten flesh, but she loved along with a stuffed toy called Snuggle Puppy Dixie brought her. Snuggle Puppy was a stuffed animal with a Velcro belly where you placed a heat pack and a battery-operated plastic heart that thumped. The purpose was to simulate being in a litter. Whoever invented this was a genius. Aggie had worn herself out napping and pouncing on twigs. So, after just a few minutes, she curled up with her Snuggle Puppy.

I went outside and got the lawn mower out. Mowing the grass wasn't my favorite thing to do around the house, but I considered it penance for the two strawberry tarts I ate earlier and marched with a good attitude. Actually, the even lines were somewhat hypnotic. Like most housework, I was able to engage my body while my mind was free to wander.

Not surprising, my thoughts were dominated by numbers. Something about the books wasn't right. The accounts didn't reconcile. Month after month, large adjustments were made to force the figures to balance. There was also a large number of disbursements to a vendor I'd never heard of. Of course, I hadn't been actively involved in the car dealership in quite some time, but the sums paid to one vendor seemed excessive. If my calculations were correct, *and I'd gone over them three times*, close to three million dollars had been paid to one vendor, MN Holdings. I needed to go to the dealership and check the invoices against the payments. I had no idea why an import car dealership was working with a Minnesota holding company, but I supposed it could be related to car parts or accessories. I hadn't been able to find out much information through my Internet searches, but lawyers had access to databases that went much deeper than anything the public could find. When Stephanie came home, I'd ask her to look in to it.

I looked up and realized I'd finished cutting both front yards and was about to tackle the backs when I heard a car behind me. I looked around and saw David pulling into the driveway.

He came up and gave me a kiss on the cheek. "Why don't you let me finish this?"

I started to protest, but he simply patted his stomach. "I could do with the exercise."

I nodded and went inside. One look in the mirror showed I had dirt, sweat, and grass clippings in my hair and all over my body. I recognized the odor that wafted to my nostrils every now and again and knew I needed a shower. I peeled my sweat-soaked clothes off and hopped in the shower for a thorough wash.

By the time I was cleaned up, David had finished the yard. I passed him on my way downstairs.

"Hope you left me some hot water. I have to get ready for my rendezvous." He smiled as he went into his room.

I went downstairs and heard Stephanie and Dixie talking in the kitchen before I saw them. Dixie's voice had the pride I'd noticed whenever she talked about her dogs.

"The girls were awesome. They visited with everyone on the ward where Marianne was resting."

"I'm surprised the hospital permits dogs. I mean, they're always so concerned about germs and things." Stephanie must have noticed something in Dixie's eyes, because she hurriedly added, "Not that your dogs have germs. They're so beautiful and clean."

She need not have worried.

Dixie merely laughed. "Oh, I understand what you're saying. Many people don't take very good care of their dogs, and they could bring fleas and ticks into the hospitals. Plus, a lot of people, like your father, are allergic to dogs. I always make sure the dogs are bathed and have their nails trimmed before we make any therapy visits. That was one of the reasons I left so early. Normally, I'd wash them myself, but one of the ladies I met at a dog show lives about thirty miles from here. She has beautiful poodles, so I dropped the girls off and she gave them baths."

"I can't believe you cut all of their hair off," Stephanie said.

"You what?" I hurried around the corner into the kitchen. Sure enough, the two poodles were standing in the middle of the kitchen without their colorful bands and looked practically naked without the extra hair.

"I've been thinking about retiring the girls from showing for quite some time. Maintaining a poodle in full show coat can be a lot of work. Two poodles multiplied the work exponentially." She looked lovingly at the dogs. "So, first thing this morning, I shaved their coats and dropped them off for baths."

"Oh, Dixie, are you sure? I hope you didn't do this because of me—"

She laughed. "Rest assured, the decision was completely my own." She petted Chyna, who I could tell from Leia by her blue harness and ribbons in her ears. "I think the girls are happy too."

Chyna wagged her tail like a fan, as though to confirm the statement.

We laughed.

"The coat is hot and summers in Chattanooga are extremely humid. Now they can enjoy their lives as pets, rather than show dogs.

I sat down at the table. "What's that amazing smell?" I looked around and noticed the large bag on the counter.

Stephanie smiled. "I passed Adamo's on my way from Charles Nelson's house and stopped and picked up a lasagna, garlic bread, and salad."

Adamo's was a wonderful authentic Italian restaurant near the beach and everything was delicious.

"Is that all?" I raised an eyebrow and stared at my daughter.

She grinned. "Of course not. I also picked up a cheesecake."

"That's my girl."

David finished his shower and came downstairs just as we finished setting the food out on the table. "Yum, that smells fantastic."

I noticed there was one extra plate on the table and looked at Stephanie.

"I invited Officer Harrison to join us for dinner. He should be here soon." She lowered her head, so her hair covered the slight flush I'd noticed come up her neck.

The doorbell rang, and she jumped up. "That'll be him now."

Within moments, Officer Harrison, Stephanie, and Turbo arrived.

Turbo joined the poodles in the kitchen at the dog bowls, while Officer Harrison sat down at the empty seat.

"Thanks for inviting me to dinner," he said.

"We're glad you could come," I said.

Initially, we ate in silence with comments about how tasty the food was, but nothing of substance. By the time the main course was finished, and Stephanie brought out the cheesecake and a pot of coffee, we were ready to get down to business.

"Who wants to go first?" I looked around the table.

Dixie raised her hand. "Well, I didn't find out much, so my report will be short." She ate a bite of cheesecake, shuddered with pleasure and then put down her fork. "Marianne has no idea who killed her brother. She was asleep in the back room. She said her brother liked to stay up looking outside and listening to the police radio and often went to bed late or slept in his recliner in the living room."

"She didn't hear anything?" I asked.

Dixie shook her head.

"I could have told you that," Officer Harrison said.

"Sorry." Dixie took a drink of coffee. "The only thing she said was she thought she heard the back door squeak."

"She didn't mention the squeaking in her statement." Officer Harrison frowned. "Did she say what time that was?"

"She thought it was around two, but she didn't bother putting her glasses on, so she can't be sure."

"Good job, Dixie. Their screen door does squeak. I've been meaning to spray it with WD40 the next time I mow, but I keep forgetting."

Dixie smiled and Officer Harrison pulled out a notepad and took notes.

"I'll go next, since I have very little to report too," David said. "I dropped the pastries off at the dealership. I talked to Chip Nelson. I thought he was just a salesman, but he was at a desk. He said he's the Assistant Manager and bookkeeper."

I nearly spit out my coffee. "Chip Nelson is the one who's been doing your father's books?"

David nodded. "He was a bit miffed when he found out you'd taken the books and the laptop."

"I'll bet he was. Anything else?"

"He wants to know if you're going to sell the dealership. He wants to buy the dealership and is willing to make an offer right away. He seems to think he has a right to it. Says he's the one that got Dad involved importing cars and not just going around to local auctions. The way he talks, he's been running things for quite some time."

"You don't say?" I drummed my fingers on the table. "Is that all?"

"Oh, and I think he's been seeing Bambi." He grinned. "He seemed a little nervous when I told him I was going back to the Purple Panther tonight."

"Why the little weasel. How dare he make a move on your father's tart right under his nose." Dixie pounded the table. "Wait, what am I saying?"

We all laughed.

"I'll go next." Stephanie took a sip of coffee. "I had a rather interesting visit with Charles Nelson. When I went to his office, he was super apologetic. 'I'm so sorry for your loss. Your father will be missed.' He *claimed*, the business hadn't been doing well and there really wasn't much left. In fact, according to him, Dad had already changed his will to leave everything to Bambi."

"But, what about—"

A gleam in Stephanie's eyes stopped me. "That's when I told him about the new will he'd left."

"Ha! I'll bet that cooked his goose." Dixie pounded the table again.

"He looked as though he was going to have a stroke. He started to turn purple and couldn't talk without stuttering." Stephanie smiled. "I got up and poured him a glass of water and asked if he wanted me to call nine-one-one."

"What did he do then?" I asked.

"At first he said it was a forgery. He claimed it couldn't be valid." She sipped her coffee. "I assured him it was in my father's own handwriting and properly witnessed. Then he wanted to see it."

"You didn't give it to him?"

I should have known better, but Stephanie's smile reassured me.

"Of course not. I told him I'd taken it to the police station because it was evidence in a murder investigation but that I'd make sure it got filed in probate once the murderer was arrested."

"You shouldn't have baited him like that. It was dangerous," Officer Harrison said.

"I'm a big girl and fully capable of taking care of myself." Stephanie gave the detective a frosty stare.

I guess things weren't totally okay between the two of them, but something told me they'd work it out. "I guess that just leaves me." I paused for several seconds to collect my thoughts. "I think someone's been embezzling money from the car dealership."

After everyone got over the shock, they started firing questions at me. *How? Who? How much money?*

I held up a hand to fend off the questions. "I'm not one hundred percent sure, but I think someone is filing fake invoices. There's a company, MN Holdings, that's been paid over three million dollars in the past year."

David whistled. "Did you say, three *million* dollars?"

Stephanie looked puzzled. "Are you sure?"

I tried not to show the hurt those words caused. "Well, it's been a while since I've done any public accounting, but there are red flags that any CPA would recognize."

Stephanie reached out and squeezed my hand. "I'm not doubting your ability or your accuracy. I just don't understand how it's possible Dad sold cars worth more than three million dollars. I mean, even if he sold a car to everyone in Lighthouse Dunes, I don't see how he could have made that kind of money."

Dixie nodded. "I see what you're saying. There couldn't have been more than twenty cars on the lot when we were there the other day."

"I don't know that I've ever seen Albert with more than that." I paused. "Plus, it's not like he's selling Rolls-Royces and Bentleys," I said. "Although, he did give Bambi that Corvette."

David snorted. "Corvettes don't come close to what he'd need to sell. He'd have to be selling the most expensive cars on the market—Bugattis, Lamborghinis, and Ferraris,"

"I've never seen anything like that in Lighthouse Dunes, let alone at your father's dealership."

"Could your husband have been involved in anything illegal?" Officer Harrison asked.

I bristled at the idea that my husband could have been involved in anything illegal. However, the reality was the man I married wasn't the same man who left me for Bambi. He'd changed a lot over the years. In all honesty, I didn't know Albert anymore. I shrugged. "I don't know."

Stephanie stared at Officer Harrison. "You know something. Spill it." How she could read his stony face and tell he was concealing information, I had no idea.

Officer Harrison paused for several moments, but we waited. "We have reason to believe there's an illegal drug ring operating in Lighthouse Dunes. But we haven't been able to figure out how they're smuggling the drugs into the city."

"Illegal drugs?" I shook my head. "No. I don't believe Albert would have been involved in smuggling drugs. He may be guilty of a lot of things, but I would stake my life that drug smuggling isn't one of them."

"I hope you're right," Officer Harrison said. "Your life and your freedom may very well be what are at stake."

CHAPTER 13

Bambi had filed a police report for the car, but the police didn't hold out much luck they'd be able to find it, at least not in one piece. We sat and talked, and Officer Harrison admonished us again to leave the actual investigating to the police. After he left, David dressed for his night out at the Purple Panther.

I had mixed feelings about sending my son to a strip club. Part of me cringed at the thought of him in a sleazy dive like that. Another part of me balked at the exploitation of women. Still another part of me tried not to be judgmental. I'd read a book about a woman who was a college student by day and danced at an exotic nightclub at night. She said stripping empowered her and provided a decent income. David was an adult and so was Bambi. I prayed the other girls performing were all old enough to know what they were doing and pushed the hesitations down.

Stephanie said she had some paperwork she needed to do for a case and went to her room to work.

Dixie took all the dogs out while I unloaded the dishwasher. When she came back in, I was sitting at the table with coffee and the last two slices of cheesecake.

"I thought we'd finished that off." She sat down, picked up her fork and took a mouthful of the creamy goodness.

"Stephanie bought two." I took a bite of cheesecake and allowed the heavenly sweetness to dissolve on my tongue. "That's my girl."

We enjoyed our cheesecake and coffee in silence and then sat back, uncomfortably stuffed.

"You know, when I took the dogs outside, I started thinking about the lights. Your neighbor's house is the only one with no lights on. That's a..."

I zoned out and didn't hear anything else Dixie said. Something she'd said triggered the memory I'd been trying to grasp for days, but this time, I caught it before it escaped.

"Earth to Lilly?"

"I'm sorry."

"You've remembered something." She looked at me expectantly.

"Remember the night before the funeral when we were on the interstate?"

"How could I forget?"

"Before we got pulled over, I noticed lights on at the dealership." I stared at her.

She looked as though she was waiting for the punch line. "And?"

"It was past midnight. There's no reason anyone should have been in the dealership that late at night. The cleaning staff would have been long gone by then."

"Who do you think it was?"

I shook my head. "In all of the excitement, I forgot about it until you mentioned lights."

"Do you think we should call Officer Harrison?" She looked at her watch.

I paused. "I don't know. I don't want to call the police because someone simply forgot to turn off the lights before they left. Given everything that has happened, it would be understandable."

"Do you remember seeing the lights on when we passed on the way?" she asked.

I thought back and shook my head. "No. I'm almost positive the lights weren't on when we passed the first time. We passed right by the dealership to get on the interstate. I would have noticed the lights. But they were definitely on when we were coming back from the casino."

"I think you should tell Officer Harrison," Dixie said.

I thought for several minutes.

"I don't like that look in your eyes," Dixie said.

"You don't have to come."

"Lilly Anne Echosby, if you think I'm about to let you run off in the middle of the night to confront a murderer without me, you've lost your marbles." She put her hands on her hips.

I hugged her. "Well, I hopefully won't be confronting anyone. I thought maybe we could do a little stakeout."

"Oh, like on television?" Dixie asked with more enthusiasm than I felt was good for her. "Should we change into black and put makeup under our eyes?"

"I don't think that will be necessary."

We prepared to head out for our first stakeout. I was nervous and excited. I had no plans to confront a killer. My idea was to park across the street from the dealership, well away from any danger. If I saw someone pull into the dealership, then I would phone the police. When I saw Dixie checking her gun before she put it into a backpack, I wondered if we had the same ideas about what would be involved in this stakeout.

I drove through a drive-thru and got two large coffees and then headed toward Albert's car dealership. There weren't a lot of businesses on the road in front of the dealership, but I was familiar with the area. The main road that led past the dealership, Highway 2, was fairly deserted, but there was another road that ran behind the building. It included an area where commuters met to carpool. There were always several cars there and one more wouldn't draw undue attention. Of course, the SUV was probably the only thing that wouldn't draw attention. Dixie and I and three poodles sitting in an SUV were an entirely different matter. Chyna stuck her head between the seat and her tongue in my ear.

I shuddered. "Remind me again why we needed to bring the dogs?"

"For protection; these are well trained dogs and, while they're not attack dogs, they will defend us." Dixie patted Chyna's head and shoved her to the backseat.

The area wasn't well lit, but there was one streetlight and I parked near enough so we could benefit from the light, without broadcasting to all passing motorists, and possible murderers, we were sitting in the car.

Once we were parked, the wait began.

"How long do you think we'll need to sit here?" Dixie asked.

"I have no idea. I'm not even sure if anyone will come. It was closer to three when we saw the lights before, but there's no telling if the person comes every night or if that was a one-time thing."

"Alright, Debbie Downer, you sure know how to throw cold water on a flame," Dixie joked.

"I'm sorry. I just don't want to set your expectations too high."

"Mission accomplished. I will expect the most dull, boring time ever." She laughed. "Want some snacks?" She pulled her backpack from the floor.

"What do you have in that thing?"

She rummaged. "Peanut butter crackers, fruit." She pulled out a banana. "Bottled water, a dog bowl, dog *T-R-E-A-T-S*."

I had seen the power of that one word with those dogs and knew she was in danger if they ever learned to spell.

"Candy bars, crackers, a summer sausage, and toilet paper." She held up the roll.

"Seriously? We aren't going into the wild. If one of us has to go to the bathroom, we'll just drive to a gas station."

"Well, it's my first stakeout, and I wanted to be prepared." She put the toilet paper back in the backpack and pushed the bag down on the floor.

I could tell by the way she avoided eye contact by looking out the window and slumped in her seat, I'd hurt her feelings. "I'm sorry, Dixie. You're right. it's better to be prepared than not." I reached over and squeezed her shoulder.

She sniffed. "Well, I guess it's just silly."

"No. It's not silly. It's actually pretty amazing."

She turned and smiled. "You think so?"

I nodded. "Definitely."

We sat in silence for a while, but it wasn't long before we started talking about old times and laughing. The time passed quickly once we started reminiscing, something we really hadn't had much time to do with all of the turmoil from the divorce to Albert's murder and then my arrest. It felt good to laugh and talk with Dixie. She told me about her life with her husband, Beau. Dixie had always wanted children but had never been blessed with them. She said it was probably the reason she pampered and spoiled Chyna and Leia. Fortunately, Beau didn't seem to mind.

"You know, I can't believe I'm saying this after that huge dinner, but I'm hungry," I said.

Dixie pulled her backpack on her lap. "What'll you have?"

"I don't know. I kind of want something more than snacks."

Dixie pulled up her cell phone. "How about we order a pizza?"

"A pizza? We can't order a pizza. We're on a stakeout."

"Why not? It's almost twelve and no one has come by. What if you're right and nobody does come tonight? "She stared at me.

"I know, but I hate to leave."

"Who said anything about leaving?" She swiped her cell phone. "Hey, Siri, get me the number of the nearest pizza restaurant that delivers."

The options that were still open in Lighthouse Dunes were slim, but Siri found one. Dixie called and ordered a pizza to be delivered to the commuter parking lot off Highway 2. As crazy as it sounded to me, the pizza company didn't hesitate but promised our pizza in thirty minutes.

Thirty minutes later, a small Volkswagen beetle cruised through the parking lot with a large neon pizza attached to the top. I turned on the interior lights. The driver, a pimply faced teen with greasy long dark hair jumped out and hurried around to my window with a greasy pizza box and a bag of napkins.

I handed him a twenty and motioned for him to keep the change, which elicited a huge smile.

Like moths to a flame, the aroma of pepperoni drew the poodles' undivided attention. If you'd ever eaten while six eyes stared you down, you would understand the state of my nerves. Dixie's standard poodles were better behaved than Aggie. They merely stared longingly at my mouth. Aggie, like Scrappy Doo, lunged forward, barked, and whimpered. Fortunately, she was only about six pounds and easily restrained. I was so focused on eating without dropping anything that Aggie could devour like a vulture, that when there was a tap on my window, I nearly jumped out of my skin.

I instinctively turned to look and saw David standing outside the car. I pressed the button to unlock the door.

David hopped into the backseat and closed the door. "Pizza, great." He reached up between the seats and grabbed a slice from the box I was balancing on my lap. He bit into the pizza and moaned.

My heart was still racing from the shock of his unexpected arrival. "David, you've just taken three years off my life." I patted my chest and tried to regulate my breathing to slow down my heartbeat. "What're you doing here?"

When David dropped a slice of pepperoni, I thought Aggie would hurt herself trying to get it. Eventually, Dixie had had enough and got out. She opened the back door of the car and hustled the dogs out. After a brief potty break, she put them in the large crate she'd loaded in the back of the SUV before we left home. Chyna and Leia climbed in without a fuss. Aggie put up a fight. She used her paws to clutch at Dixie's neck. However, Dixie managed to extract herself and tossed her in the crate with the big poodles.

David quickly chewed his pizza and swallowed. "You got anything to drink?"

Dixie handed him a bottle of water from her backpack. He twisted off the cap and drank half the bottle before he came up for air. When he did, he reached up to grab another slice. It was the last one. He hesitated. He looked from me to Dixie. We both nodded. He took it and ate it so quickly I would have thought he hadn't eaten in a week if I hadn't seen him devour a good amount of food during dinner. When he finished, he drank the rest of the water. "Thanks. I was so hungry, and that really hit the spot." He patted his stomach. "You two really know how to have a stakeout."

"Glad we could help," I said. "Now that you've replenished yourself, perhaps you can answer my question. Why are you here?"

"I went to the Purple Panther as planned." He leaned between the two seats as he spoke. "I was a little early, so I thought I'd check out the back parking lot, where Bambi's car was stolen." He shook his head. "I don't know what

I was looking for. I guess I wondered if maybe she was making it up, just reporting the car stolen so she could get insurance money or something." He shrugged. "Anyway, I was just about to walk around the back corner when I saw them." He paused for dramatic effect.

"Who?" Dixie and I both asked.

"Bambi and Chip." Even in the semi-darkness of the car, I could see his face very clearly. He raised an eyebrow and tilted his head down in a way that said Bambi and Chip were up to no good.

"What were they doing?" I asked.

He sang the playground song. "Chip and Bambi, sitting in a tree. *K-I-S-S-I-N-G.*" He looked from me to Dixie. "Although they moved waaay beyond kissing, if you know what I mean?"

Dixie whistled.

"In the parking lot? I asked.

"I'm sure it's not the first time," Dixie said.

I shrugged. She was probably right. "I wonder how long that's been going on," I mused.

Dixie nodded. "Exactly what I was thinking."

David looked puzzled.

"I wonder if this started before your father died or after."

David nodded. "I get it. You're thinking Dad found out Bambi and Chip were…getting busy and confronted them."

"And if Chip or Bambi shot him," Dixie said.

"Or both," David said.

"Right." I pondered the possibility. More and more evidence was piling up against Chip. He had access to the books. He was probably guilty of embezzlement. If he was having a fling with Bambi, he would have access to the apartment. Even if I didn't have evidence to prove one or both of them killed Albert, maybe I could at least prove there was someone else with a strong motive. Reasonable doubt was what Matlock always said on television. I turned to David, "But that still doesn't explain why you're here?"

"When they finished, Bambi got out and went inside. She was dressed in her costume and I knew she would be there for the next few hours. Chip, on the other hand, drove away. So, I followed him."

"Followed him?" The reality of what he'd just said took a few moments to sink in. "You mean…"

He nodded toward the dealership.

That was when I noticed the light on inside.

CHAPTER 14

We sat staring at the building for several seconds. That's when the seriousness of the situation hit me.

It must have dawned on Dixie at the same time because she turned to me and said, "Now what?"

Good question.

"Do we call the police?" Dixie whispered.

"And tell them what? One of the employees is at the car dealership at night?" I realized how stupid that sounded when spoken aloud.

"Well, he shouldn't be there," Dixie said.

"Mom's right. He works there. He could say he forgot something and went to pick it up."

I looked at the time on my phone. "At three in the morning?"

David shrugged. "I don't know, but I think we're going to look pretty stupid if we call them now. I think we need more evidence."

I nodded. "I agree." I opened the car door.

"Where do you think you're going?" Dixie asked.

"I thought I could sneak in and see what he's up to. For all I know, he might be shredding documents that would prove he's embezzling money."

"You're not going without me." Dixie jumped out of the car.

"You're crazy if you think I'm going to let you two go in there alone." David said as he got out of the car.

"Well, we can't all go," I said.

"Why not?" Dixie opened the door and grabbed the pizza box and her backpack. "But let me throw this garbage away first."

"What about the dogs?" I asked.

We looked at each other, and I could tell by the look in her eyes what she was going to say before she opened her mouth. "Oh no."

Dixie hurried to the back of the SUV and got the dogs out and put them on leashes. "Why not? Chyna and Leia are well trained and might be protection."

"And Aggie?" I pointed at my little toy poodle as she stretched as though she'd just worked a twelve-hour shift.

Dixie smiled. "She's got a big heart and that might just come in handy." She walked the dogs over to a grassy area and waited while they relieved themselves. "Besides, she's got to learn some time."

"We can't just march over there," David said.

"Why not? It was your father's business. Now that he's dead, we own it," I said more to convince myself than him.

"I mean, what's the plan?" David stepped in front of us. "Two women, a man and three poodles are just going to walk up to the building at three in the morning and confront the person who most likely killed my dad. And say what? *We were out for a moonlight stroll?"*

"We happened to be in the neighborhood and noticed the light?" Dixie joked.

I shrugged. "Why do we need an excuse? It's our business. If we want to come by, why do we need to explain to Chip Nelson or anyone else?"

David stared with raised eyebrows and a smirk.

I chose to ignore the smirk. "Dixie, give me Aggie." I took the leash from her. "Will the girls let David walk them?"

She nodded and handed the leashes for the standard poodles to David.

"Wait. Why am I bringing the dogs? Aunt Dixie is the professional dog whisperer," David whined.

"Because Dixie is the only one of us with a gun and the knowledge to use it, unless you're packing heat?"

David shook his head.

I looked at Dixie and she nodded and pulled her gun out of the backpack. "She'll need her hands free, so she can focus if it comes to that."

The skepticism I'd seen in David's eyes was now replaced with respect and a healthy dose of fear. "Good point."

We walked over to the dealership lot. Even though it was dark, the moon was exceptionally bright. My pulse was racing. The dogs were surprisingly quiet. They kept their noses to the ground, looking more like hound dogs tracking a scent than retired show dogs. As we got to the building, there was a noticeable change. Chyna and Leia pulled ahead of us. Their steps were deliberate and stealthy. They crept around corners, always sniffing as though they were tracking. We followed their examples and were more cautious, being careful to make as little noise as possible. When we approached the back of the building, the small hairs left unshaved rose across their shoulders and down their backs. It wasn't easy to see, but it was obvious something changed, and the dogs were wired.

There was a small garage in the back of the lot. Albert referred to it as his barn. It was used for parts storage. There was a metal garage door, but the tin building didn't have heat or air-conditioning. There was a motion light on a pole near the barn. That was where the light was coming from. We snuck around the side of the building near the opening. We stopped. A low rumble resonated from the dogs. Even Aggie seemed to sense danger. She stood tall and straight next to her canine sisters. We huddled together.

"What now?" David asked.

I quietly peeked around the corner of the building.

Inside, Chip Nelson had parked two cars. Both cars were imported sports cars. One car already had its tires removed, while the other one sat nearby.

"What's he doing?" Dixie whispered in my ear.

I shrugged then motioned for them to follow me to the back of the building, farther away from the door.

"What's he doing? Stealing car parts?" Dixie asked.

"Now can we call the police?" David asked.

I nodded. "Dixie, call Officer Harrison. He's not stealing parts, he's—"

A growl rumbled through the dogs like thunder rolling over Lake Michigan. The growls started deep inside and by the time they made their way out, there was a great deal of energy behind them. The noise caused us to turn and look at the same time. Bambi stood in front of us.

"Bambi, what are you doing?" I released the breath I'd been holding. "Get over here." I motioned for her to come away from the door.

The dogs lunged and growled. David strained to keep them from pouncing on her.

She laughed. "What am I doing?" She smiled and then reached out and grabbed me. She pulled me to her chest and then whipped out a large gun. "Apparently, getting the drop on you, old lady."

Dixie was balancing her cell phone and her gun and was late in getting her weapon pointed.

"Hand it over." Bambi put the muzzle of her gun to my head. "Or I'll blow her brains out."

"Damn!" Dixie slid the gun toward Bambi.

"And get control of those beasts or I'll shoot all of them." She did something to the gun that made a clicking sound.

I jumped at the noise.

"Plotz," Dixie commanded.

I had never seen the dogs disobey a direct order, but there was a delay that made me wonder if they were thinking about it. The dogs eventually laid down in sphinx-like poses. Neither took their eyes off Bambi and the rumbling was still there. Aggie was still growling, and I leaned down to pick her up, but Bambi got nervous and jerked me back against her.

"I was just going to pick her up. She hasn't been trained like the other dogs," I explained.

"Let Granny take her." Bambi kicked Aggie and sent her flying across the ground toward Dixie.

Aggie screamed. As long as I live, I don't think I will ever be able to forget that sound.

Hearing Aggie squeal lit a fire inside. My blood boiled, and rage rose up in me just as the growls rose up in the poodles. I turned my head and saw Bambi with a large grin on her face. That smile was the spark that started the fire.

I remembered the self-defense classes Bradley Hurston taught us years ago. "SING." I put all of my weight into an elbow to her solar plexus. Then I stomped down on the instep of her foot with all of my weight. When she doubled over in pain, I took the heel of my hand and thrust upward as hard as I could to her nose. As soon as my palm hit the soft cartilage of her nose, I heard a crunch and knew I'd broken her nose. The blood gushed down her face. She squealed like a pig from the pain and dropped like a rock. I never got a chance to administer a final kick in the groin, which probably wouldn't have been necessary with a woman anyway. Solar Plexus, Instep and Nose, SIN, had done the trick.

One of the poodles, Chyna, was in the air before my final blow fell. Like a gazelle, she leapt into the air and knocked Bambi to the ground. Then she stood on her chest with her teeth bared and growled, inches from her face.

Chip Nelson came out of the barn when Bambi screamed. When he turned the corner, Leia shot past me. She flew through the air and landed on Chip, who screamed and cried like a baby. "Get off. Help."

"Mom, are you okay?" David hugged me.

"Yes. I'm fine." I looked to Dixie. "How is Aggie?"

Dixie held her shivering body close. "I think she'll be okay, but we should get her to a vet."

I reached out and took my quivering dog into my arms and my heart broke. She held onto me with her little paws and put her head on my shoulder.

Sirens blared and at least five police cars pulled into the dealership. Officer Harrison and Turbo led the pack. The officers ran up to us, weapons drawn and pointed. Everyone was shouting, and the scene was chaos. Once the police were on the scene, Dixie called Leia, who reluctantly left Chip and pranced over to her owner. Chyna took a bit of coaxing before she could be convinced to relinquish her prisoner. Eventually, Dixie took her by the collar and pulled her off Bambi, who lay quiet, probably passed out from the shock and blood loss.

Officer Harrison pointed out who the bad guys were. Chip was rolled onto his stomach and handcuffed. They had to call an ambulance for Bambi.

"Do you want to tell me what the—" Officer Harrison started, but something in my face must have warned him to proceed with caution. He took a deep breath. "What happened?"

Still cuddling Aggie to my chest, I walked to the garage. "I remembered seeing a light on the night before the funeral, but in the excitement, with nearly getting arrested, I forgot about it. Tonight I remembered and we decided to come down and see for ourselves." I skirted around some of the details. He didn't need to know about our pizza party stakeout. "We came over and saw Chip taking the tires off of these cars. Before we could call the police, Bambi showed up and pulled a gun on us."

Officer Harrison looked in the barn. Something in his jaw got hard and taut. He looked down at Turbo by his side, but his ears were set back and he paced nervously. "Stay here." He gave an order in German and Turbo got to work.

Turbo immediately went to one of the cars and started to aggressively dig at the tire. Officer Harrison called to one of his fellow policemen lined up near us. One of the officers entered the barn and inspected the tire rim. After a few moments, he pulled out a large plastic bag full of a white substance.

"Sweet mother of God," Dixie whispered.

Turbo went to each tire and did the same thing.

After he finished with the first car, the officers had a powwow. When they were finished, Officer Harrison and Turbo came out to where we were. He removed the dog's vest and pulled out a white towel. Instantly, Turbo changed from the super serious drug sniffing police dog into an oversized puppy. His ears went back, and his tail wagged. He looked as though he smiled. Officer Harrison played tug of war with him with the towel for a few seconds. Eventually, he released the towel and Turbo took off. Chyna and Leia stood with tails wagging and looked longingly after their new friend and his towel.

"Is it okay if they play too?" Dixie asked Officer Harrison.

He nodded.

She unhooked their leashes and they took off after Turbo. The three dogs chased each other and played tug of war and keep away with the towel.

I watched for a few moments and then turned back to Officer Harrison. "Aggie was injured when that B…Bambi kicked her. I need to find someone to make sure she's okay."

He looked at the dog in my arms and nodded. "There's an emergency vet on Lakeshore Drive." He pulled out his cell phone. He pushed a button and spoke. "This is Officer Harrison. I have an emergency. A lady is going to bring a toy poodle in who was injured apprehending a suspect." He grinned. "She might have internal bleeding or a broken bone." He listened and then thanked the person and hung up. "It's all set. Take Highway 2 toward the lake and then left onto Lakeshore Drive. It's about two miles down on the left."

Dixie called Chyna and Leia and we headed back to the commuter lot. David took the standard poodles home in his car. Dixie drove while I held Aggie and we sped down the road to the emergency vet.

The vet's office was fairly busy, considering it was nearly five in the morning. I saw from a sign on the door, the emergency vet opened after most vet's offices closed at nights and on weekends. The staff was waiting for me and rushed us back into one of the examination rooms immediately. Dr. Shah was a short woman with a dark complexion, dark hair and soft, kind eyes. She was gentle and smiled at me and then immediately examined Aggie. She was gentle and spoke with a soft voice that reassured as her hands probed.

She turned to me. "I don't think anything is broken, but we won't know for sure unless we take x-rays. We'll need to sedate her to make sure she stays perfectly still," she explained.

I nodded and handed Aggie over to the assistant, a young girl with pink hair and a nose ring.

When she took Aggie out, it was as though someone had opened the flood gates. In an instant, I was crying like a baby. Dr. Shah looked stricken and reassured me Aggie would be perfectly fine. I tried to nod I understood, but nothing coherent came out.

Dixie said, "She's had a rough week."

Something about the total inadequacy of her words and her tone made me laugh.

"Am I going to have to slap you?" Dixie asked.

I shook my head. "I'm okay. It's just...'a rough week' has to be the understatement of the decade."

Dr. Shah hurried out of the room. The look on her face showed she thought we were a few fries short of a happy meal.

While we waited for Aggie, I filled out nearly as much paperwork as I did the last time I went to the doctor. "Insurance? This form is asking about insurance."

"You should consider it. I have insurance for both of the girls. It can save thousands."

"You're serious."

She reached in her backpack and pulled out two insurance cards; each had one of her dog's pictures.

When the paperwork was completed, Dr. Shah came back in with the x-rays. She put them on a machine and explained Aggie had no internal bleeding but did have a small fracture in her leg. She would put a splint on and wrap the leg. With rest, she should be fine within four weeks. She was almost finished and would bring Aggie out shortly.

Within the hour, I carried a groggy poodle with a bright pink gauze-wrapped leg home with medicine for pain and instructions to see my vet. By the time we drove home, the sun was up. We'd been up all night.

CHAPTER 15

When we pulled into the driveway, there was a car parked in the driveway that I recognized as belonging to Detective Wilson. In addition to that one, Officer Harrison's car was there. Since Turbo wasn't pacing in the back, he must be inside, hopefully getting some rest with Chyna and Leia. The garage was blocked, so Dixie parked on the street. By the time we got to the front porch, Stephanie opened the door and rushed out. She flung her arms around my neck and hugged me, careful not to crush Aggie, who was curled up on my chest.

"Oh, Mom, I was so scared when Joe told me what happened."

"Joe?" I must have looked as puzzled as I sounded.

Her neck flushed. "Officer Harrison."

I nodded. "I'd forgotten his first name. I'm sorry we worried you, dear." I stopped before entering the house. "What's with all of the cars?" I motioned at the cars lining the driveway.

She rolled her eyes. "Detective Wilson arrived a few minutes ago with a warrant. She wants the books, laptop and the evidence about embezzling you found."

I nodded and walked into the house.

Officers wearing gloves were rummaging through drawers and cabinets.

"Is that really necessary?" I looked at Detective Wilson. "The books are upstairs. If you give me a minute, I'll go and bring them down."

"That won't be necessary." Detective Wilson waved off my assistance. "That's not how this works."

If I hadn't been awake all night and been through a roller coaster ride of emotions, I might have taken offense at the offhand manner in which she dismissed me. But I was too tired to care. "Fine. I need coffee." I walked toward the kitchen. A police officer who had been standing in the living room extended an arm to prevent me from entering the kitchen.

"The items you're looking for aren't likely to be in the coffeemaker." Stephanie argued.

Detective Wilson nodded to the policeman, who dropped his arm, allowing me to enter my kitchen. However, after a half second, he followed me into the kitchen. I put Aggie down on her dog bed and watched while she curled up into a ball and slept. The officer stood by and watched while I made coffee.

In a previous life, several centuries before my husband tried to divorce me, before I was not only accused of murdering him, but arrested for it, and before I discovered a long-time family friend had not only embezzled money from us but had used the business to smuggle drugs, I would have offered the police coffee too. I had been a different woman back then. The new Lilly Echosby still believed the police were my friends, but I had developed a tougher shell.

The new Lilly Echosby sat at the kitchen table with my daughter, best friend and our new friend, Officer Harrison, and drank coffee. I looked around and saw Chyna, Leia and Turbo curled up on the floor under the window. Aggie whined, and I picked her up and cuddled her for a few seconds until she settled down again. When she was still, I sat back down and drank coffee with her on my lap. It didn't take long before she was back asleep. Every time I looked at the pink gauze around her leg, my heart skipped a beat. I caressed her leg absentmindedly while I sipped my coffee.

After about fifteen minutes, David and a policeman came downstairs carrying a laptop and the box of books and papers I'd taken from Albert's office. The officer gave David a receipt for the items and the search warrant. David escorted the police from the premises. Detective Wilson stopped before leaving and stared at Officer Harrison for several seconds, as if to mark his presence as one of us rather than one of them. Officer Harrison, true to his training, didn't blink.

She then turned her attention to me. "You'll need to come down to the station later and make a statement."

I nodded.

Detective Wilson stared again at Officer Harrison. After a few moments, she turned and walked out.

When David closed the door on the last policeman, he grabbed a cup of coffee and sat down. We all breathed a collective sigh and then laughed that we all felt the same emotional release.

"I hope you won't get in trouble." I looked at Officer Harrison. "I don't think Detective Wilson liked your being here."

He shrugged. "I'll be fine."

Stephanie poured the last of the coffee into Detective Harrison's mug. Then she went to the coffeemaker and made another pot. When she was finished, she filled all of our mugs. She sat down and looked around the table. "Okay, somebody needs to fill me in and start at the top."

We spent the next hour going through the details. By mutual consent, we left the details of our pizza party out. When we got to the part about Bambi kicking Aggie, tears welled up in my daughter's eyes.

"Oh my God. What a monster. How could she do that to a poor defenseless creature?" Stephanie dabbed at the tears that filled her eyes.

David reached over and patted Aggie as she slept on my lap. "I'm not disagreeing with you, but this little dog has the heart of a lion. She may be little, but she proved she's pretty fierce too."

"She's not the only one." Officer Harrison's lips twitched as he tried not to smile.

"Aggie apparently takes after her mama." Dixie smiled.

"Remind me never to get on the wrong side of Mom. She's got a mean right hook." David joked.

"I've never hit another human being in my life…well, I hadn't until this whole thing with your father and Bambi." I patted Aggie but then looked up. "How is Bambi, anyway?"

"Two black eyes, a broken nose, bruised ribs and a broken foot. She's pretty beat up, but she'll live." Officer Harrison's lips twitched.

"How did she get the black eyes?" I asked. "I didn't hit her in the eyes."

"When you break your nose, the bruising often shows under the eyes," Officer Harrison explained.

"Was she involved with Chip and the drugs and everything?" I asked.

"Looks that way, but we haven't gotten much from her yet. She's still in the hospital and pretty heavily sedated," Officer Harrison said.

I felt bad about breaking her nose for about five seconds and then Aggie shuddered in her sleep and the remorse I felt moments earlier vanished. Aggie was just a six-pound dog. She hadn't deserved the way she was treated. Bambi, on the other hand, held a gun to my head and threatened to shoot three human beings. She deserved everything she got.

"So, Chip was using Dad's business to ship drugs into the United States?" Stephanie looked at Officer Harrison.

He nodded. "That's what it looks like. We knew there was some drug ring that was getting drugs into the area, but we didn't know how they were doing it."

"I don't understand. How on God's green earth were they getting all those drugs into and out of the country," Dixie asked.

"Where there's a will, there's a way. We know drug traffickers use Interstate 94 that goes from Detroit to Chicago as one main thoroughfare. Turbo and I have been involved in quite a few stings on that stretch of highway." He sipped his coffee and looked over at Turbo, who looked up when he heard his name but immediately went back to sleep. "We didn't know they were shipping directly to Lighthouse Dunes. So, that has the Vice Squad and the DEA boys really excited."

"Great." I sipped my coffee.

"You don't think Dad knew?" Stephanie asked the question I'd been pondering ever since Turbo discovered the first bag of drugs. How much had Albert known? Despite all of the changes over the years, I still found it impossible to believe Albert would be involved in anything as serious and shady as drug trafficking.

I shrugged. "I don't believe he knew. If he did, I don't think he would have given Bambi the Corvette."

"But, if she knew about the drugs, that would explain why she was so freaked out when the car was stolen. Maybe they hadn't gotten the drugs out of the car yet." David yawned.

I nodded. "I don't think Chip expected your dad to take the Corvette. However, once he gave it to Bambi, he probably figured he had plenty of time to get the drugs."

"Why wait?" Dixie asked.

"Maybe he thought the police would be watching them." I looked at Officer Harrison. "Especially, after you gave him the ticket and gave him the evil stare down."

He smiled and took a sip of coffee.

"I don't think Albert would have given Bambi the car if he'd known, but…" I shrugged again.

Detective Harrison stared at me. "Something else is bothering you. What?"

I smiled. Detective Harrison was either very good at reading people, or he had been around me long enough to notice when something was bothering me.

"Well, I just feel like I'm missing something. Chip was smuggling drugs using Albert's car dealership, *and* he was embezzling money." I stared into my cup for a long time. "It just strikes me as odd. I mean, I don't know a lot about Chip, but, to be completely honest, he's never struck me as smart enough to pull something like this off."

"I know what you mean." Stephanie leaned forward. "Chip used drugs. I could see him being involved in this business, but he certainly wasn't smart enough to mastermind the whole thing."

Officer Harrison raised an eyebrow. "You think there's someone else involved?"

I shook my head and stifled a yawn. "Frankly, I don't know what to think. I'm tired and my brain is all muddled up."

Dixie leaned forward. "Well, I've been trying to figure out why he killed Albert."

"Why or if?" I stifled a yawn.

"What do you mean, IF?" David asked. "Who else could have done it?"

I looked at Officer Harrison.

"As far as I know, Chip Nelson hasn't confessed to killing Albert. In fact, he vehemently denies killing him." He shrugged. "But then he's vehemently denied being involved in drug trafficking too."

"How can he deny it? He was caught red-handed?" Dixie asked.

"He claims he was set up." Officer Harrison stood up. "He lawyered up and refused to say anything."

"Lawyered up?" I asked.

"It means he executed his sixth amendment right to legal counsel," Stephanie said. "And, I'd be surprised if his father will let him say anything." She rubbed her neck. "I know I wouldn't."

"He's been crying like a baby for his daddy, but, for some reason, Daddy hasn't come running," Officer Harrison said.

My yawns would no longer be stifled. I yawned and started a chain reaction of yawns with David and Dixie.

"Don't do that." Dixie yawned.

"Sorry." I blinked. "What time do I have to be at the police station?"

Officer Harrison looked at his watch. "Get some rest. I'll let them know you'll be in this afternoon."

I nodded. "Thank you. Thank you for everything."

"Yes. Thank you. I've never been so happy to see the cavalry come riding in as I was at that moment," Dixie said.

He nodded. "My pleasure."

Stephanie went to let him out and the rest of us went upstairs to get some sleep.

Having been up all night, I thought sleep would come easy, but unfortunately, it proved elusive. I tried to empty my mind and lie still, but try as I might, my mind would not shut down. Instead, the events from the past week tumbled through my head like a tennis shoe in a dryer. The images and events from the past few weeks tossed and tumbled around. I tried to lie still and not wake Aggie, who was snuggled up next to me.

Seriously, had it only been one week? I thought back. Pictures flashed through my mind. The picture of Albert sitting across the table from me telling me he not only wanted a divorce, but he wanted to move his skinny girlfriend, who was younger than our children and dumber than a box of rocks, into our home, my home. That was followed by the picture of Albert walking out of the house with Bambi the night before he was killed. The next picture was the look on Stephanie's face when she learned her father had been killed. The picture of Albert in his casket was followed by the picture of Chip Nelson standing in line to give his condolences after the funeral. That picture infuriated me more than all the others. In fact, I was so angry, I got up and paced to relieve the stress.

I had only taken two passes around the room when I heard a faint knock on the door. "Come in."

Dixie opened the door a crack and stuck her head in. "Did I wake you?"

"Not at all." I motioned for her to come in and continued to pace.

"I thought I heard you moving around. You couldn't sleep either?"

I shook my head. "Something's not right, and I can't put my finger on it. My brain won't shut down and allow me to sleep, so I just stopped trying."

"What's bothering you?" Dixie sat on the bed and stroked Aggie.

I stopped to think if I could put my finger on what was bothering me, but eventually I just shook my head and kept pacing. "I can't describe it, but something's missing. Stephanie's right about Chip Nelson. He's a drug addict, but I can't believe he managed a drug trafficking operation. He just wasn't..." I searched for the right word.

Dixie nodded. "I get what you're saying. He isn't the sharpest knife in the drawer."

I nodded. "Exactly. He's much more likely to have thrown a big party on his yacht for his friends and consumed all of the...whatever he was importing."

"So, you think he had a partner who was working behind the scenes to arrange everything?"

I nodded. "It's the only thing that makes sense."

Dixie lounged back against the headboard. "I don't think any of this really makes sense." She caressed Aggie. "What were you mumbling about when I came in?"

"Oh. I was just thinking about what a total hypocrite Chip Nelson is. He came to the house and stood in line to give condolences when he had, in all likelihood, shot Albert in—"

I stopped abruptly.

"What?" Dixie sat up. "I know that look. You've thought of something."

"It's just…at the repast, the Nelsons were all standing there together, Marilyn, Charles and Chip. Charles cleaned up the mess Chip made. He'd always cleaned up after Chip and Marilyn. Albert used to call him the 'Cleanup Man' because he cleaned up everybody's messes." I paced.

"Well, with a son like Chippy and a lush for a wife, I'm sure he's had a lot of practice cleaning up messes."

"There's something else." I thought. "Several years ago, Charles Nelson ran into some financial trouble. He nearly lost his house, his yacht… everything. Then, something happened, and he was back on his feet and right as rain."

"What happened?"

I shrugged and then turned and continued to pace. "No idea. Whatever it was, he was richer than ever…He used to make frequent trips to Paris and the Riviera."

Dixie whistled. "You don't think…"

"I don't know what to think, but I do know his financial turnaround coincided with Chip working at the car dealership," I stopped abruptly and stared at Dixie, "and Albert turning his business into an import car dealership."

"But he's an attorney. Surely he wouldn't be involved in anything illegal!"

"He is an attorney. He's a very smart attorney. He's certainly smart enough to mastermind an international drug trafficking ring."

"He may very well be the mastermind behind this whole business, but how are you going to prove it? You don't have any evidence."

I paused. "That isn't entirely true. I just might have the proof after all."

CHAPTER 16

We gave up trying to sleep. Instead, we showered and headed to the police station to give our statements. Stephanie notified my attorney, and Christopher met us at the station. I had a brief moment of panic when I got to the front door of the Lighthouse Dunes Police Station. The last time I was brought here, I was handcuffed. I took a deep breath and walked up to the counter.

Dixie and I were taken back to the cubicles, where the detectives sat. I couldn't help turning to look at Officer Harrison's desk as I passed by on my way to Detective Wilson's desk. In years gone by, employee status could be determined by the size of the office. In the cubicles of the twenty-first century, status was determined by how close those cubicles were to windows. Detective Wilson's desk was next to a window and well lit.

Once we were all seated, we relayed our stories to a young man who typed it up. Detective Wilson asked very few questions, only interrupting to clarify a point periodically. I felt bad about dragging Christopher out as he had very little to do. He barely spoke and mostly sat with his legs crossed and listened. While we waited for the policeman to print the statements, I stared at Christopher's shoes. He had one of his legs resting on top of the other, and his shoes were very visible. Christopher was immaculate, even in casual attire. Today he wasn't wearing an expensive, hand-tailored suit, but a pair of slacks and with soft leather shoes. Something about those shoes captured my attention.

"Anything wrong? Did I step in something?" Christopher looked at the bottom of his shoe.

"No. I'm sorry."

"You've been staring at my shoe for five straight minutes," he joked.

"It's just...well, you dress really well."

Christopher smiled. "Thank you. I guess we all have our vices. For some it's cars or jewelry."

"For me, its dog shows," Dixie added. "One year my husband added up the amount of money I spent on dog show competitions and…well, he cringed."

Christopher nodded. "I love nice clothes and shoes." He held out his leg. "Berluti, hand burnished, made from a single piece of leather, without visible seams, from Paris."

"Beautiful." I tried not to stare, but they were works of art, rather than mere shoes. I forced my brain away from Christopher's shoes. "You have a point about vices," I mused. "For Chip Nelson, it was drugs. Marilyn Nelson went for alcohol, and…Charles Nelson…"

"Yes?"

I nearly jumped out of my skin as I hadn't heard Charles Nelson come up. "Oh my God. I didn't hear you come up." I stared. "Dear God, Charles, are you okay?"

He looked horrible. He had two black eyes and a white bandage covered his nose and he used a cane. One foot was in a compression boot that looked like something Herman Munster or Frankenstein would wear. "Yes, Thank you. Just a little accident."

I waited, but no explanation came. Underneath his tan, I saw a slight flush. "What happened?"

"I fell…down a flight of stairs at the house."

"I hope you're going to be okay."

"Broken nose, bruised ribs and a broken foot. I'll heal."

Even with all of his injuries, I had to admire the way he dressed.

Charles Nelson was immaculately dressed in a suit I could tell wasn't purchased off any rack in Lighthouse Dunes. In fact, I would bet money that suit had been purchased and handmade for him. I looked at his shoes and noticed the same, hand-crafted leather as Christopher Williams.

"Are those Berluti shoes?" I asked.

Charles Nelson seemed slightly taken aback but nodded. "Yes, they are."

I remembered Dixie mentioning he was a snazzy dresser, but I didn't think I really had thought about Charles Nelson or his clothes very much previously. However, now I noticed. His fingernails appeared to have been manicured, and he had a large watch that caught the light from Detective Wilson's window and cast a shadow on the wall.

Christopher noted my interest in the watch. He raised an eyebrow. "Nice watch. Is that a Hublot Berluti watch?" He mused. "Platinum case with eighteen karat white gold screws and a Venezia leather-embossed dial and strap."

Charles Nelson tilted his head in surprise. He pulled on the cuffs of his handmade shirt sleeves. "Yes, it is." He buttoned the jacket of his suit like a naked man concealing his body.

"I love Hublot." Christopher stared admiringly.

Charles Nelson pulled at his collar. "Yes, well, I was looking for Detective Wilson."

Detective Wilson came around the corner. "Detective Milton will have your statements ready shortly. Please review them and sign." She then turned and escorted Charles Nelson down the hall.

"What a snazzy dresser," Dixie said.

"I see what you mean about vices," Christopher said. "That Hublot Swiss watch is five figures." He held out his arm and exposed his watch. "Rolex, no diamonds, four figures. His suit was tailor-made, British."

"How can you tell it's British? I mean, I could tell by the quality of the material and the way it fit that it wasn't an off-the-rack suit he picked up at a department store, but what specifically told you the suit was made in Britain?" I asked.

Christopher smiled. "It's the cut mostly. Did you notice the ticket pocket?"

"What the heck's a ticket pocket?" Dixie asked.

"It's a small flapped pocked above the right hip pocket on a jacket. It's a very British look. I think it dates back to a time when businessmen took the train from their country estates into the city and needed a convenient place to put their rail ticket. The buttons are distinctive. Henry Poole, Savile Row. Plus, the hand stitching around the lapel and before he buttoned his jacket, I noticed the lapel buttonhole and boutonniere loop."

I shook my head in puzzlement.

"It's a hand-stitched loop behind the buttonhole of the lapel to hold the base of a flower."

"Wow. Do men still wear flowers on their lapels?" Dixie asked.

Christopher shook his head. "Sadly, most men don't, but it's a nice touch." He paused for a moment. "The shirt was bespoke Charvet." He leaned close. "Bespoke, custom made in French." He kissed his fingertips to his lips. "Absolutely the best shirt in the world. The detail…" He shook his head. "Did you notice the way the stripes all matched. The left cuff was the slightest bit shorter than the right to allow for the watch. The workmanship was magnificent."

We nodded knowingly.

"The shoes were Berluti, also bespoke and hand burnished. Premium crafted patinated soles and hand-wrought Berluti ankle motifs." He took off one shoe and pointed out details as he talked. "Similar to mine, they're made from a single piece of leather to avoid seams. Colored lining and leather soles are like walking on a cloud." He put his shoe back on.

"I have no idea what you just said, but it doesn't matter." I shook my head. "The bottom line is Charles Nelson wears really expensive, hand-made, *bespoke*," I used air quotes, "clothes and shoes."

"Heck, his clothes have been to more foreign countries than I have," Dixie said.

"In a nutshell, he's wearing over fifty thousand dollars," Christopher said, knowingly.

Dixie whistled. "Fifty thousand dollars?"

Christopher nodded. "Conservatively. The watch could be worth that by itself."

"How did you get to know so much about clothes?" I couldn't help asking.

He grinned. "I love clothes, and I have a twin brother who's a buyer for a high-end store in New York. He travels to Paris and Milan several times per year and keeps me updated on the latest fashions." He looked serious. "But, what does that tell us? I mean, so what Charles Nelson likes to spend a lot of money on clothes?"

I bit my lip and stood up. I needed to think. I paced. I shared what we knew about the troubles Charles Nelson went through several years ago and how he managed to turn things around about a year ago.

"That was the same time your husband's car business started importing cars, isn't it?" Christopher asked.

I nodded. "The embezzlement was too sophisticated for Chip Nelson to have worked through on his own. I'm a certified public accountant, and it took me a bit to recognize some of the accounts and the holding companies."

"I doubt if Chippy could tell the difference between a liability and an asset," Dixie said.

Christopher leaned back. "You think Charles Nelson was involved?"

I nodded. "Not only involved. I think he masterminded the entire thing."

Christopher whistled. "Do you have any proof, other than the fact he likes to wear expensive clothes?"

I shook my head.

We talked until Detective Wilson returned. When she returned, Christopher shared our theory with her. Detective Wilson listened, skeptically at first, with her arms folded across her chest and a *yeah right* expression on her face. As we continued to explain, her facial expression relaxed, as did her body language. Her arms unfolded. Instead of leaning back, she leaned forward. I thought she would dismiss my theory as crazy, especially as we talked about the custom clothes, but surprisingly, she seemed excited. Her eyes sparkled, and she asked questions for clarification, rather than challenges. When she had exhausted her questions, she went to talk to the police chief. When she returned, we were invited into an office just a few steps away from Detective Wilson's cubicle.

Chief Paul Russell was a large, burly redheaded man with a thick mustache and beard. He had a loud booming voice, but he used it sparingly. He listened to our theory and then picked up the phone and called the district attorney.

The district attorney invited us to come to his office. If I still believed in Santa Claus, I would have sworn Jeffrey Alex Matthews was him. He was a plump, older man with white hair, a white moustache and a long white beard. He was jolly, with dimples and rosy cheeks, and he wore old-fashioned spectacles.

I told my theory for the third—or was it the fourth time. The excitement had worn off, and the lack of sleep had finally caught up with me. My brain was foggy, and I missed some of the details I'd included in the previous two or three run-throughs. Thankfully, Dixie or Christopher were well-acquainted with the details and filled in when I missed anything.

"Wait, you didn't mention the fancy Savile Row tailors," Detective Wilson added.

Sleep deprivation and hunger made me blind to some of the unspoken communication between the detectives, but I suddenly woke up and realized there was more going on here than my theories. "What's the big deal?" I looked from Detective Wilson to Chief Russell and finally to Santa Claus. "As much as I'd like to believe I'm brilliant with all of the deductive abilities of Sherlock Holmes and Agatha Christie combined, the truth is, I'm not a genius, like Nero Wolf. I'm just a housewife...a widowed former CPA who likes to read mysteries. Now, twenty-four hours ago, you were convinced I'd killed not only my husband, but my neighbor. Something's up, and I want to know what."

Dixie's shock was reflected in her eyes, but she kept her mouth closed and waited. Christopher had to work to keep from smiling.

Detective Wilson and Chief Russell exchanged looks and then he nodded.

Detective Wilson looked as though she would rather eat glass than explain, but eventually she took a deep breath and got to it. "None of what you're saying would be enough to convince a jury Charles Nelson, attorney and pillar of Lighthouse Dunes, is a drug-trafficking mastermind. Most of this wouldn't get you anywhere. But…"

"But?" I asked.

She sighed. "There's one piece of information we've been withholding."

I waited.

Chief Russell took over. "Bradley Hurston was a retired cop. He didn't go down easy. He put up a fight."

I looked from the chief to Detective Wilson.

Eventually, she continued. "We found a button under his body. The killer must have lost it in the struggle and didn't notice."

"A button?" I asked.

Detective Wilson nodded. "A very distinct button."

"Let me guess. Henry Poole?" Christopher shook his head. "I should have guessed. That's why you asked about Henry Poole when you interrogated her?"

Detective Wilson nodded again. "We've been looking into it, but one button isn't much to go on. We can't get a warrant to check the buttons on every suit for every man in Lighthouse Dunes."

The district attorney gave a Santa Claus chuckle. "No, but I would feel comfortable asking for a warrant to search Charles Nelson's suits to see if one of them is missing a distinctive *Henry Poole* button. We may not be able to get him for the drug trafficking, but your information certainly opens up a couple of other areas for us to investigate."

"The embezzlement might be something we can use to tie him to the murders. We'll get our nerds working on those holding companies," Chief Russell added.

The district attorney sat on the edge of his desk. "There's bound to be a trace of some kind. Detective Wilson will work on the button." He looked in her direction.

She nodded.

"It would be great if we could get either Chip or Bambi to turn state's evidence, but I doubt if Chip will turn on his father." The district attorney looked sad. "He's been a very naughty young man."

Dixie leaned over and whispered in my ear, "Did he just say naughty?"

"Maybe Bambi would prefer to testify against Chip and Charles Nelson in exchange for immunity?" Christopher asked.

"SING," I shouted.

"Excuse me?" Santa Claus looked puzzled.

"SING, S-I-N-G. Bradley Hurston used to teach self-defense classes to the women in the neighborhood when he was a policeman. He taught us the SING self-defense method."

Detective Wilson rolled her eyes. "It's a common technique."

"That's what I did when Bambi put a gun to my head and then kicked my dog. I remembered what Bradley Hurston taught me, and I used it to defend myself. SING, minus the groin. I skipped that."

"That's great," Chief Russell said, with a look that implied my elevator didn't go to the top floor.

"But don't you see, the injuries Charles Nelson has are the same as Bambi's. Broken foot, bruised ribs and a broken nose. And when you break your nose, it causes black eyes. I'll bet when he tried to attack Bradley Hurston, he got more than he bargained for. Instead of a frail old man, he got an ex-policeman who put up a fight."

"But wasn't he in a wheelchair?" Dixie asked.

"He was, but he wasn't paralyzed. He could stand with help. The wheelchair just made it easier to get around. He also had a cane, and I'll bet he used it to beat the crap out of Charles Nelson."

Detective Wilson looked from the District Attorney to Chief Russell. Something passed between the three of them and we were ushered out of the room

Normally, I would have been curious and resentful of the dismissal, but I was too tired and too sleepy to care. Dixie and I went through a fast-food drive-thru. I finished a sandwich and fries before I pulled into the garage and went upstairs and crashed. If Charles Nelson entered my thoughts again, I don't remember. I slept long and hard and woke up only once during the night.

CHAPTER 17

The morning paper was full of news of the arrest of prominent attorney, Charles Nelson, his son, Charles Nelson III, and a stripper from Southwestern Michigan, Bertha Jones.

"Bertha? How do you go from Bertha to Bambi?" Stephanie asked.

"I don't think too many men would be titillated by a stripper named Bertha." Dixie took a bite from the pastry she'd picked up earlier.

I looked across at Officer Harrison, who'd stopped by to tell us about the arrests.

"She's singing like a canary now. She's rolled over on both of the Nelsons in exchange for immunity."

"Ah, so Santa Claus took my advice." I sipped my coffee.

"Santa Claus?" Officer Harrison asked.

"The district attorney." I heard Aggie whimper and I picked her up from her dog bed and put her in my lap.

He was silent for a moment. "I can see the resemblance." He smiled. "How does it feel to be a free woman?"

I thought about it. "I don't know. I feel like so many feelings have gotten mashed together. I'm glad the police no longer believe I killed my husband or poor Mr. Hurston."

"Is it really over?" Dixie asked.

Stephanie nodded. "All charges have been dropped and Mom is completely in the clear."

"Bambi...ah, I mean Bertha said Albert discovered her and Chip together in a...um...compromising position. He went irate. He fired Chip and said he wanted him gone. He knew something wasn't right at the dealership, but he didn't know what."

"I'll bet he suspected something, that's why he changed his will and left everything to Mom," Stephanie said.

Officer Harrison looked from Stephanie to me and sipped his coffee. "Chip panicked and shot Albert."

"But why did they kill Mr. Hurston?" David wandered downstairs and poured himself a cup of coffee.

"Chip told his dad what he'd done. So, when Mr. Hurston said, 'I saw you. I know what you did,' he panicked. Chip was afraid to kill a second time, so Charles said he'd take care of it."

"Charles had made a lifetime of cleaning up Chip's messes," I stroked Aggie and watched as she laid her head down on my lap.

David joined us at the table. "What'll you do now?"

"You and Stephanie are going to be leaving soon." I noticed a look pass between Officer Harrison and Stephanie but ignored it. They were both adults and they would either figure things out, or not. I sighed. "There are too many memories here." I had gotten up early this morning and watched the sunrise and thought about what I wanted to do with my life. "If neither of you are interested in the dealership..."

Both David and Stephanie shook their heads.

"I thought maybe I'd sell it to your uncle Vinnie."

David gave a half shrug and a nod. Stephanie merely nodded her approval.

"I'd already decided to sell the house and start over someplace new." I looked at Dixie.

"I'm glad. I think you'll like Chattanooga."

"I hope so." I thought about Miss Florrie as I stroked Aggie. She looked up at me with her big trusting brown eyes. "But, if I don't, I'll move again. and I'll just keep moving until I find my happy place."

Please turn the page for an exciting sneak peek of

V.M. Burns's

READ HERRING HUNT

now on sale wherever print and e-books are sold!

Mystery bookstore owner Samantha Washington is about to find out it's not so easy to play Monday morning quarterback when it comes to murder...

To the town of North Harbor, Michigan, MISU quarterback Dawson Alexander is a local hero. To Samantha Washington, owner of the Market Street Mysteries Bookstore, Dawson is more than a tenant—he's like an adopted son. But to the police, he is their prime suspect after his ex-girlfriend is found murdered. It's more than enough real-life drama for Sam to tackle, but her role as a mystery writer also calls. Returning to the English countryside between the wars, she finds Lady Daphne Marsh in quite the quandary. Someone has tried to murder the scandalous American divorcée Wallis Simpson, for whom Edward VIII so recently abdicated his throne. It seems finding a suspect is no small challenge when most of England has a motive...

While Sam's lawyer sister Jenna rushes in to build Dawson's defense, Sam and her lively grandmother, Nana Jo, huddle up to solve the mystery and blow the whistle on the real killer. With the tenacious members of the Sleuthing Senior Book Club eager to come off the sidelines, Sam and her team just might stop a killer from completing another deadly play...

CHAPTER 1

"Did you see the getup that little floozy had on?"

"Shhhh." I glanced around to make sure the "little floozy" was out of earshot. Tact wasn't Nana Jo's strong suit.

"Don't shush me. I've seen Sumo wrestlers wearing more fabric."

Nana Jo exaggerated, but not by much. Melody Hardwick was a supermodel thin, heavily made-up college senior who had attached herself figuratively and literally to my assistant, Dawson Alexander.

"Surely that boy knows she's nothing more than a little gold digger." Nana Jo had taken an instant dislike to Melody.

"You don't know she's a gold digger. You just don't like her." I locked the door to the bookstore. "Besides, it's not like Dawson has any money."

"He may not have a pot to pee in now, but the boy has PEP." Nana Jo wiped down the counters and bagged the trash.

"What's PEP?"

"Potential Earning Power. That boy is the best quarterback MISU's had in at least a decade. They're undefeated and if things keep going like last week, they have a shot at a bowl game and maybe a championship."

My grandmother had always been a sports enthusiast, but ever since the Michigan Southwest University, or *MISS YOU* as the locals called it, quarterback started helping out in my bookstore, she'd become more of a fanatic.

"He was embarrassed. Did you see how she clung to him?"

"Dawson's a big boy. He can make his own decisions."

Based on the look she gave me, she wasn't convinced. Frankly, I wasn't convinced either. I was concerned about him too. School was a challenge for Dawson. At the end of his freshman year he was placed on academic probation. Thanks to a lot of hard work and tutoring from me and Nana Jo throughout the summer, he'd raised his grades, avoided academic suspension, and turned his life around. He didn't have to work at the bookstore anymore. His football scholarship covered room and board. I never wanted to charge him for staying in the studio apartment I created in my garage, but student athletes had to pay the going rate for housing and get paid fair market wages for work.

"Girls like that ain't nothing but trouble. You mark my words. Just like Delilah, she'll come after him with a pair of scissors first chance she gets. That woman is nothing but trouble."

Nana Jo's words broke my reverie and brought back the worry I thought I'd eliminated. I tried to shake it off, but it lingered at the back of my mind.

We cleaned the store and then she hurried off for a date with her boyfriend, Freddie.

I took a quick tour around the store. I looked at the books neatly stacked on each shelf. It was still hard for me to believe I owned my own mystery bookstore. Market Street Mysteries had been a dream my late husband and I shared for years. After his death over a year ago, I was finally living our dream. I walked down each aisle and ran my hands across the solid wood bookshelves that still smelled woodsy and fresh and shined with the oil polish Andrew, my Amish craftsman, gave me. After six months, the store was doing well, and I still got a thrill walking through and realizing it was mine. My four-legged companions on these strolls trailed along behind, toenails clicking on the wood floors. Toy Poodles, Snickers and Oreo, might not share my love of mysteries, but they definitely approved of the baked goods that made their way under tables and counters.

The back of the bookstore was enclosed to provide a yard for privacy and an area for the poodles to chase squirrels and bask in the sunlight. As fall hit the Michigan coastline, the weather had turned cool. The leaves were starting to darken from bright shades of yellowy green to deeper, rich hues of amber, burgundy, and russet. Lake Michigan was also undergoing a change from the deep, blue calm of summer to the pale blue that blended into the horizon and was only discernible from the sky by the choppy white swells that danced across the surface and pounded the shore. Autumn was my favorite time of year, and I lingered outside and enjoyed the sunset until Snickers reminded me she hadn't been fed by scratching my leg and ruining my tights. I needed to remember to make an appointment with the groomers first thing tomorrow or give up wearing skirts.

When my husband, Leon, and I dreamed of the bookstore, we planned to make the upper level into a rental unit to offset the cost. After his death, I sold the home we'd lived in and turned the upper level into a two-bedroom loft for me and the poodles. Nana Jo moved in after a dead body was found in the back courtyard, but she still had her villa at a retirement village. I never dreamed how much I'd enjoy living in the space.

Next week would be one year since Leon's death. The pain was less crippling. The bookstore kept me busy during the day. But the nights were still difficult. I started writing to help occupy my time and my mind. Six months ago, I'd finished the first draft of a British cozy mystery and spent the last few months editing. Nana Jo wanted me to send it out to an agent, but that would involve allowing someone besides me and my grandmother, who loved me, to read it. I wasn't ready for that type of humiliation and rejection yet. Besides, in the unlikely event that a publisher was interested in my book, they'd want to know what else I had. What if one book was all I had in me? The only way to find out would be to try again. So after dinner I made a cup of tea and headed to my laptop.

* * * *

Wickfield Lodge, English country home of Lord William Marsh–November 1938

Thompkins entered the back salon where the Marsh family was having tea and coughed. "I'm sorry, but the Duke of Kingfordshire is on the telephone."

Lady Daphne was in her favorite seat by the window. She started to rise but was stopped when Thompkins discretely coughed again.

"His grace the duke asked to speak to your Ladyship." He turned toward Lady Elizabeth.

Lady Elizabeth Marsh glanced at her niece, Daphne, noting the blush that left her cheeks flushed. She placed her teacup down and hurried out of the room. In the library, she picked up the telephone. "Hello James dear is there—"

"Thank goodness you're home. I'm sorry but I don't have time for pleasantries. Time is of the essence." Lord James FitzAndrew Browning, normally calm and composed, had a slight tremor in his voice, which reflected the urgency of his call even more than his words and lack of propriety. The duke took a deep breath and then rushed on. "This is going to sound strange, but I need you to trust me. You're going to get a call from the Duchess of Windsor asking for permission to move her hunting party to Wickfield Lodge this weekend. It's vital she be allowed to do so."

Whatever Lady Elizabeth expected, it hadn't been this. She stood frozen for a moment before recovering herself enough to respond. "Well of course, James. We…we have no plans this weekend."

James released a huge sigh and she could almost see him wiping his brow.

"James, you know we're happy to help any way we can, but you mentioned this was 'vital.' Vital to whom?"

James hesitated a moment before responding. "Vital to England. The Crown. Maybe the entire world."

CHAPTER 2

Saturdays were busy days at the bookstore and I was thankful my nephews, Christopher and Zaq, were home from college for fall break and helping out. The twins were invaluable in getting the bookstore up and running over the summer. The boys were twenty and while they were identical, their personalities were so different it was very easy to tell them apart. Both were tall and slender. Christopher was business oriented and preppy, while Zaq was technology inclined and edgier. Neither was a mystery lover, but they each had their own gifts and I was thankful they were willing to spend time helping out their aunt and earn extra pocket money.

Nana Jo was a mystery lover and was great at helping match customers with authors and mystery subgenres like hardboiled detective stories, cozy mysteries, or police procedurals.

Today was a home football weekend for MISU and a bye week for the twins' school, Jesus and Mary University, or JAMU to the locals. When Dawson started working at the bookstore, I toyed with the idea of putting a television in the store so we could watch him play on Saturdays. However, a television in a bookstore seemed paradoxical. I compromised by foregoing the smooth jazz I normally piped in and tuned into the sports channel instead, at least for MISU and JAMU games. I expected complaints from people who liked to sit and read in peace and quiet. But so far, the comments were all positive. I suspected the lack of protest was due to the customers' desire to support a hometown boy combined with their affection for Dawson's baked goods. They were willing to give up a little peace and quiet to support someone they knew.

Thankfully, Dawson and the MISU Tigers had today's game well in hand with a healthy lead of three touchdowns. Home team wins made for happy customers, and happy customers spent more money. As locals discovered Dawson lived and worked here, I'd noticed an increase in traffic. Many were football fans who wanted to congratulate him, talk sports, and get autographs for wide-eyed kids. The others were infatuated young girls who glanced shyly at him when he was working and then hid behind books, giggling whenever he looked at them. Regardless of the reason, the extra traffic was good for business.

MISU won handily and I had a very good day in sales. The twins had dates and hurried out immediately at closing.

"You should go to the casino with me and the girls," Nana Jo said.

"Thanks, but I think I'll stay home. I want to get some writing done." We reshelved books and cleaned the store.

"Great. You started working on the next book in the series? You know, I'm really proud of you. But you still need to start sending your book out to agents. I hear getting published is a long process. I read somewhere Agatha Christie was rejected for five years before she got her first book deal."

"I know. I—"

The alarm system I'd installed this summer startled me and I dropped the books I was shelving. The alarm buzzed whenever a door or window was opened, even if the system wasn't armed. Nana Jo stepped around to see who had entered and I picked up the books I'd dropped.

I placed the books on a nearby table and headed for the front of the store. I could have sworn I'd locked the door. Just as I came around the corner, I heard Nana Jo.

"We're closed."

"Oh, I know. I just thought I'd wait for Dawson."

I struggled to recognize the voice. As I got to the main aisle, I saw Dawson's scantily clad girlfriend, Melody. Today's ensemble included more fabric than the one she wore yesterday, but not by much. A short black skin-tight miniskirt with a deep V-neck mesh cut top with fabric that barely covered her breasts and red, six-inch heels that Nana Jo's friend Irma called hooker heels.

"Lord, have mercy. What're you wearing?" Nana Jo stared open mouthed.

The shocked expression wasn't lost on Melody, who laughed and twirled to insure Nana Jo got the full effect. "You like?"

"Is someone watching your pole?"

Melody flushed and cocked her head and took a step forward as though she were about to say something insulting.

Younger people often thought of the elderly as feeble and weak. However, my Nana Jo was over six feet, two hundred pounds, held a green belt in Aikido, and could shoot a bat off the top of a building at three hundred yards. *Don't ask me how I know that.* Despite the difference in their ages, in a fight, my money was on Nana Jo.

"Dawson isn't here, and the store is closed." I stepped in between the two women. "If you're looking for Dawson, I suggest you try campus."

For a moment, Melody looked at me as though I were gum she'd scrapped from the bottom of her shoe.

"What's going on?"

I was so intent on preventing an altercation between Nana Jo and Melody I hadn't heard Dawson enter through the back door.

Apparently, Melody hadn't either. "Dawson. How long have you been there?" She smiled big.

"Long enough." The chill in his words made me turn to look at him. His eyes were hard, and his face was set like granite. "What're you doing here, Melody? I told you we were finished yesterday."

Melody kept her smile in place as she sauntered around me. "I knew you couldn't really mean that. We both said things we didn't mean yesterday." She stood inches from Dawson and placed her hands on his chest and leaned close. "Let's go up to your room and talk things over."

Dawson didn't move for several seconds, but I could see the vein in the side of his forehead bulge with each breath. Finally, he grabbed Melody by the wrist.

She winced in pain. "Ouch. You're hurting me."

Dawson turned and walked out the way he came, dragging Melody by the wrist along with him.

"I guess he was smart enough to see through that little cheap hussy after all," Nana Jo said. "I think that's the last we'll see of her."

I hurried to secure the front door. Something in the way Melody looked and a flutter in my spine told me Nana Jo was wrong.

* * * *

Normally, Sundays were spent with my mom. Church, lunch afterward, and girl time. This Sunday was no different. Today we were shopping downtown South Harbor.

Unlike North Harbor, South Harbor had a bustling downtown with picturesque cobblestone streets and brick store fronts that sold everything from fudge and truffles to overpriced coffee. Mixed between quaint soda shops and antique stores were clothing stores with shoes that cost more than a month of my salary when I was a teacher.

"Honey, isn't this cashmere sweater lovely? It would look great on you." My mom held up a bubble gum pink garment that looked as though it might fit one of my thighs.

"Mom, I couldn't fit my imagination in that sweater."

"They have larger sizes, dear. I really think you need to upgrade your wardrobe. Everything you own is black or brown. You look like you're still in mourning." She placed the fluffy concoction up to my neck.

I glanced at the tag and nearly choked. "Are you joking? That sweater costs more than my house payment."

"You really should put more effort into your appearance. You've really let yourself go since Leon died. I think you're hiding behind your mourning and it's time you started living again, and maybe dating."

I stared open-mouthed. "Not all of us can live the life of a princess. I don't have the time or money to waste getting my nails and hair done and buying over-priced sweaters. I have a business to run."

The sales clerk, who had walked up with a bright smile on her face, turned and walked away.

My mom sighed and replaced the sweater. She walked to the back of the store. That sigh spoke louder than any words could have. Obviously I had disappointed her again. I stood there for a moment and then sorted through the rack of sweaters, looking for one that would fit over my head without making me look like an overstuffed sausage. I could afford the sweater. That wasn't the problem. Finances had always been tight when Leon and I were working. A cook and an English teacher didn't buy cashmere sweaters. But I'd sold the house and used the insurance money to buy the building. The bookstore was doing well, not *Fortune Magazine* worthy, but thanks to low overhead, frugal spending, and hard work, it was making a profit. One cashmere sweater wouldn't break me, and it would make my mom happy. But, as a grown woman in her mid-thirties, I shouldn't have to buy a sweater I didn't want to make my mom happy. I wished Nana Jo had come with us today. She would have understood and helped intercede between me and my mom.

My mom was so very different from Nana Jo; it was hard for me to imagine my grandmother gave birth to her. They were polar opposites. Josephine Thomas was tall and hardy. My mom, Grace Hamilton, was five feet, less than one hundred pounds dripping wet, and delicate. My mom was like a dainty porcelain figurine you keep on the tallest shelf behind a glass door, locked away from harm for fear of breaking it. Nana Jo blamed my grandpa, who always called my mom his little princess, for planting the *princess seed* in her head. In her mid-sixties, my mother had never had a job outside of the home. She'd never paid a bill until after my dad died. She was the princess.

I dropped my mom off at her South Harbor condo and headed back over the bridge to North Harbor, where I belonged. I glanced at the pink shopping bag on the seat that contained a white cashmere sweater I would be too afraid of spilling anything on to ever wear and swung my car into the parking lot of a nearby liquor store. I glanced at my watch. Thankfully, it was after twelve, when alcohol could be purchased. I looked at the license plates of the cars parked in the lot, noting the majority were Indiana residents who had escaped across the state line into Michigan, where they could buy alcohol on Sunday. We were all escaping from something, but I didn't have the time or energy to figure out what at the moment. A bottle of wine would have to substitute for therapy for now.

* * * *

During the summer, I saw quite a lot of Dawson. When the fall semester started, we barely saw each other, despite the fact he lived in the apartment over my garage. Twice daily football practices, weight training, and classes took up a lot of his time. But Dawson loved baking and he was really good at it. His apartment was a tiny studio with only a one-burner stove, which made it challenging to bake on a large scale. Dawson had gotten into the routine of using my kitchen to bake enough goodies to get us through the week at the bookstore. So, when I entered through the back door, I smelled a sweet delicious aroma wafting down the stairs to greet me.

I climbed the stairs without my normal escorts. Snickers and Oreo usually heard the garage door and bounded to the bottom of the stairs to greet me. However, the possibility of a cookie or treat dropping to the floor was a greater enticement than seeing me.

I placed my pink bag on the counter with less care than I used for the bottle of wine. Dawson had his back to me as he lifted a tray of cookies out of the oven and placed them on a rack on the counter.

"What an amazing smell." I breathed deeply and allowed the smell of vanilla, almonds, and sugar to fill my senses.

"Thanks. You're just in time to try one." Dawson turned to face me.

"Oh my God! What happened to your face?"

He didn't say anything, merely hung his head. I hurried around the counter and turned his face toward the light to get a closer look. Three red scratches trailed across both cheeks. There was a gash under his left eye and a bruise on his forehead. His eyes were bloodshot and dark circles underneath indicated he hadn't slept.

He tried to turn away, but I held his chin and forced him to look at me. "What happened to you?"

We stood like that so long, I didn't think he would answer.

Eventually, the silence grew too much for him. "I'm fine."

I snorted. "Well, you sure don't look fine."

Dawson shrugged. "It's nothing." He forcefully, but gently, pulled my hands away and walked to the back of the kitchen. He leaned against the wall and folded his arms, providing a barrier.

I took a deep breath and tried to steady my breathing. "Was it your father? Is he out of jail?"

He shook his head.

"Then who?"

He hung his head. "Let's just say Melody didn't take our breakup well."

"You should go to the doctor. Those scratches look deep, you—"

He was shaking his head before the words were out of my mouth. "If I go to the doctor, the newspaper might find out."

Sad that at nineteen you had to be concerned about the newspapers running a story about a girl who lashed out when her boyfriend broke up with her. But, this season the MISU Tigers were getting a lot of publicity, Dawson in particular.

I went to the bathroom and got a cold compress and mercuric acid. He didn't balk when I made him sit at the dining room table and didn't say one word when I started to treat the cuts. "Newspapers are the least of your worries. Wait until Nana Jo finds out!"

He winced, but I wasn't sure if it was the mercuric acid or the thought of what Nana Jo would say.

* * * *

"What an unusual request. James didn't have any other information?" Lord William asked as he absentmindedly broke off a piece of his scone and fed it to Cuddles, the Cavalier King Charles Spaniel positioned at his feet.

"Not that he told me. Although, I'm sure he'll fill us in when he gets here." Lady Elizabeth picked up the knitting she kept nearby, which she said helped her think clearly.

"Is Lord James coming too?" Lady Daphne Marsh picked at an imaginary string on her skirt and avoided making eye contact with her aunt.

"Well, I suppose so, although I didn't ask him. I just assumed he would." Elizabeth looked at her husband. "You don't mind do you, dear?"

"No. No. Of course not." Lord William tossed the remains of the scone down to the dog and pulled out his pipe. "I'm sure James wouldn't have asked if it wasn't important."

"My thoughts exactly." Lady Elizabeth resumed her knitting.

"I don't suppose you know anything about this?" Lord William asked his niece.

Lady Elizabeth Marsh sighed. Sometimes her husband could be rather slow to read the signs, or he would have noticed his niece, Daphne, had said very little since Lord James Browning's name was mentioned. The two met six months ago when he came to help out his friend and old classmate Victor Carlston, Earl of Lochloren, who was accused of murdering one of Daphne's beaus. At the time, Victor believed he was in love with Daphne and chivalrously stepped in to protect her by allowing the police to believe him guilty of murder. Lord James helped to reveal the true killer and insured his friend's freedom. Victor was now living in wedded bliss with Daphne's sister, Penelope, down the road at his family estate, Bidwell Cottage. The Marshes hoped another announcement of marriage would be forthcoming as Lord James and Lady Daphne seemed destined for the altar. However, the duke's visits of late had been fewer and far between.

"No. I haven't spoken to James…ah, the duke in nearly two weeks," Daphne said almost in a whisper.

"I suppose you better tell Thompkins and the rest of the staff to prepare for guests," Lord William said.

"I would, but I think I want to wait until we're sure," Lady Elizabeth said. "Technically, she hasn't asked yet. I don't even know how many people to expect."

"Do you suppose David will come too?" Lord William asked.

Lady Elizabeth knitted. "I have no idea. The last I heard, he was in France."

"I don't suppose there will be a problem with the Queen Mother and the rest of family," Daphne asked.

"Well, I guess that depends on what type of problem you mean." Lady Elizabeth knitted silently for a few moments. "Bertie and Elizabeth are still very angry, and the Queen Mother is disappointed in David. I still feel rather badly that none of the family attended the wedding."

Lord William sputtered. "But really, how could we attend? It would have been a sign the family agreed with his abdication to marry a divorced woman—an American." Lord William waved his pipe while he spoke, flinging ashes across the sofa.

Lady Elizabeth looked up and shook her head. The sofa was starting to show bare patches from the maids brushing off tobacco. It would have to be recovered soon. "Well, I don't know if the fact she was twice divorced or an American was the objectionable part. I might have considered attending if the wedding were one day earlier or one day later."

“I agree. It was as though they were thumbing their noses at the family by getting married on King George’s birthday,” Daphne said. “Really, his own father’s birthday.”

“Bad form.” Lord William refilled his pipe.

“Regardless of the circumstances, David and Bertie are brothers, and I believe they’ll work things out in the end,” Lady Elizabeth said. “Besides, James said it was vital to the Crown that she hosts her hunting party here. So, that must mean the king is at least aware of the event.”

Lord William nodded and puffed on his pipe.

“At any rate, it doesn’t appear we’ll find out how the Crown feels about things. The duchess hasn’t called. What if she’s found another place to hunt?” Daphne asked.

Thompkins entered the room silently and coughed. “Her Grace, Wallis Duchess of Windsor is on the telephone for your ladyship.”

CHAPTER 3

Nana Jo's response when she saw Dawson's face was loud and littered with old-fashioned words like *floozy, harpy, tart,* and *shrew.* When she calmed down, she mixed up a concoction with Aloe Vera gel, honey, vitamin E oil, and baking soda. Dawson looked like he had leprosy most of the day Sunday, and he had to fight off Snickers, who kept trying to lick off his mask, but Monday his face looked so much better, it was like night and day. The scars were still there. Only time would truly heal them, but the improvement was amazing.

"Mrs. Thomas, you're a miracle worker." Dawson kissed Nana Jo on the cheek.

"Well, you need about two more days before the scars will disappear completely." Nana Jo stared at her handiwork. "But at least you don't look as though you've been in a cat fight."

"You never cease to amaze me," I said after Dawson hurried off to campus.

Nana Jo and I sat at the breakfast bar and drank coffee.

"Where on earth did you learn to mix up your healing paste?"

Nana Jo smiled as she sipped her coffee. "I grew up on a farm. There was always some kind of accident that happened on a farm and most people were too poor to go riding off miles to a doctor. My grandmother used to be the local midwife and well…medicine woman. She mixed all kinds of things up in her kitchen and grew herbs for healing everything from the croup to rheumatic fever."

"I never knew that." I stared at my grandmother. I'd known this woman all my life and she was still able to surprise me.

Nana Jo shrugged. "I never thought it worth talking about. Most of those old remedies would be considered nothing more than old wives tales nowadays."

"Scientists are discovering that a lot of those old remedies actually worked. I read an article recently that chicken soup really does help with a cold. Although scientists aren't sure if there is some ingredient in the chicken soup itself or if it's in the person's mind. Whatever the reason, it works."

We sat for a few moments and talked about poultices, plasters, and herbal teas. Then we went downstairs to the bookstore.

I had a lot of fears when I quit my job as an English teacher and opened the bookstore. Would I be able to handle things alone? Would I be able to make enough to support myself? Did people still read books? The answer to all of those questions was yes. Recently an old friend I hadn't seen in over twenty years asked if I found working in a bookstore monotonous and boring? I didn't even need to think before I answered. Market Street Mysteries was a lot of things, but monotonous and boring certainly wasn't one of them. New people came in every day. Boxes of books arrived weekly. Some boxes included books from writers I'd read for years, which were like old friends. Familiar series from Victoria Thompson, Emily Brightwell, Jeanne Dams, and Martha Grimes sent a thrill of excitement through my body as I gazed at the bright covers and anticipated the joy of figuring out whodunit. There was also the joy of discovering new writers and wondering which ones would be added to my list of favorites. On those rare moments when the store was quiet, I sometimes went for a walk downtown North Harbor and stepped into shops owned by my neighbors. The bookstore had helped me through one of the worse times of my life, the death of my husband and best friend. I'd created a new life for myself with new friends and I hoped a new career as a writer, one day.

A few doors down from Market Street Mysteries, a new restaurant had opened. I stood in front of the window and stared at the menu taped on the door. I looked at my watch and realized it was after two and my stomach growled as I read the menu. I stepped inside and waited while my eyes adjusted to the darker interior.

"I'm glad you decided to come in." A man with salt-and-pepper hair and beard, cut close in the style worn by the military, soft brown eyes, and a big smile came out from behind the bar.

I must have looked puzzled because he motioned to the window. "I saw you outside."

"Oh. Yes. Sorry."

"No need to apologize. That's why I put the menu up. I was hoping it would entice people to come inside."

"Well it worked." I laughed.

"How about a nice table by the window?"

I nodded and took a seat in the chair he held out for me.

"I have a lovely white wine from a local vineyard."

"Oh no. Just water with lemon please."

When he left, I looked around. The restaurant was clean and decorated with an urban edge. Exposed brick walls, stained concrete floors, and iron fixtures created a modern, hip atmosphere. Televisions lined the wall behind the bar. My waiter returned with a glass and a carafe of ice water with lemon.

He smiled as he placed the carafe of water on the table. "You own the mystery bookstore a few doors down, don't you?"

I took a sip of water and nodded.

"I thought so. I've been trying to meet all of the other store owners around here. I'm Frank Patterson."

He held out his hand and we shook.

"Samantha Washington, but you can call me Sam."

"Sam, I'm pleased to meet you. How long have you been down here?"

I knew he was asking about how long my bookstore had been open. I looked at him and started to respond when my attention was caught by the picture on the television behind him.

Melody Hardwick's picture filled the screen. Then it was replaced by pictures of a body covered by a blanket.

I gasped.

The words that scrolled across the bottom of the screen said Melody's body had been found by early morning joggers. The police believed her death was the result of *foul play*. The picture that next filled the screen and nearly stopped my heart was of Dawson getting into the back of a police car.

* * * *

I didn't remember the walk back to the bookstore. Nana Jo said I came in looking like a whirling dervish. I did remember marching into the South Harbor police station with Nana Jo. The brick two-story building was downtown and not far from my bookstore. North Harbor and South Harbor shared the same Lake Michigan coastline. The two towns were separated by the St. Thomas River that zigzagged through northern Indiana and southern Michigan for over two hundred miles and ended as it wrapped around North Harbor in a U and flowed into Lake Michigan.

The county police station and courthouse were attached and comprised a sprawling complex located on an area that sat on a small street in between North and South Harbor. Other than field trips as a child, I had only been to the complex as an adult when I was summoned for jury duty. My memory of the facility was prior to 9/11 and didn't include security cameras and metal detectors that would rival those at the nearby River Bend airport.

I was so concerned about Dawson I didn't remember a number of things from the time I saw his face on the television to the moment I walked into the police station. However, the memory that would live with me until my death would be when Nana Jo set off the metal detectors and we were instantly swarmed by police officers with guns drawn, all shouting for us to raise our hands and lay down on the floor. I remember the officer who pulled my wrists behind my back and the feel of the cold metal handcuffs as he placed them on my wrists. I looked over at my grandmother as she lay by my side, also cuffed and on the ground. My heart raced, and my blood pounded in my head. Yep. That was a memory that would stay with me forever.

Thankfully, my nephews hadn't been idle after we left the bookstore. One of them must have called their mother. Never had I been so happy to see and hear my sister, Jenna, as I was at that moment.

"What do you think you're doing?" Jenna said in the cold, steely voice I dreaded. "You have ten seconds to get my sister and grandmother off that floor or as God is my witness, I will sue every last one of you." Jenna was a criminal defense attorney well-known by the police for her tough, no-nonsense attitude. I'd once heard that the district attorney's office referred to her as a pit bull and I had to say, as her sister, I thought it was pretty accurate.

"You know these women?" One of the officers stepped up from the pack.

"I just said that, didn't I? And you have two seconds to lower your weapons," Jenna said between clenched teeth. Then she turned her back to the officers and looked directly into the camera that was positioned over the door. "As you can see, these imbeciles have my sister and elderly grandmother handcuffed and laying on the cold concrete. Obviously they aren't a threat, yet these officers continue to point their weapons."

The officers put away their guns. One of the officers helped me to a standing position. It took two of them to help Nana Jo to stand.

"Your 'elderly' grandmother set off the metal detector." He turned Nana Jo's purse upside down and all the contents flew across the floor. His cocky smile turned into a sneer as he looked at Nana Jo's iPad, phone, notebook, brush, holster, makeup, and about twenty other items lying on the ground. He kicked the empty holster and looked around the floor. But there was no weapon.

"Hey, Barney Fife, you break my iPad and you're buying me another one," Nana Jo said.

Jenna smiled and continued to address the camera. "No weapon, just an empty holster. And if she had brought her weapon, you'd find her permit to carry in her wallet."

The smirk vanished as the officer looked at the wallet and found the permit. He returned the wallet and other belongings to Nana Jo's purse and nodded to the officers holding us and the handcuffs were removed.

"I guess it was the iPad that set off the detector. Anyway, she should have announced she had a weapon and shown her carry permit immediately," he said as though he were educating a child—bad mistake.

"I'll keep that in mind the next time when I actually have a weapon. Of course, you would have known that if you nincompoops would have waited a minute before Wyatt Earp and the rest of the posse drew their guns like they were about to shoot it out at the O.K. Corral." Nana Jo snatched her purse away from the officer.

* * * *

"I intend to subpoena the videotapes, so make sure nothing happens to them. If my sister or grandmother is injured due to this incident, you will be hearing from me."

The officer looked as though he wanted to say something, but the look in Jenna's eyes showed him silence would be his best defense.

"Now where have you taken Dawson Alexander?" Jenna's question brought me back to the reason for our visit.

We were escorted to a reception area. We signed in and were then led to a small conference room. Jenna was allowed to go with the police officer, but Nana Jo and I were left to wait. I wanted to protest, but the look in Jenna's eyes convinced me silence was my best defense as well.

Still flustered from the experience of being handcuffed and having guns pointed at me, I was glad for an opportunity to sit down. I hadn't realized how nervous I was until I poured myself a cup of water from the pitcher on the table and my hands shook so badly I spilled most of it on the table.

"Are you okay?" Nana Jo grabbed some napkins from her purse and helped me clean up the water.

"No," I answered truthfully. "But I will be. That was scary."

Nana Jo smiled. "That was pretty nerve-wracking. I'm sorry, honey."

"I'm glad you thought to leave your gun at home."

She smiled. "I didn't."

"What?"

She shook her head. "Honestly, I was as surprised as that policeman. I must have left it at home, but it was an oversight. I was so upset about Dawson I didn't even think about my peacemaker."

"Lucky for us." I smiled and leaned across the table. "I'm pleasantly surprised to know you have a permit to carry."

Nana Jo grinned. "Well, we can thank Jenna for that too. To be honest, I've been carrying a gun for more years than you've been alive. But after everything that happened in the summer, Jenna convinced me I needed a permit."

We waited for what felt like an eternity but was only twenty minutes. Jenna returned with Detective Bradley Pitt. Detective Pitt had been the lead investigator in the murder of Clayton Parker, a realtor who was found in the backyard of my building over the summer. He was an unpleasant man with a knack of jumping to the wrong conclusion, like when he thought I murdered Parker. Detective Pitt was short with a bad comb over and polyester pants that were too short and a bright, flowered polyester shirt that was too tight. His certainty that I was a murderer forced me, Nana Jo, and her friends from the retirement village to become sleuths to figure out who murdered Parker.

"Stinky Pitt, I should have known you'd be behind this debacle. Once again, you've got everything bass-ackward, upside down sideways." Nana Jo taught Detective Pitt in elementary school and loved to embarrass him by using his childhood nickname.

Detective Pitt's jaw clenched, and his ears got red. "I wish you would remember that no one calls me that anymore." He glared at Nana Jo, who contrived to look innocent.

She loved to goad him and knew exactly what she was doing. But she was careful never to call him Stinky Pitt around other police officers.

"Look. Dawson Alexander is *absolutely* not a killer," I said. "You've arrested the wrong person."

"We haven't arrested anyone *yet*. We just brought him in for questioning." Detective Pitt walked around the small conference table. "But, that's not to say we won't be pressing charges. We've barely had time to talk to him."

"And from now on, you won't be talking to him without legal counsel present," Jenna said. "Now, I want to talk to my client."

Detective Pitt looked as though he wanted to comment but, to his credit, he kept silent. He merely shook his head and mumbled something about lawyers meddling or muddling, I couldn't really tell, under his breath as he left.

"Wow. You're tough," I said with more than a little awe.

Jenna laughed. "They don't call me pit-bull for nothing. I earned that title."

We waited for several minutes and then the door opened, and Detective Pitt returned with Dawson.

Detective Pitt looked as though he intended to stay and listen, but Jenna wasn't having it.

"Thank you, Detective. I'll let you know when we're done."

His only response was to turn and leave, but the door did seem to close with a bit more force than I remembered him using previously.

Dawson looked as though he'd aged ten years since this morning. Could it only have been a few hours? His eyes looked tired and the scars that seemed faded this morning looked more prominent now; although I might have been more attuned to them, given our current situation.

"Dawson, I've told Detective Pitt I'm your legal counsel. However, you don't have to accept me. If there's someone else that you—"

"No. I really want you to represent me. I was just too embarrassed to ask." He hung his head and looked up sheepishly. "I don't know how I'm going to pay you."

"Pshaw. Don't worry about that. I don't charge family."

Dawson looked surprised and misty eyed.

I was a bit misty myself. Dawson was like family. Leon and I were never blessed with children, but Dawson had come into my life during a time when I was in need of someone to focus my attention onto. He'd allowed me to mother him and had slid into one of the holes that Leon's death had opened up.

"Now, I need to know, what have you told them?" Jenna looked at me and Nana Jo. "Normally, I wouldn't do this in front of you. Conversations between a client and an attorney are privileged."

"That means you can't tell anyone what he says to you, right?" I asked.

"Pretty much. It's complicated, but that's the general idea. Legal counsel is charged with giving the best advice possible. However, if someone comes to a lawyer for advice, they need to feel free to communicate everything without fear anything he says will be used against him. If he holds back, because he's afraid, I can't give the best advice." She looked at Dawson. "Do you understand?"

He nodded.

"Now, understand only the conversation between an attorney and a client are privileged. If Sam and Nana Jo stay, they could be compelled to reveal it. That's why I would recommend they leave."

Nana Jo and I both started talking at the same time, but Dawson overrode us. "It's okay. I didn't kill her. I don't have anything to hide. They can stay."

"I don't care what the law says. I'd never tell them anything," Nana Jo said.

"Neither would I."

Jenna merely shook her head. "Am I the only law-abiding citizen in this family?" She smiled. "My family would apparently lie under oath." She shook her head.

"For someone I care about, I'd lie like a rug," I said.

"Darned straight," Nana Jo agreed. "That's why we keep you and your husband, Tony, around. Two lawyers in the family come in pretty handy."

Jenna shook her head then turned her attention to Dawson. "I need you to tell me everything you've said to the police."

"I didn't really say anything. They kept me waiting in a room for almost an hour. Then Detective Pitt showed up. He started asking me a lot of questions, but I'd had a lot of time to think when I was waiting." He paused and then shook his head. "My dad didn't teach me much, but he always said, 'never say nothing to no cops, boy, not without a lawyer. They've gotta give you a lawyer in this country. Ain't America great?' That's what he would say." He looked around at us. "So, I didn't say anything. I just said I wanted a lawyer."

Jenna breathed a sigh of relief.

"Atta boy," Nana Jo said.

Dawson smiled. "I didn't think they'd do it. Detective Pitt kept saying I didn't need an attorney because I wasn't under arrest. When that didn't work, he said innocent people didn't need attorneys. If I wasn't guilty of anything, then I should want to help them." He looked at Jenna. "I have to admit, I was starting to crack. If you hadn't come, I probably would have started talking."

Jenna looked as though she wanted to spit nails. She got up and started pacing around the small room. "Why that no good dirt bag. I'll have his badge," she mumbled. After a few minutes, she sat down again and smiled at Dawson. "I'm sorry you had that experience. In this respect, your dad was right. If you ask for an attorney, they are supposed to stop and immediately call for a public defender." She sighed. "However, now on to business. Do you have a dollar?"

Dawson looked puzzled but didn't question Jenna's request. He pulled out his wallet and took out a dollar and handed it to her.

She took the dollar. "Thank you. This is my retainer. That means you are retaining me to represent you and be your lawyer. I'll write you a receipt and have you sign a document to that effect. Okay?"

Dawson nodded.

"Okay. Now you are not to talk to the police at all unless I'm with you. Understand?"

Dawson nodded.

"I called your coach on my way here. He's aware of the situation. He doesn't know the university's position yet. But, I'm guessing the university will want to distance themselves from you until this whole mess is cleared up. There's been so much negative publicity about football players and other athletes getting arrested, I'm sure the university counsel will recommend they take a neutral stance. But, we'll deal with that hurdle when we get there."

Jenna pulled a notebook, tape recorder, and pen out from her brief case. "Normally, I wouldn't do things this way. But, I need to know everything. Start from how you met Melody to today." She turned on the tape recorder.

He paused and took a couple of deep breaths before beginning his tale. "I met Melody on campus. One day she came up to me in the quad and asked for my cell phone. When I gave it to her, she put her number in my contacts and handed the phone back. She told me to call her."

Nana Jo whistled.

"Shush. I'm willing to let you two stay, but you need to be quiet and let him finish," Jenna said.

We nodded.

She looked at Dawson. "Go on."

"Well, she was hot, and she was a senior and…she was *really* hot."

"We get the picture. She was hot and easy, and you got involved. Is that right?" Jenna asked.

Dawson nodded. "Yeah. We were involved."

"How long?"

"Only a couple of months. The season started in late August and she came up to me in September."

Nana Jo made a sound that sounded like, harrumph. "Figures. MISU was on a winning streak and your picture was on the front page of the *River Bend Times*. She saw her chance to latch onto a meal ticket and she took it."

"Nana Jo please." Jenna looked irritated. "Stop interrupting."

"It's okay. She's right. At first, I was flattered. Guys looked at me different when I walked around campus with Melody on my arm. Girls too. But, she didn't really care about me. She only wanted to be seen with me. She just wanted to go to parties and have her picture taken. She wanted me to move out of my apartment." He glanced at me shyly. "She went to the owner of Harbor Point Apartments and convinced him to rent the penthouse apartment to me."

"Harbor Point?" Despite Jenna's warning, I couldn't stop myself from interrupting. "Those units are really expensive. They look right out on Lake Michigan. The penthouse must cost a fortune."

"Normally, they lease for three thousand a month."

Nana Jo whistled, and I nearly choked.

Even Jenna seemed surprised. "How could you afford that?"

"I can't. The owner is a big MISU fan and a friend of hers. She said he was willing to lease it to me for two hundred a month."

Jenna looked as though she could barely believe her ears. "Two hundred? That's ridiculous. Sam could get more than two hundred a month for the garage studio. Why would he do that?"

Dawson shrugged. "I don't know, but it seemed shady. I didn't like the guy. He seemed slimy. He was older and wore polyester shirts with all these gold chains. He had really dark chest hair and big fake-looking hair that looked like a toupee. I just didn't trust him." Dawson looked down.

After six months, I knew Dawson pretty well. Nana Jo and I exchanged glances. There was more to this. Jenna hadn't spent nearly as much time with Dawson as we had, but her instincts must have kicked in because she remained quiet and waited. Most people didn't recognize the power of silence and tried to fill it in quickly. As a former teacher, I can honestly say silence generated more results than anything else I'd ever said or done. It worked this time too.

"He reminded me of my dad. I knew there would be something in it for him later. One night I was playing pool with some friends by the old HOD."

"The HOD?" Jenna stared. "That trailer park owned by the House of David?"

Dawson nodded.

The House of David was a religious commune that flourished in North Harbor during the early twentieth century. At one time the area thrived with an amusement park, baseball stadium, and fruit and vegetable market. Practically all their businesses had closed long ago when their founder, Benjamin Purnell, was tried for fraud and accused of child molestation. The molestation charges were never proved, but the rumors did plenty of damage. Purnell died not long after the trial and the House of David split into two factions.

"I saw him there. Virgil Russell was at the bar, drinking."

Either Dawson had learned to read my mind, or I'd let my thoughts show on my face, because he hurried to add, "I wasn't drinking. I just like to go there and shoot pool. It's quiet. No one there talks football or knows who I am." He hung his head.

I hadn't realized how much pressure he was under. I thought his biggest worry was keeping his grades up and staying on the team. I hadn't realized how much the pressure of the media and the fans was weighing on him. As I scanned his face now, I saw what I hadn't before.

"So, you saw this Virgil Russell at the pool hall." Jenna continued. "Did he see you?"

"No. I snuck out as soon as I saw him. But, he looked like he was waiting for someone. I don't know why, but I waited in the car until he came out. When he came out, he wasn't alone."

Dawson's voice got very soft. He was obviously reluctant to continue, but he took a couple of deep breaths and plowed forward. "That's when I saw them. Melody and Virgil were together."

Jenna looked at me.

I shrugged. Obviously she knew Virgil since she introduced Dawson to him. Again, my face must have revealed my confusion.

Dawson fidgeted and refused to make eye contact for several seconds. Then he looked at me. "Don't you see, they were *together*."

Finally, it dawned on all of us at the same time.

"It was disgusting. He had to be old enough to be her father. He had his hands all over her and she was wrapped around him like a…like a…" Dawson struggled to find the right simile to describe what he'd seen.

Nana Jo didn't have any trouble conjuring up the right comparison. "Like an octopus."

"Yeah. That pretty much says it all."

I studied Dawson's facial expressions and body language, and I knew there was more. He was holding something back. But I refused to entertain the thought he murdered that girl.

Jenna took a couple of deep breaths. "Okay, so you saw your girlfriend with another man. Did that make you angry?"

Dawson seemed to think about the question before answering, "Maybe for a few seconds. But, honestly, I think I felt relieved."

"Relieved? Why relieved?" Jenna asked.

"I knew things wouldn't work between Melody and me. I knew she didn't care about me. This gave me the excuse I needed to end things with her. And, that's what I did. I broke it off."

"When was this?"

He was silent for a few moments. "Friday night, right after the pep rally."

"How did she take it?"

Dawson rubbed his face. "Not so good. At first, she tried to deny it was her. Then, when that wouldn't work, she said I was mistaken about their relationship. She claimed they were just friends." Dawson shook his head. "She must think I was the biggest hayseed on the planet. There is no way I mistook their relationship when he had his hands all over her. He was groping her like a…like a…"

"Like a blind man at a produce stand." Nana Jo again came to the rescue.

"Nana Jo." Jenna was not amused, and her voice said, either be quiet or you'll have to leave.

Nana Jo used her hands to indicate she was zipping her mouth shut and throwing away the key.

Jenna turned back to Dawson. "Okay, so three days ago, you broke up with her. She didn't take it well. What happened next?"

"Saturday was the football game. Later that evening, she came by the bookstore. She said she wanted to talk. I took her up to my apartment. We got into an argument."

"Did you hit her?" Jenna asked.

Dawson shook his head. "No. I never hit her. Although she hit me several times. She scratched me. I had to grab her wrists to protect myself." He held up his hands to show how he had grabbed her. "She kicked and spit and lashed out with everything she had. I held her down on the sofa until she calmed down. Then I picked her up and put her out. She screamed and cussed and beat on the door for a while. I was afraid she'd wake up the whole neighborhood, but I never opened the door. She finally must have gotten tired and left. That was the last time I saw her."

"Sounds like she really made a big racket." Jenna looked at me. "Did you hear it?"

I shook my head. "No. I didn't hear a thing." I turned to Nana Jo. "Did you?"

Nana Jo shook her head.

Jenna sat and stared. "Dawson, is there anything else you want to tell me?"

He paused and eventually shook his head. "No. That's everything."

"What about yesterday? Did you see her Sunday?"

"No. I stayed home. I baked."

"That's right. I was there with him," I said eagerly.

"But you weren't there all day. You went to church with Mom yesterday. I know because she told me. You went to church and dinner and then shopping."

"Well, yeah, but he was home baking when I got home."

Jenna didn't look relieved. "What about you?" She turned to Nana Jo.

"Ruby Mae's granddaughter sang a solo at their church. I went to hear her and then I went to brunch with the girls."

The girls were Nana Jo's friends from the retirement village. They were feisty, active, and sweet each in their own way.

Jenna frowned. Then she got up and paced. "I'm going to be honest. It doesn't look good. We need to find out when she died. The police will most likely arrest you."

Dawson looked terrified and, I have to admit, something clutched my chest that seemed to be restricting my airway and forcing tears to my eyes. "But he's innocent."

"I know, but he has a really good motive. Plus, he had an altercation with the deceased. It's just a matter of time before they find Dawson's skin cells under her fingernails. Even a fool like Detective Stinky Pitt could get a conviction with that."

The thing clutching at my heart made it hard to speak. With effort, I managed to squeak out, "But what are we going to do?"

"I'm going to work on a defense."

Nana Jo stood. "And we're going to figure out who killed that floozy."

About the Author

V. M. Burns was born and raised in South Bend, Indiana. She currently resides in Tennessee with her two poodles, Cash and Kenzie. Valerie is a member of Mystery Writers of America and a lifetime member of Sisters in Crime. Readers can visit her website at www.vmburns.com.

Printed in the United States
by Baker & Taylor Publisher Services